THE
FERRYMAN WILL
BE THERE

Also by Rosemary Aubert

Free Reign
The Feast of Stephen

THE FERRYMAN WILL BE THERE

AN ELLIS PORTAL MYSTERY

Rosemary Aubert

McArthur & Company
Toronto

First published in Canada 2001 by
McArthur & Company
322 King Street West, Suite 402
Toronto, Ontario M5V 1J2

Published in the U.S. by Bridge Works Publishing Company

National Library of Canada Cataloguing in Publication Data

Aubert, Rosemary.
 The ferryman will be there

An Ellis Portal mystery
ISBN 1-55278-201-8

I. Title.

PS8551.U24F47 2001   C813' .54   C2001-930112-X
PR9199.3.A9F47 2001

Book Design by Eva Auchincloss
Cover Illustrator by Caty Bartholomew
Cover Composition by Fortunato Design
Printed in Canada by Transcontinental Printing Inc.

The publisher would like to acknowledge the financial support of the
Government of Canada through the Book Publishing Industry Development Program (BPIDP) for our publishing activities. The publisher
further wishes to acknowledge the financial support of the Ontario
Arts Council for our publishing program.

10 9 8 7 6 5 4 3 2 1

This book is dedicated to my brother, David Proe,
and to all his loved ones.

Sincere thanks to

Barbara Phillips
Warren Phillips
Les Petriw
Tony Proe

and especially to Kerr Spiers
for the story of The Ferryman.

They then came to the black river Cocytus, where they found the ferryman, Charon, old and squalid, but strong and vigorous, who was receiving passengers of all kinds into his boat, magnanimous heroes, boys and unmarried girls, as numerous as the leaves that fall at autumn, or the flocks that fly southward at the approach of winter.

—*Bulfinch's Mythology: The Age of Fable,*
"Chapter XXXII"

THE
FERRYMAN WILL
BE THERE

CHAPTER ONE

I've been a sinner and a saint, a criminal and a judge, an altar boy and a blasphemer. And now, at the age of fifty-eight, I'm an old man, or at least an *aging* man obsessed about growing old, about wasting my life, about time passing, about setting things straight. The life I've led tells me that a man is as apt to get what he doesn't want as to get what his heart is set on. I wanted things to be right between me and my son. I did not want the terror of facing Jeffrey again after not laying eyes on him for eight years.

Waiting for the light to change at the intersection of Bloor and Yonge, I caught a glimpse of myself in the side window of a BMW stuck in morning rush-hour traffic. My salt-and-pepper hair had turned completely gray since I'd seen Jeffrey last. My once well-muscled slightly overweight body had turned gaunt, then nearly skeletal, then back to muscled again. My clothes had gone from Armani to Goodwill, then settled somewhere in between.

I stepped off the curb but jumped back when a turning taxi screamed its horn at me. I almost welcomed the rush of fear that set the blood pounding through my chest. Some things are easier to be afraid of than others.

A sweet, soft, sunny September morning, definitely the kind of morning for the remembrance of things past. The last time I'd crossed the threshold of Blane Tower, the office high-rise John Stoughton-Melville had named for his father-in-law, Stow had dismantled his legal practice to become a Justice of the Supreme Court of Canada and move to the capital in Ottawa. I had no idea what he was using Blane Tower for these days, but I was about to find out.

The elevator sped through twenty-nine floors without stopping. I was alone, alone enough to contemplate that it, like everything else in Stow's life, was elegant. Oak panelled, carpeted in red, mirrored on the ceiling and softly lighted. Stow, it seemed to me, had appropriated all good things to himself: wealth, intelligence, a stellar law career, a stunning wife and now — I was beginning to understand — Jeffrey, my own son. As the elevator door slid noiselessly open, I realized that all the careful words I rehearsed to say to the boy — not boy, Jeffrey was now twenty-nine — had fled.

"Good morning, Mr. Portal. It *is* Mr. Portal?" I nodded. A gray-haired woman about my own age extended her well-manicured hand the moment I stepped into a reception area decorated in dark cool tones that obliterated the autumnal warmth of the morning, replacing it with seasonless sterility. The last time I'd been here, I had sneaked glances at treasures from Stow's personal collection: a madonna from the Italian Renaissance, a golden goblet encrusted with rubies, a portrait of the mother of Harpur Blane Stoughton-Melville, Stow's dead wife,

2

another person whose love I always felt Stow had robbed me of.

"Mr. Portal, I mean the *other* Mr. Portal," the woman said with an awkward smile, "has had to take an unexpected conference call. He's asked me to inquire as to whether you'd like breakfast while you wait for him. He regrets the delay."

At the thought of placing anything into the gurgling cauldron of acid that was my stomach, I felt bile rise at the back of my throat. "No thank you," I managed. "I'll just wait."

She smiled again and motioned me toward the smoothly upholstered curve of a dark blue chair. It looked as inviting as a wave of the sea. I gingerly lowered my posterior into its unwelcoming embrace.

I don't know how long I sat there. Time, as Mr. Einstein could probably have explained, expands and contracts and twists itself to its own purpose. There was no clock visible and no hint of the passage of time in the silent motions of the woman as she worked behind another dark curve of furniture that served both as her desk and a protective barrier between Jeffrey and all intruders. I stared at the sea-blue carpet and wondered how Jeffrey had ended up here.

If he had ever told me what he intended to do with his life, I couldn't remember. He was twenty-one when I left the family and I had not been exactly a homebody during his adolescence. There was an ocean of regret between me and my son but we had always bridged it with silence and denial. Even now as I struggled to think of what to say to him, I found my thoughts veering away from Jeffrey and this morning.

"Ellis, I've called to congratulate you," Stow had said last week instead of hello. Justice J. Stoughton-Melville never wasted a word on preliminaries.

"Congratulate me, Stow? What for?" Stow always seemed to know more about what was happening in my life than I did. I no longer questioned how he managed that. He had to know, for example, that when he called me at home, he was calling from the chambers of a Supreme Court Justice to the chambers of a rooming house boarder.

"Ellis, surely you've seen the papers. Jeffrey's firm has won the competition for the renaturalization of Nathan Phillips Square in front of City Hall." Not only had I been unaware of this good news, I had not even known Jeffrey *had* a firm, though Stow had told me my son was an architect, had warned me that it was to my own detriment that I refused to mend the breach with Jeffrey. Being devoid of shame himself, Stow could not comprehend how shame hampered others. A major failing in a judge, it seemed to me.

"I thought Jeffrey was an architect," I said weakly. "Doesn't renaturalization involve tearing structures down? Why would an architect want to do that?" For all I knew, Jeffrey hated Nathan Phillips Square. I used to take him there to skate on the public ice rink when he was a child. He would go around and around always seeming to stare at the buildings surrounding the square. I wondered why he didn't get dizzy but I'd never asked him how he avoided it.

"Really, Ellis, you appal me. Jeffrey had the whole front page of the urban affairs section of yesterday's *Daily World*. His proposal will make a senseless expanse of concrete into a living urban forest. It's a courageous and

4

highly innovative design." There was a breath, but only a breath, of silence. "I would be immensely proud if he were my son," Stow said in his deep, level, confident voice.

Well, he's not your son.

"He's expecting you to meet with him," Stow had announced.

I felt the fury rise in me before I was even sure I'd heard correctly. "What do you mean 'expecting'?"

"Monday morning at 9:15. I told him you'd be there."

"You're a liar!" I gasped at my own insolence.

But Stow had laughed. "Only if you make me one, Ellis. Be there and keep me honest." He laughed again and hung up. And made me spend the whole weekend wondering what to say to my son. After forty-eight hours the only words I'd definitely decided on were, "I'm sorry."

I was brought abruptly back to the present at the sudden sound of a door opening in a place in the blue-gray paneled wall that I hadn't realized contained a door. As if in slow motion, a man stepped from behind it and began to make his way toward me across the expanse of dark carpet.

I rose, not surprised to discover my knees were shaking. I extended my hand, steadying it. The man's fingers were grasping mine before I looked up and saw that this stranger could not be Jeffrey. He was the right age but too stocky, too dark, too warm. He shook my hand with genuine enthusiasm. "It's an honor to meet you, Judge Portal," he said. "I'm Jeffrey's attorney."

All at once I realized what this meeting was about. It had nothing to do with Jeffrey's award or Stow's interest in my son's career. Above all, it had nothing to do with reconciliation. It had to do with money. "Look," I said, politely withdrawing my hand and stepping back. "I'm not in a position to discuss the financial settlement that Jeffrey's mother and I have finalized."

The man looked startled, perhaps embarrassed. He shook his head. "No," he said. "No, of course not, Mr. Portal. I've only come out to apologize for the delay. Jeff was really looking forward to speaking to you this morning but you know how it is." He shrugged.

"How is it?" I asked, no longer having the slightest idea what I was doing there.

"Jeff wants to talk to you. He really does. But since he got that award the phone's been ringing off the hook. He's just up to here." He lifted his hand to his chin and I saw he wore a college ring, which meant he was probably American. Was "Jeff" so successful that he needed international legal advice?

"Yes," I said. "Up to here. Good for him." I was being sarcastic but the young lawyer took me completely seriously.

"Gee, thanks for understanding," he said, reaching, I thought, to slap me on the back, but thinking better of the idea in time to stop himself from touching me. "Jeff figured you'd be willing to set up another appointment and I said I'd come out here and take care of you myself because I've been a fan of yours for a while now."

I could not imagine how this young man could know one good thing about me. No doubt because, I realized later, I could not imagine how Jeffrey could know one good thing to tell him. "I'm a little up to here myself at the moment," I said ridiculously. "So why don't I give Jeff a buzz and we'll rebook. I'll run my eye over my daybook."

A look of surprise flashed across the young man's friendly, open features but he was too much of a lawyer to let me know what was on his mind. He probably understood that my careless tone was completely fake. There was no way in the world I would call my son. I had spent forty-eight hours wringing my hands. Now I was reprieved.

It didn't occur to me until I was back out being honked at on Yonge and Bloor that the *other* Mr. Portal was probably behind his blue wall feeling exactly the same way.

Later that day in the canyon of buildings further south on Yonge Street, the afternoon sun didn't make it all the way down to the sidewalk, but the breeze was still soft when I arrived at Police Headquarters in the hope I'd find Matt West.

Nobody bothered to ask me to sign for a visitor's pass. The assistance I'd rendered in my two so-called murder cases had made me known to the police in ways more congenial than in my earlier roles as assault perpetrator and vagrant. The duty sergeant at the front desk nodded in recognition when I began ascending the wide marble staircase from the lobby to the offices on the upper floors. This Gargantua in the heart of town was the newest in a long line of Toronto Police Headquarters and it looked more like an intercontinental hotel than a cop shop. I supposed that was appropriate for a sophisticated city of more than four million people, nearly half from other countries. The Toronto police offered emergency services in one hundred and forty languages. I appreciated the present cosmopolitan nature of the city, even though I could still remember when Headquarters had been a run-down hulk on grungy Jarvis Street and the language of service had been English.

"You wanted to see me, Matt," I asked a little sheepishly. Detective Sergeant Mattheson West glanced up at me from behind his unusual desk, an old enamel-topped kitchen table. His eyes are a shade of dark green I've only seen in a person whose blood is a mixture of Negroid and Caucasian. In New Orleans they call coffee-colored skin like his "Creole". His black hair, marked now by a few strands of gray, is curly, thick and short-looking even when he tells me he hasn't had a haircut in four months.

In one of those rare moments in which a civilian is granted a peek at what goes on behind closed doors at Headquarters, I heard Matt's male colleagues tease him that Detective West was promoted to Sergeant solely because he has a double "handicap". He's black and he has only his left hand. Females say his success is because he is so good-looking, and I suppose he is. Nobody mentions that he's gay.

"What's your hurry, Portal? It's only been four days since I called — the first time. Don't tell me you've been busy. I hate to see a man of the law tell a lie."

"Since when?" I retorted.

Matt didn't smile but that did not mean he didn't enjoy our bantering or appreciate the rapport we share. Because of a brush with homelessness in my own past, he often calls on me for what he terms "participatory consultation". I feel right at home in his office. Matt heads up the task force for Reduction through Early Action of Crimes against the Homeless, which the police call REACH and everybody on the street refers to as "the homeless bureau". Though it had been a long time since I decorated my own home — unless you counted a packing crate — I served as Matt's interior design consultant in addition to my other contributions. He liked to encourage visits from the down-and-outs of the city, so we kept his office looking as sloppy as the shelters, flophouses and community centers frequented by most of his clients. Photos of street people were tacked to his wall in a careless disarray that nevertheless managed to convey his dedication to those he served.

He rose and offered me a cream-filled chocolate doughnut and a coffee from a supply he always kept nearby. He understood that some of the homeless who visited him would have nothing else to eat that day. I took them and sat in the battered chair in front of his desk. "Thanks, Matt. Are you sure you can spare this? You wouldn't want to run out. What would a cop be without a doughnut?"

"What would you be without a wise mouth?"

I took a sip of coffee. It wasn't latte or cappuccino. It tasted like the institutional glop of jails and mental hospitals. Fine by me. "Do you need me for something?"

"I needed you last week, Ellis. Where have you been?" Matt's green eyes shot me a speculative glance tinged with concern or suspicion. I couldn't tell which. Either way I didn't feel like telling him the truth, which was that between my anxiety over Stow's interference and my confusion over my financial situation, I felt gripped by immobility. Matt wanted me to work for him, but I didn't think I was ready. When I was a judge, I was known for being sensitive to the problems of the disadvantaged. I got even more sensitive when I became a bum. Still, it's one thing to befriend a cop and quite another to work for the police.

With his strong left hand, Matt pushed away from his

desk and swivelled toward a beat-up paint-stained cabinet that, with the flick of single button, swung open to reveal a computer. He positioned the mouse and clicked a few times. I had to get up and stand behind him to see what was on the screen. It looked like a simplified map of Toronto with a number of black dots randomly scattered across it.

I hated to display my ignorance but I had to ask, "What is this, Matt? What do the dots represent?"

"Catacombs," was his terse reply.

I've been to Rome like any good Catholic — or lapsed one. "Catacombs? In Toronto?"

Matt indulged me with a faint smile. "These are underground squats, places where street kids live."

I studied the map over Matt's broad shoulder. Most detectives are proud not to wear a uniform. Matt in this, as in all things, was different. He had on the regulation light-blue, short-sleeved shirt the street constables wear in warm weather. I didn't want to follow the line of his muscled arm where it ended in the brown stump of his wrist. I kept my eyes on the screen. "Why do you want me to see this?"

Without answering, he clicked a few more times. The map changed into a grid and then the grid changed into some sort of three-dimensional graph that I couldn't understand. "This," Matt said obligingly, "is something brand new we're working on."

"It looks like calculus, those equations I had to do when they put me in the wrong class at the university." If Matt wanted me to do something that involved math, he had to count me out. I was having enough math problems with money.

"Take it easy, Portal, we don't need you to do math."
He fiddled with the mouse again and the graph changed
shape and color, from a green mound to what looked like
a rugged blue mountain range with sharp red peaks.
"This is geographical criminal profiling," Matt explained.
"We plot known vacant buildings in the city on one axis
and petty crime statistics on another axis, along with
some sort of third variable, usually a time factor, on the
remaining axis. Then we . . ."

"Matt, I can't work with stuff like this, I . . ."

With one motion of his powerful left index finger,
Matt clicked it all away. The screen went blank. "Forget
this part of it, then," he said.

"Part of what?" I asked, going back to the seat I'd
vacated.

"This part of what Deputy Chief Corelli has asked me
to talk to you about."

I tried to hide my surprise but I've always found it
hard to keep my thoughts from a police officer. Even
when I was a judge, police witnesses for the prosecution
often anticipated my questions. "You may be wondering,
Your Honor," they would say, and then they'd answer the
very question I was about to ask. I used to have to remind
myself not to take this trick into consideration when
rendering a verdict on the accused, whose witnesses
were not mind readers. If top brass were interested in
my work, the force must be quite impressed with me,
unless . . .

"She's kind of desperate for good publicity because
of proposed budget cuts," Matt broke into my thoughts
and he laughed, a deep, rich laugh. "She's sent down a
directive instructing us to enlist the services of 'valuable

members of the community'. That would be you, my man."

"I don't think Corelli would be thrilled to have a disgraced judge and former tenant of a large cardboard box working for her."

"As a matter of fact, Portal, she would." Matt rolled his chair back to his desk and with swift movements of the practiced fingers of his remaining hand, flipped open a manila folder and pulled a document, then a photograph. But he didn't say anything. He was baiting me. I tried to resist but was tempted.

"Did you have a particular situation in mind?"

"Situation?" He didn't look up.

"I mean did Corelli have something definite she wanted you to ask me about?"

"Yes." He turned over another piece of paper. He was exceptionally deft with his single hand. I admired that, especially since he'd lost the other hand guarding the late object of my unrequited love, Harpur Stoughton-Melville . . . I also admired his cop-like trickery. The longer he made me wait, the more eager I was to hear what he had to say.

"Do you mind giving me a hint?" I edged forward on the rickety old chair, which creaked under my weight.

Matt wrinkled his wide shapely nose at the paper as though it held deep clues. "Last week," he began, "as I'm sure you're aware, there was a fatal shooting at the fall film festival."

The Toronto Film Festival was one of the biggest in the world. With a nickname like "Hollywood North", Toronto could not help but be proud of its film industry. It was hard to walk down the street without tripping over some clown in a director's chair with a crowd of clip-

12

board holders hovering around him. Early-morning newscasts included the location of traffic-snarling film shoots along with those of accidents and water main ruptures. All in a day's work.

"Charington Simm," I said, and Matt nodded. "I guess there isn't a person in town who hasn't been following that case. It isn't every day that the top director in Canada is shot dead in front of eight hundred witnesses."

"Not one of whom saw a thing," Matt said with a sigh.

"But the Simm case is a homicide. Why would you be working on that?" I popped the last bite of doughnut into my mouth and glanced over to the box to see if there was another.

"Like just about everybody else in this sorry world," Matt said, "Simm wasn't what he appeared to be. A week is plenty of time to check into a man's business dealings, and Simm's were a little, shall we say, complicated."

In my days as a judge, I'd considered investing in films. Who among my friends hadn't? I knew all about the rate of return on what we used to call "creative goods". "His films cost millions — tens of millions," I observed. "But they must have made that much, too."

"I don't know how much they made," Matt replied. "But what I do know is that our forensic accounting experts are having a look at things and from what I hear, they're not exactly happy about what they see." I feared he might click on more graphs but mercifully I was spared.

"What does this have to do with your department?" I asked. "Charington Simm was not the sort of man to find himself without a home."

Matt gave me that world-weary glance that cops offer

to people who aren't using their brains. "If there's one person in the city who should know that homelessness can strike anybody, it's you, Portal. But whatever the situation with the Simm investigation," he said, "it's not him I'm concerned about. It's his daughter, Carrie."

The newspapers had been full of articles about the girl. I cringed to think that I'd probably bought the tabloids to read about Simm's child instead of the more respectable paper that had carried the article about my own child. "She's certainly a tragic figure," I offered. "She can't be older than about sixteen."

"Fifteen." Matt said, his even voice beginning to show the slightest trace of excitement as his story unfolded. "The deceased makes a film in which his teenage daughter plays a starring role. The two of them attend the premiere of the movie together, almost as though she's his date. They get out of the limo. There's a scuffle. He's down and she's at his side screaming for help. And nobody sees the shooter or even hears a shot."

I clicked my tongue in disgust. "That's impossible," I declared. "I've heard the 'I didn't see a thing' line in court a thousand times."

"No," Matt answered, leaning toward me. "Not impossible. Whoever killed Simm used a small-caliber handgun, a .25 ACP. What some people on the street call a 'raven', either because to them it's a bird in the hand or because it's easy to conceal at raves. A .25 ACP is the smallest center-fire semiautomatic available. Discharged in an empty hallway, it might sound like a cannon. But under most circumstances, it wouldn't make much noise. And in a crowd yelling its admiration for a couple of good-looking celebrities, plus reporters and photographers shouting for attention, the gun might not seem to make any sound at all."

"I don't know much about guns," I demurred. Matt loved to talk about guns, knives, poison. He was what people call a "sensitive" police officer. But he was a cop's cop when he wanted to be. I usually let him go on about weapons. "So if it's that small, could it have inflicted much damage?"

He gave the question a moment's thought. "Shot in the head at close range," he said carefully, "a man is likely to be damaged. Even with a small gun. Even with a peashooter, for that matter."

"But what about the shells? If it's a semiautomatic, wouldn't there be ejected cases at the scene?" I never liked to admit my interest in firearms. That would have been unseemly for a judge and dangerous for a bum. But sometimes I couldn't help myself. I'd seen plenty of weapons in my years of sitting on the bench and my years of sleeping on benches, too.

"I thought you didn't know anything about guns?" Matt challenged.

"I'm not totally ignorant. I was a judge. Still am, legally. I might still be a lawyer, too, if I paid my dues to the law society."

Matt consulted his papers again, though I knew he didn't really need to. "The reports show that no ejected cases were found on the scene. There was one single shot fired and the shells for that gun are tiny. There were hundreds of people present. The case could have landed anywhere. Underfoot. In the street. Even in somebody's clothing or hair. If somebody in that crowd had found it, they might not even have known what it was. They might have thrown it in the garbage without thinking."

"But none of this has anything to do with you, Detective. *You're* not investigating a homicide." Neither, of course, was I, but I was beginning to feel excitement rise.

"Right. We're talking about Carrie Simm. Seconds after her father was shot, she was photographed kneeling beside him, begging for help. She was with him in the ambulance. She was with him at St. Mike's when he was pronounced dead twenty minutes after arriving. By the time the coroner left, though, everybody seemed to have forgotten about Carrie. There are no photos of her outside the morgue, though there were plenty of reporters present. Carrie Simm was last recorded beside her newly declared-dead father. She hasn't been seen since."

What Matt was telling me was pretty much what had appeared in the papers. I began to feel annoyed. No matter how friendly cops sometimes are, the street wisdom holds that you should never forget they're the ones in charge. Did Deputy Corelli want me involved in this case as "window dressing", an empty gesture of community support, or was Matt going to tell me something I didn't already know?

"Who reported her missing, Matt?"

"Family," he answered, "Charington Simm and his one and only wife had been divorced for several years. Carrie lived with her father, more or less."

"More or less?" I didn't like the sound of that. It rang a bell, reminding me of the times, whole years, when I'd put my legal ambitions far ahead of the needs of Jeffrey and Ellen, his sister.

"Yeah. Off and on," Matt said. "Carrie and her mother never got along, seldom saw each other. But the mother knew how close Carrie was to Simm and how

16

upset the girl would be at witnessing his violent death, so she went looking for Carrie to offer support. Only she couldn't find the girl. After two days, she came to me."

"You knew this kid when you were on the Youth Bureau, didn't you?" I asked. "Was she one of the street kids you met when you were working undercover?"

"Yes. Like her father, little Carrie Simm was not exactly what she seemed. She's fifteen now, but she ran away the first time when she was nine years old. I scraped her off Yonge Street and toted her home on a pretty regular basis before I got promoted to this job." He leaned back and gave me another typical police glance. This one was conspiratorial. "I guess when you were involved in that Second Chance matter you heard a few things about me and the kids."

Second Chance was a halfway house for fugitive girls that had run a shady operation on the side. Only three years had gone by since I'd figured out what was going on there and who was behind it, but it seemed longer. Breaking up that operation had been my first "case". I'd sworn it would be my last, but I was wrong. "Yes, Matt," I answered. "Some of the girls you helped, the ones who got off the street and moved on to better things, said they'd run into a tough pimp with a heart of gold. 'Solomon', I think you called yourself. The girls never exactly said your name, but it was clear to me who they were talking about. Clearly, too, they trusted you, which is remarkable for that group."

If he was pleased at this accolade, he didn't show it.

"And the street people trust you, Portal. That's what this is all about."

I tried to be cop-like and not show I was pleased

at Matt's compliment. Then I remembered he had something up his sleeve, so to speak. "You think Carrie Simm might be back on the street? Is that what you're saying?"

"Where else would she be?" Matt replied. "She and her father had bumpy times. But things were straightening out. Surprising as it seems for the daughter of a filmmaker, she actually deserved to be in his films. She was good. I'm not artsy-fartsy, but she had presence on the screen. You looked at her but you were never sure what you were seeing. Young, old. Boy, girl. She sort of shimmered. You couldn't take your eyes off her." As if he were suddenly embarrassed by this flight into film criticism, Matt caught himself. I think he blushed. I remembered that before he met a lawyer named William Sterling, Matt had been a married man. His voice flattened. "She's a kid," he said. "If her father got shot, I'm sure she'd flee back to the only people she really trusted."

"And that wouldn't be her mother," I agreed. And it wouldn't be any social worker or family counselor, either, I didn't bother to add.

"No. It would be other street kids she'd turn to." Matt hesitated as if he hated to say what came next. "Could be she'd go back to a gang."

Tourist boosters aren't going to include the fact in any brochure, but for all its genteel loveliness and clean, lively urban charm, Toronto also has gangs, including violent girl gangs. "The Spiders?" I ventured. The Spider gang was the first and the worst of the girl gangs. Its members came from every ethnic group: WASP, Asian, Black. And as many middle-class girls as poorer ones joined up. There were some girls who joined the Spiders instead of going to college. Girls wore the gang's Black Widow tattoo in obvious places. One was rumored to sport it in the middle of her forehead. But the more devious were tattooed in secret places on their bodies and only revealed the spider in moments of intimacy or intimate danger for their victims. The majority of Spiders contented themselves with shoplifting, picking pockets and the occasional mugging. Those capable of multitasking robbed tricks, while the truly talented robbed banks.

"The Spider gang strikes me as a good guess," Matt replied. He swiveled his chair so that he was no longer facing me.

Here it comes.

"You knew a couple of girls from the Spiders," he said, as though talking to the air. We were moving closer to the point. Closer to the real reason he wanted my help.

"You mean poor little Moonstar, Queenie Johnson's daughter?"

Queenie is Cree and the widow of a Cree, but she bears the last name of an English Canadian missionary. Queenie was my best friend on the street, though she was living out of town at the moment. Her daughter, a victim of life on the skids, had died violently before she reached legal adulthood.

"There's another Spider among your close associates." Matt hesitated. "Tootie Beets," he finally said.

"Are you serious?" Though she was probably not yet twenty-one, Tootie was one of the oldest and wisest people I'd ever met. She was an ex-street kid turned landlady. *My* landlady, though daily I told myself that had to change. She ran her rooming house the way others ran multinational corporations.

"Yes."

"I've never seen her tattoo," I said. Then it was my turn to go red in the face.

"I don't know how current her gang involvement is," Matt said, turning back to face me. "And like you, I hope it's not current at all. But she knew the Spiders. So did Moonstar. So did Carrie. It's possible that Carrie, stricken with fear and grief over the murder of her father, perhaps feeling that her own life is in danger, is with that gang right now."

I was still trying to figure out how the police thought I could be of assistance. "You want me to grill my land-lady?"

Matt coughed into his hand. "I think a simple conversation might suffice," he said. "Adolescent girls are reported missing all the time. They usually turn up in a few hours or the next day, having given the parents a good scare. But sometimes there's a lot more involved than a teenage temper tantrum. Missing girls who join the Spiders are serious trouble. The really tough ones, girls who were born on the street, are quick to teach crime to the more innocent ones, ones who come downtown from the suburbs, from Scarborough, Etobicoke and North York. But those suburban kids know a few tricks of their own. And sometimes they're the ones with the weapons, guns stolen from Daddy's collection or even, sorry to say, Mommy's purse."

I could have feigned outrage at this, but why bother? I had lived on the street and in the ravines of the city for five years. I knew the score. "What am I looking for, Matt?"

"For now, just watch and listen. Any mention of Carrie or the Spiders would help us out. Any indication of a change in girl-gang activity might also be useful."

"Change?"

20

"Yeah. Names. Locations. Report back whatever you get."

I smiled. "That's all it will take for you to gain a few extra brownie points with the brass?"

Matt didn't answer that question. "If you agree to work with me on this, Portal, I can put you on the payroll. And who knows, helping us out again, you might make 'Citizen of the Year'."

I decided to give the matter some thought. I didn't want to be "Citizen of the Year" and I was starting to feel the hot breath of the taxman on the back of my neck over the money I already had, but I needed to find something to do with my time before I began to behave like a bum again, or worse, gave into the temptation to write a book about my life.

"I've got to sleep on it, Matt. I might talk to Tootie. But I don't need to be on the payroll and I don't need to get awards."

"So now you're rich and you've already been 'Citizen of the Year'?" He said it as if both ideas were the greatest joke. And they should have been. Except they were true. I couldn't expect Matt to remember the contribution to society I'd made when I was a judge but I was beginning to understand I'd best remember it myself.

CHAPTER TWO

After I got to know Tootie Beets as a good landlady, I asked her where she got her name. She said "Beets" came from the dark red lipstick she wore that made her look as though she'd been eating beets and "Tootie" came from a mystery novel one of her friends stole from the library. It was as good a street name as any. Like all the street names I'd ever heard, it somehow fit for no reason anybody could define. There *was* something mysterious about Tootie. She started out as one of the suburban kids Matt had mentioned. I calculated that she must have about an eighth-grade education, since she ran away at fourteen. Her grammar and her values amalgamated the middle class she'd been born into and the street class she'd chosen for herself. Sometimes she avoided profane language so strenuously that I wondered whether she might be religious. Other times, she let loose with the profanity beloved of her peers. I found it fascinating to listen to both Tooties. She liked rules and people who knew how to obey them. But she was also a wild one and her china-smooth, powdered-white skin, thick jet-black hair and blood-red lips marked her as a child of the streets.

My own street name was "Your Honor", and that suited me just fine. My complicated professional history had commenced in an immigrant Italian neighborhood in Toronto's west end and came to a screeching halt in front of a judge who found me guilty of assault causing bodily harm, no small embarrassment to me who sat for ten years in the criminal courts at Old City Hall Courthouse before alcohol, drugs, illicit sex and overwork destroyed my life. The judge discharged me on several conditions, which I felt I could best obey by disappearing into the maw of the city. After six months in a mental hospital and six months sleeping on the downtown streets, I hit on the idea of living in one of the wilderness ravines in the Don River Valley that cuts through the city core. One day I discovered part of a human body and became a reluctant detective. The attention that caper garnered led to a temporary job with the city. A second murder case brought me back downtown and one day, taking a nostalgic trip through my old Italian neighborhood, I was startled to find that a house I'd once owned and lived in with my wife and children was now owned by Tootie Beets.

I had mixed feelings about Tootie, but for the most part, I felt protective and paternal. I couldn't deny, though, that she protected me, too. As long as I was her tenant, which I'd now been for a year, I could put off finding a real home, a real future. I asked myself how I could live in a rooming house and have to properly dispose of my divorce settlement of 3.5 million dollars, struggling to prevent half of it from being grabbed by the CCRA, Canada Customs and Revenue Agency. The old name "Revenue Canada", like a street name, had been shorter, scarier and more honest.

I found Tootie in the front parlor of the house sitting

23

on a worn leather armchair, her long legs thrown over the arms of the chair and her slender body draped across its seat. She was dressed as always like Elvira, Queen of the Night, the sexy, ghoulish TV movie hostess. Black pants, black T-shirt, black boots with a dozen silver buckles. A silver chain with a slew of silver keys dangled from her neck. Her face was wrinkled in intense concentration. She didn't look up when I let myself in, but she called out to me before I reached the first landing.

"Mr. Portal, I need you to tell me what this means." I turned and faced the young woman as she stood near the bottom of the stairs. Tootie was almost as tall as I. I liked the fact that when she spoke, she locked you with her dark brown eyes. Most judges consider direct eye contact to be a sign of honesty. Sometimes it's a sign of an exceptional ability to lie. She clutched a piece of letterhead from the Sheriff of the County of York. "They're going to take my house." Her red painted nail tapped the paper as if to eliminate the miserable news.

"What?" I said, not sure I had heard her correctly. "Why? Are you behind in your mortgage or are there liens on the property?"

"Nothing's leaning on it. I keep it in good shape and nobody else's house touches mine." The dark eyes glistened. Was tough Tootie about to weep?

I smiled despite myself. "A lien is a claim against the property by a person to whom money is owed."

"No! I don't owe money," Tootie claimed emphatically. She stamped her heavy boot, setting her various metal accessories vibrating with an incongruously merry tinkle. She shoved the letter at me.

I found my glasses and took a look at the letter. Tootie stood close enough to me that I caught a whiff of her perfume, a blend of coconut and lime. I was surprised to notice the scent and slightly embarrassed, as if the fresh, youthful zing of it were indecent in my old nostrils. Wilfully, I applied myself to the document at hand. The letter was complicated and it took me a few minutes to understand it. "The Sheriff's office is informing you that a property development firm, in cooperation with the city's non-profit housing commission, has bought up every house on this block except yours," I explained. "This letter says you have a right to name a fair market price for your house within the next ten days. The developer is about to have your house appropriated by the city so that his housing project can commence."

"You mean the city and them are tearing down my house to build houses for poor people?" Tootie asked. "That's freakin' stupid, plus not fair. My grandmother bought this house and left it to me. It's mine and it's all I got."

I studied the letter again. "I think it's worse than that, Tootie. This developer isn't building homes for the poor on this street. He's building million-dollars-a-unit condominiums. There's a unit allotment for low-cost housing. That means he builds twenty expensive homes here and one cheap home in another part of town."

"I don't get this crap. Fair value? What's that supposed to mean? And what's 'appropriate' or whatever you said?"

I tried to think of a clear way to explain how the city was approving the destruction of low-cost housing to replace it with luxury accommodations. Words failed me. "If you don't sell your house to the city, Tootie, they'll take it and give you what they want to give you rather than what you ask for."

"So I don't have a choice?" A tear slid down her

25

smooth white cheek making her look like the sad clown paintings that decorated every wall of the house.

"You have no choice at all about the appropriation," I told her. "And little choice about the method of determining compensation unless you go to court. You'd need a lawyer."

"But I can't afford one!" She yanked the letter out of my hand. She bit her bottom lip, her teeth white against the reddened skin. She was the picture of an outraged citizen. "You used to be a judge. Doesn't that mean that you used to be a lawyer?"

"Tootie, I can't help you. I'm not a lawyer anymore." I felt helpless and hopeless — worse, ashamed. "Even if you had a free lawyer, it would be a long fight and it might be nearly impossible to win if everybody else on the block has sold. Besides, would you want to be the only house on a street full of condos?"

"Don't act like such an old loser!" She scowled and I caught a glimpse of an anger that probably had served her in confrontations with weaker people on the street. I wasn't inclined to mess with it myself. "At least you could tell me somebody I could call!"

I spent the next hour on the phone and I did manage to get her an appointment with a real estate lawyer who was a friend of a friend from the old days. I was pretty sure the consultation would prove futile, but Tootie was so pathetically grateful that I didn't have the heart to discourage her. But I had no scruples about using her gratitude to get her to open up about the Spiders.

"Today I saw a police officer who says he knows you," I began.

She gave me a look that said, "Big deal." Girls like Tootie know a lot of policemen. I didn't want to risk mentioning the name "Solomon". There would be young people around who didn't know Matt had used that cover. For all I knew he might still use it from time to time.

"The officer's name is Matt West," I went on. "He said you might be able to help me out if I asked you about the Spiders."

I thought she flinched slightly, but I couldn't be sure.

"I don't know any cops anymore," she said. "Why would I? I'm a honest landlady. And I don't know about gangs, either." She shrugged and a long earring made of linked metal objects I once knew as roach clips softly brushed her white neck. "Anyway," she added, "nobody I know gets a Black Widow tattoo these days or any tattoo unless they're onto the Ferryman. Some people get a Ferryman tattoo."

Surprised at this gratuitous information and fairly sure it was being offered only to keep up my interest in her appropriation problem, I pressed for more. "I never heard of the Ferryman. Does he have followers? Is this a new gang?"

She flashed me a look of pure unadulterated rage. I recognized it even though I'd not seen it in years. It was the rage of the little hookers and shoplifters and check bouncers I'd sentenced in my court. It was the look of my lawyer-daughter Ellen before she grew up. It was the look of a person not yet twenty-one who still thinks the young are entitled to keep their secrets from the old. I knew when to back off.

Alone in my room, I wished I could talk to Queenie. Not because her late daughter Moonstar had worn the Black Widow tattoo, but because Queenie was my friend, possibly my only real friend. Sometimes I thought about the two of us, drunk and half-frozen, huddled in Yonge

Street doorways silently shaking with laughter when some self-righteous passerby asked us why we didn't get a job. Now we were on the mend together. It was I who had helped Queenie get back on her feet, using part of the small fortune from the shared marital assets I thought I had forfeited when I hit the skids.

I'd also accumulated sick pay because my friend Stow had looked after my interests. I'd sat on most of the money now for the six months since my divorce became final. It gained interest by the hour but it was building up a big tax bill I didn't have the cash to pay. This could be solved by investment — but in what?

Until I could straighten this financial problem out, I eased the shock of having some funds again with a few small extravagances and one major one. I sent Queenie back to her home in the Cree Indian settlement of Moosonee, Ontario, nearly a thousand miles north of Toronto. She was attending the College of the North, had begun only a few weeks earlier, after having studied all summer on a crash course to catch up on the basics missed in her scanty early education. Queenie didn't have a phone, nor were her literacy skills yet good enough for correspondence. I felt I had sent her away without thinking enough about what I was doing. I wanted her back. Maybe I wanted something I couldn't admit to. The brisk, insolent perfume of Tootie Beets had stirred me in an unexpected way.

I glanced around. My once-plain room was stuffed with my new possessions. A compact, expensive television with built-in VCR and DVD sat on top of the ancient chest of drawers Tootie had provided. On the floor crouched the menacing black mass of my stereo system, complete with speakers I couldn't work, and disk players

I didn't need. I had a notebook computer and a complex phone system that recorded every message along with the time, date and name of the caller. It could tell me how many times in the last twenty-four hours the same caller had phoned even if the number was unlisted or blocked. Glancing at the digital display, I saw that someone seemed to have been trying to get me all day. I pressed a key to display the phone number of the caller. It was a local number I didn't recognize. I pressed another button. "Caller's name unknown," read the screen. I assumed it was the tax department harassing me.

I was so intent on reading the display that I wasn't expecting the phone to ring and I jumped when it did. The digits in the box showing the number of calls from the same source advanced by one. Afraid to lift the receiver, I pressed a button labeled "monitor".

I heard a raspy male voice, a voice damaged by age, illness or drugs. "Ellis, please don't be alarmed. I realize you cannot have expected to hear from me. I don't mean you any harm, I assure you. But we must talk as soon as possible. I don't expect you to return this call, though I imagine you have ways of tracing the number. I will call again."

The voice sent a shiver along my shoulders. A judge never forgets that there are people who have reason to hate him. And a man who has been down and out but who has suddenly had a reversal of fortune is never forgotten by his old pals from the street. I reached down to erase the message and the record of the eighteen times this man had called. In the shiny surfaces of my electronic equipment, I saw myself reflected for the second time that day, looking almost civilized. One rainy autumn night, Queenie and I sat on the curb and watched to see whether her piece of floating trash or mine would win a race in the gutter. That night I caught my reflection, too, and was filled with humiliation. Then my piece of trash beat hers and we went and had a drink to celebrate and I forgot my humiliation. I no longer had the consolation of drink or the consolation of Queenie. I fiddled around with my radio until I found a station that could put me to sleep.

The next day Tootie Beets shed a few more tears. She called a house meeting and as her six tenants sat around the same table where we'd celebrated the last Christmas, she announced, "I talked to a lawyer today and she said I better tell you that everybody here has to find a new place in one month. A rich developer is forcing me to sell my house and pushing us out like we are just nobody." She took a deep breath and her voice didn't falter, but once again rivulets made tracks in her pale face powder.

Hers were not the only tears. The single woman tenant began to weep, too. The men seemed subdued. I sympathized with the marginalized lot of them. "I tried to give a decent home to people who just had to obey the rules and pay the rent," Tootie said, "and you guys were real good. I'll give out letters to prove it. Just ask if you want one. I really hope nobody gets shafted by some grabby old landlord who makes you pay a lot of money to live in a crummy dump. If I ever get another house, you guys are gonna be number one on my list."

For one wild minute, I thought of buying a house for Tootie to run so that we all would still have a place to live. It was going to be hard for these people to find housing in Toronto without proper bank letters and proofs of employment. I didn't want to think what sort of impression a reference letter from Tootie would make on a prospective landlord.

But I realized that the purchase of a rental property was not the best use of my funds. Maybe I *did* need a paying job that I could use to satisfy the taxman's claim on my interest until I could decide what to do about my principal. It was time to get serious about Matt West's offer.

"Sit down, Portal, and take a look at this," was all Matt West said when I told him I was interested in learning more about the Charington/Carrie Simm case. One-handedly he slid a DVD into a slot in his computer, and I realized he was better at operating his system with one hand than I was with two. I knew him well enough to know what he'd say if he had caught me grimacing. *A. Don't be patronizing, Portal. B. Anybody could operate better with one hand than you can with two.* He clicked away with his mouse while he explained, "This is a disk we had our visuals people put together. They compiled every clip shot by TV crews covering the film festival the night Simm was shot. The guys edited out scenes without the victim or his daughter and they cut the sound, so we can follow the strong visual narrative."

Suddenly the screen was completely filled with a crowd of formally dressed people, men in tuxedos, women in the sleeveless, low-cut gowns of late summer. I recognized the usual film gala types from my pre-decline days as a potential movie investor and budding coke aficionado. The camera lingered now and then on a beautiful, unknown face, but it seemed impatient for celebrity and hounded the stars, capturing the toothy smile of any famous face it could snare in the press of people outside the Yonge Street theater. Anybody could buy a ticket to the film festival opening-night gala if he had the necessary money, but almost nobody could get close enough to the real heroes of the evening, the producer/director of the featured premiere, Charington Simm, his star, Carrie Simm, and her co-stars, two American actors who were household names. The four were visible for a fraction of a second as they exited from a gray Rolls Royce before being swarmed by screaming admirers. Even with expert editing, the police DVD changed viewpoint abruptly, showing that the camera had been jostled by fans. Fans even crowded around several bodyguard types who arrived simultaneously in a separate limo and whose well-cut suits didn't hide their exceptional muscles.

"I can hardly see Simm at all!" I said, staring at the feeding frenzy.

"Keep watching."

The crowd parted for a moment and the camera zoomed in on a tall, lean gray-haired man in a tux the color of the Rolls. "There's Simm," I said, "but where's the daughter?"

Matt clicked on a "pause" button. "Up at the top of the screen," he said. "Simm and the girl got separated for a minute when they stepped out of the car. You can see one of the bodyguards trying to get her back to her father's group."

I studied the screen. I had once owned a painting that for a short time was suspected to be an unknown Manet. It wasn't, but it was beautiful, full of the light of early evening reflected from the silks, satins, jewels and eyes of a glamorous, excited crowd. The frozen clip was like that and at the very top, a tiny face surrounded by a spiky halo of coppery hair was just barely visible. Even as a blurry oval the size of half of my smallest fingernail, the face looked perfectly symmetrical, as exquisite as if painted by a master.

Matt clicked again. The camera closed in on Charington Simm. Since there was no sound, I had to guess what he was saying, but I'm sure he was touting his film, praising his people. Square-jawed, lightly tanned, blue-eyed and intelligent looking, Simm was conventionally handsome, but there was something hard about his face as well, a mask thinly veiling wariness or wiliness. I felt I wasn't seeing the real Simm at all.

But that was not how I felt when the camera finally caught Carrie.

"How old did you say she is?" I asked Matt.

"Fifteen."

She looked much older than fifteen and somehow at the same time, much younger. As if it had no color of its own but had taken on the glow of the rapidly setting sun, her hair was a flaming cloud of golden red. Her skin seemed almost translucent in its pale flawlessness, her cheeks tinged with a peachy pinkness like the cheeks of a babe, but drawn tautly over fine high bones. And her wide eyes, the same blue eyes her father had, burned with an intense inviting light. She was young and old, innocent and knowing, smiling but harboring some secret sorrow.

In an instant the beguiling face on the screen was gone and I was again staring at the pushing, screaming crowd. They all seemed to be trying to get into the inner double doors of the theatre at once, moving as one squirming mass toward the funneling front foyer.

There were several overhead views of this, and I began to wonder why the editor hadn't cut them when, for no visible reason, the motion of the crowd suddenly shifted dramatically the way I had often seen the wind shift the ripples of the river or a flock of birds turn as if on a pivot and fly as one in a direction entirely opposite to that they had been taking only moments before.

"What's happening?"

"Watch." Matt didn't freeze the film this time. Moving with the cohesion of a thick liquid, the crowd flowed away from the theater and back toward Yonge Street. I sensed Matt watching me as I watched the DVD. He reversed and played the segment again. And again.

And then I saw what he wanted me to see. There was one small portion of the crowd that was forming a circle, like a whirlpool in water.

"That's where Simm went down," I speculated.

"Right. See how the crowd is circling around him —"

"Did you get those people?" I asked. "They must have seen something or somebody, despite the fact that no witnesses have come forward."

"I've been told Homicide identified every one of the immediate circle. No one heard a shot. There was so much shouting . . . And everybody claims to have had his or her eyes only on Simm, not on anybody else in the crowd," Matt replied.

I tried to make out who was where in the seething crowd. "Where's the daughter now?" I asked. "I don't see her anywhere near him. I —"

Before I could finish my sentence, I saw her. Here too there were several views of the same scene. The cameras that captured her were so close together and the editing so expert I felt I was watching an art film. A man lies on the sidewalk. A lovely young woman in a flowing white gown throws herself on top of him and cradles his bleeding head. And then she does it again and again and again, each time from an angle only slightly different from the last until the scene seems like some tragic, repetitive dance.

Without saying anything, and as if he'd done it several times before, Matt froze the next frame. It showed the face of Carrie Simm looking directly into the camera. A face on which grief and regret mingled with shock and disbelief. It was so clear a picture that you could see her eyes overflow with tears, so compelling a sight that at that moment, I felt I knew her. Like any father, any right-thinking bystander, I wished I could wipe the suffering from Carrie Simm's young face. Compelled by an overwhelming sense of powerlessness, my eyes unable to leave the screen, I watched the picture jerk and jump back into action. The camera appeared to be shoved aside by an authoritative arm and for a few seconds all that was visible was a long shot of the prone body sprawled on the sidewalk, visible between the kneeling, grieving daughter and an officious medic who was dramatically taking the pulse of the victim in a gesture that looked futile. Carrie leaned over and put her cheek against her father's chest as if her tears could restart his heart. Then the monitor went blank.

There was a moment of silence during which I had plenty of time to recall the rage of Tootie Beets and the secretiveness it indicated. "I'm not sure how I can help you," I said, "but I'm willing to give it a try. I talked to my landlady yesterday and she certainly knows something about the Spiders."

"What did she give you?"

"Not a lot. But she did let it slip that nobody uses the Black Widow tattoo anymore. Then she volunteered the name of what sounds like another gang. She said, 'Some people get a Ferryman tattoo.'" Matt nodded as if this bit of information was no news to him. He perpetually received tips of every kind, so it was always hard to know whether you might be telling him something he had already heard from someone else sharper or faster, or had simply figured out for himself. I wondered sometimes whether Matt's reticence was a result of his being homosexual. More likely it was the result of his being a cop. I wasn't in a position to ask him. "I'm willing to talk to Tootie again," I offered. "But now my time with her is limited. She's preoccupied with a major problem of her own. The city has authorized a commercial expropriation of her house."

"What does that mean?" Matt asked the question as he smoothly removed the video and replaced it into its precisely labeled case. I noticed someone had removed the front of the case so that Matt didn't have to wrestle with it. I imagined the Toronto Police Service provided a pretty thorough rehabilitation program for injured officers, and good sensitivity training for the officers who worked with them. But I still couldn't understand how Matt managed to always appear so calm. His lover, William Sterling, had disappeared three years earlier, the same year the madwoman had hacked off his hand. As if he knew I was thinking about him, he looked up at me impatiently. "Well?"

"A developer bought every house on the block but Tootie's," I explained. "She acted surprised, but I suspect she had opportunities to negotiate and either turned down the offers or ignored them. I talked to a real estate lawyer and she told me that the city is a partner with the developer on the new housing project. The developer was able to apply a municipal bylaw forcing the sale of Tootie's house."

"So now you're out of a place to live, too?"

"Yes," I said, changing the subject. As curious as I was about Matt's private life, I didn't like him asking questions about mine. "Simm was murdered a whole week ago. Homicide must have good leads by now."

"Forget the killing," Matt said. "That's Homicide's lookout. I'm not interested in who offed the prick. I'm sure there are plenty of people who figure he had it coming. I might even be one of them."

I was surprised at Matt's uncharacteristic display of emotion. I wondered whether he'd had run-ins of his own with Simm. Parents of runaways are sometimes allies of the police. But more often, in my experience, they are adversaries. You don't deal long with kids before you start taking their side. I'd had to watch myself when I had extremely young criminals in adult court. I had to remind myself that criminality can be full-blown at a very tender age. Sympathy under the wrong circumstances not only erodes justice, it can also allow a public danger to roam the streets unfettered.

I suspected Matt knew a few things about Charington Simm and his daughter that he didn't see fit to impart to a civilian, even a civilian he was intending to employ.

"What's my next step on this?" I asked.

Instead of answering, Matt studied a 4-by-5-foot wall map of the city like a king gazing with patient fondness over his own domain.

"Carrie Simm is out there somewhere," he said. "She's scared. She's already alienated every teacher, social worker, police officer, doctor, truancy official, Children's Aid worker and halfway house volunteer who ever dealt with her. In the whole city there was only one man who could control her once in a while and now he's dead. Where did she go?"

"It shouldn't take a genius to figure it out," I offered.

"Too bad, Portal. I heard you're a genius." Matt gave me a look that was half sneer, half smile.

I guessed it was appropriate to smile back. "I don't like to make promises, but maybe I can at least find out whether Carrie is connected to the Spiders or the followers of the Ferryman, whoever that is."

"That would be a start," he answered. "And —" He rose, which I took to be a sign that our meeting was over, "your working for us will get Deputy Chief Jayne Corelli off my back."

I walked with Matt to the top of the stairs. As his left hand reached to shake my right, there was a nearly inaudible clink. The detective wore a large, heavily embossed gold ring and so did I. His had been given to him by William Sterling, missing and presumed dead. I had been given mine by Stow the day we both became lawyers. A lot of water had flowed under the bridge since then, including that of the raging Don River that had swept William to his death.

My world was full of people with complicated pasts and uncertain futures

CHAPTER THREE

I'm known to be an arrogant man and one of the advantages of arrogance is that you don't have to take expert advice.

Maybe Matt West thought solving Charington Simm's murder would not necessarily lead to finding his daughter. I couldn't see it any other way. In my experience, police pride themselves on their ability to focus, to zero in on a fact or a suspect. Judges are different. They like to see the larger picture. And at the center of the picture of Carrie Simm was the cadaver of her father.

Against Matt's advice, I set out the day after our chat to learn what I could about the dead director, especially about his final days and his last film, which, I noted from the arts pages of the big dailies, was being hailed as that twenty-first-century paradox, the "instant classic".

From window displays on trendy Yorkville Avenue, the unofficial commercial headquarters of the fall film festival, I saw the ten-day event was still in full swing. In one window, a mannequin dressed like Marlene Dietrich, with her foot up on a kitchen chair that looked like Tootie's furniture, held a placard announcing that the closing gala would be that very night. Common knowledge told me tickets to the gala were sold out months in advance. The papers were still splashing "Director's Killer on the Loose — Daughter Remains Missing" headlines across their front pages, turning even devoted festival fans into ticket scalpers. The top seats were being hawked in front of the refurbished Yonge Street 1920s theater, the Splendour, the way ice hockey scalpers used to hawk them at Maple Leaf Gardens before hockey moved out and condo dwellers moved in. A thousand dollars wasn't enough for the front row at the closing ceremonies. Even a thousand dollars American.

So I had to figure out a way to get in without a ticket.

Fortunately, both judges and bums have experience at attending events without the trouble of paying. In my old life, to accept a large gift that would influence judicial decisions was illegal and unethical. But there were plenty of small gifts extended to me as a prominent member of my community, gifts that it would have been ungracious not to accept. Everything from baseball tickets to Christmas breads came my way and I took such tokens of support openly. Of course, when my luck ran out and I had to figure out how to sneak into shelters and soup kitchens and sometimes people's garages and basements, different ethics applied, or so I thought.

The crowd in front of the Splendour was neither as large nor as boisterous as the crowd had been in front of the theater when Simm met his end. In fact, this was a somber group. Word had apparently got around that mourning was the appropriate attire for the evening. Almost everyone was dressed in black, gray or white. The official security team for the event wore black jackets over dark trousers. I was in black slacks and a white shirt myself.

Both the high-profile nature of the event and the added publicity meant that extra security had been hired to monitor the entrance to the theater. The top-notch people — personal bodyguards, Toronto Police, even the RCMP — would be assigned to celebrities and dignitaries. But there were enough non-celebrities around, plus enough of the general public standing on the sidewalk trying to get a glimpse of the stars, that more additional security officers were needed, men and women like the officers whose regular jobs were in the courts. They wouldn't be going through any special background checks or complicated identity procedures. They wouldn't be wearing uniforms or carrying weapons, either. But they might have a password or special instructions when they reported to the security office for duty.

It took me a few minutes to figure out that the security office was a little booth off the south side of the inner lobby. I saw that the southern door to the lobby seemed to be the one a number of service people, including the extra security, were using to get into the building. I stood in line, faked a company name that sounded like a security firm, said I'd been lent by them, added a meaningless code number and flashed my library card for good measure. That not only got me in, it got me the use of a black jacket only one size too small.

My disguise allowed me to mill around until I could get my bearings. The crowd soon grew to fill the three tiers of the lobby, each level lushly carpeted in red and reached by a massive central staircase. Gold-and-white heavily embossed wallpaper, accented with scrolled white plaster molding, gave the huge auditorium a theatricality that robbed it of elegance. Marlene probably felt more comfortable in her store window than she would feel here.

The imagination of the movieland mourners seemed unlimited, as lavish in understatement as in flamboyance. A solidly built woman in black denim cut-off jeans and a white stretch-lace tank top traded condolences with a tall thin man in a white satin tuxedo. A young woman with upswept black hair and a long gown made entirely of feathers the color of a raven lifted a champagne flute to touch the lip of a similar flute held by an old man in gray silk army fatigues. A plethora of well-dressed people, too. Plenty of Ralph Lauren, Armani, Donna Karan. But on the whole, the Toronto movie crowd, at least those at the final festival gala, looked a little unsure of itself. As if Cannes mixed with L.A. was being interpreted by people who had been to neither.

I was beginning to think that Matt had a point and that I was wasting my time with the Simm crowd, when I caught sight of a familiar face. They say on the street that if you stand still long enough, sooner or later, somebody you know is going to hit you up for something.

"Your Honor! An unexpected pleasure . . ."

Everything about Sammy Lito was small-time, including his ability to turn a profit on his cocaine-dealing business, but he did get around and he was clever in a limited sort of way. His black jeans and well-cut black suit jacket didn't look secondhand until you got close. The outfit, and his thinning black hair pulled back in a long, narrow pony tail, along with his single gold ear loop were appropriate wherever Sammy might find himself, in a business meeting, at a posh reception like this one, or in jail.

The first time I saw him, Sammy stood arraigned before my bench in a tight black T-shirt intended to show muscle but showing instead the skinny arms of a man who was going to be in danger from tougher men in jail. He gave me a long speech about how he promised never to touch coke again. I calculated it perfectly safe to grant him bail on the 20-piece (20-dollar) drug deal he was up on. I also calculated I'd see him again and I had, a hundred times on the street. He always treated me the same, with a sort of amused contempt that didn't hide the fear he harbored of displeasing me, as if I still had the power to make things easy or hard for him.

"What are you doing here, Sammy?" I asked him. "Did you strike it rich?"

A waitress went by with a tray of cucumber slices topped with anchovy paste and some red objects that looked like bloodshot eyes. Sammy reached out but instead of taking a canape, he gave my shoulder a little squeeze that I understood to be an awkward show of camaraderie.

"Hey no, man," he said, "I got a little work now, but I'm not rich." He paused and looked around the room with his perpetual nervous eagerness. "You, though, I hear you won the lottery."

"Not exactly."

He smiled, a tentative little crescent that revealed the browned teeth of a man who can't keep his hands off the inventory. "You won something, man. You're looking good." He let his hand slide from my shoulder along the front of the collar of my shirt.

"This is a security guard's uniform . . ." I moved a step back, which wasn't easy in the crowded lobby. He moved too.

"No, man. No. You're a dresser. Always were. Good summer-weight wool slacks. Hand-sewn shirt. Nice."

I almost expected him to finger the fabric of my

trousers, but he restrained himself. He was right about the quality of the clothes but they were as secondhand as his own. I wasn't about to waste time talking fashion, though. I needed to work the room. He was in my way.

"Are we finished here, Sammy?"

"Hey, Your Honor, don't be so unfriendly. It's been a long time. Friends should talk, if you know what I mean."

"About what?"

Sammy raised his eyebrows and made a little waving gesture with his outstretched fingers. "Let's have a drink, a little chitchat. For old times' sake."

"I don't have any old times, Sammy. All I'm interested in is today. If you'll excuse me, I've got to move on."

The place was getting hot. I discarded my borrowed jacket and trying unsuccessfully to likewise shed Sammy Lito, I shouldered my way through the thick crowd. We ended up in front of a bar featuring a pyramid-shaped mound of crystal cupids whose mouths spouted streams of champagne. I couldn't tell whether this remarkable object was a leftover from the original movie theater or had been especially rented for the occasion.

Lito sipped complimentary Moët while I nursed a twelve-dollar orange juice. Even with money in my pocket I resented that being on the wagon cost more than being a lush. "See anybody you know?" I asked him.

He smirked and inclined his head. "There we have the grieving widow."

I followed with my eyes to a small group of people near a large potted flowering fig. I would have thought that Simm would have been married either to a willowy blond actress acquired later in life or else a well-preserved matron who had managed to hang in for the long haul. I

44

was surprised to see that the ex-Mrs. Simm was instead an attractive dark-haired woman in her early forties. She was one of the few not dressed in mourning. A simple natural linen suit set off her high cheek bones that were an older, tawnier version of Carrie's. The widow Simm looked composed, but sad. I reminded myself that she was technically not a widow.

"How long were she and Simm divorced?" I asked Sammy. A waiter passed with a platter of fat pink shrimp and a thick rosy sauce for dipping. I popped a shrimp in my mouth, then helped myself to another before the waiter disappeared into the crowd.

"Couple of years," Sammy answered, watching me chew.

I swallowed. "Was there a large settlement?"

"No. And first she was pretty mad about that, but then she settled down." He took a gulp of champagne. "Simm was better at spending money than making it," he added.

"But I thought his films were immensely popular."

"Yeah. They made millions, but mostly in video releases and foreign markets. It takes a long time for that money to come home to roost, if you get my drift. Plus Simm was an all-or-nothing kind of guy. He liked to hire top stars and shoot for months in weird locations. It all costs, man. It costs." Sammy shook his head. "I wouldn't want to owe some of the people he owed."

"Mafia?"

Lito laughed out loud. "Pal, the big money these days, like the sun, rises out of the East."

I didn't know what he was talking about, but he seemed to be studying the ex-Mrs. Simm's group, one of whom suddenly stepped from behind the big showy

45

ficus and into clear view. Able to keep lean only by diet-
ing, exercise or that most efficient of weight-management
programs, poverty, I recognized a man who was natu-
rally thin. I guessed this man to be about the same age as
Mrs. Simm, although it was hard to tell because he was
Asian, Chinese probably. His slim, olive-toned silk suit
hugged his slender body like a sheath hugs a knife.

"Who is that man?" I asked Sammy.

"Beats me," he answered, shrugging.

I knew he was lying and I also knew he wasn't going
to stick around much longer. Liars don't put themselves
in the way of questions.

I took a good pinch of the cloth of Sammy's jacket so
he'd have to embarrass himself if he tried to get away.
"Who was Simm close to, Sammy? Give me some names."

"Hey, Your Honor, take it easy. You got nothing on
me. And I got nothing on Simm. But if I was interested,
I'd check out his people — you know, his production
company. Maybe pay a little visit to his assistant. Talk to
some of the people in his office. I can give you a couple of
names if you'll take your hand off my jacket."

It sounded like a fair exchange, though I felt immediately guilty, as if I had reverted to the same bullying tactics of the final days before my burnout, times when I
terrorized court clerks, for example, by insisting in open
court that they go wash up if I detected cheap perfume or
aftershave and then recessing court until they complied. I
dropped my hand and with exaggerated slowness,
Sammy brushed his jacket, the way a cat licks away
unwanted petting.

I was losing what little patience I had. "Come on,
Sammy. Give me the names."

He gave his skinny shoulder one more little swipe

before he replied. "Simm's main assistant was his partner, Linda Stalton. You don't see her and Simm's ex in the same room, I'll tell you that. As for secretary-types and little wanna-be actresses, most of those babes flew the coop so fast you couldn't see 'em go. They were all lookers." He leered at me. "You could chase down a couple of those babes. You seem awful uptight, man. A bit of time with a chick might loosen you up."

I felt like punching the little worm. I clenched and unclenched my fist.

"Hey, look man," Sammy said, "I don't mean no disrespect. The word on the street is you're looking to get involved in investing, that sort of thing. Simm left some things hanging. Maybe you could get in. Why don't you just chat up a couple of his people? Tell them Lito sent you."

"Yeah, Sammy," I said, "maybe I'll do that." I turned away and this time he didn't follow. I didn't stick around for the speeches. I didn't want to hear Simm's devotees gushing about the contributions he'd made to the art of the film.

September in Toronto is warm during the day and cool at night. I was in my shirtsleeves, but I decided to walk off the shrimp and the sugary orange juice. I cut across town on College Street and ended up near a coffee bar where I stopped in for a cappuccino. The cafe was full of Italians, elderly men chatting in the flowing tones of the old tongue and young men using the clipped, wise-ass, tough English that is somehow the descendant of Italian in this town. I took the only table left, a tiny round circle of marble with iron legs, at the front of the shop. I cracked open a fresh copy of the *Corriere Canadese* and struggled through articles about soccer and politics, understanding about three-quarters of what I read. I glanced up to give my eyes a rest and to idly scan the late-night crowd parading by the window. Suddenly, beside my own face reflected in the glass, I saw the face of a corpse.

William Sterling was dead, drowned. To all appearances, Matt West had mourned him and moved on. So why did the dead lawyer seem to be standing not two feet away on the other side of the pane? His wispy hair, almost totally white, hung in long straggly strings around his gaunt face. His eyes were sunken into dark circles in his sallow skin and in the light filtered through the cafe window, his pupils looked opaque. His mouth was slightly open and I could see his perfect, white teeth. But because his face was so terribly yellowed and thin, the perfection of his teeth made them seem false. He looked a hundred years old.

But he had been born the same year as I. Like Supreme Court Justice John Stoughton-Melville, William had gone to law school with me. At the time, he'd been a champion rower, a man of exceptional physical strength. He'd also been brilliant and after passing the bar had become a successful lawyer and eventually a respected member of the gay community. He'd been devoted to the cause of equal legal rights for same-sex couples. I had gone to a memorial service for him at which the most poignant elegy had been delivered by Detective Sergeant Matt West.

Ironically, the specter on the other side of the glass was more appropriately attired for the evening than I was. He wore a clean, stylish tan trench coat, and a gray-and-tan scarf circled his throat. But so convinced was I that William Sterling had been lost in the flood in the Don River Valley, I could only assume that like Scrooge who thinks that Marley's ghost is but an undigested bit of undercooked potato, my apparition seemed the result of bad shrimp. I thought I'd better investigate. But when I rose from the table, the look of fear on the figure's face deepened and he turned and fled.

I ran after him as fast as I could. He had not disappeared like a ghost, but was running only a block ahead of me. His gait was a pathetic, loping half-hop and involuntarily, my mind sped back to when we were both young. Then, pudgy Ellis Portal couldn't have caught up with lean William Sterling on a bet.

I caught up with him now. He was only a few yards ahead of me when he stumbled, tried to right himself and ended up down on one knee. I could have run right up to him but some instinctive respect for his dignity made me stop and keep my distance until he was able to pick himself up.

He was brushing the sidewalk dust from his coat when I approached. "William?" I asked softly, "Can it possibly be you?"

He didn't say anything at first, just looked at me. I reached out and touched his shoulder. Through the fabric of his coat I could feel nothing. No warmth. No proof that he was real. "You're supposed to be dead," I said weakly.

He pushed my hand away — strongly. Rather than rejection, I felt relief. "Where have you been? What's happened to you?" I asked.

He just stared. I wondered whether he had been rendered deaf and mute, but after a moment's further silence, he swallowed, coughed and in the same breathy, raspy voice I'd heard on my elaborate telephone answering system, spoke. "I've been sick," he choked out. "I've been sick for three years."

Although I now understood he was not a product of my excitable imagination, he seemed so devastated, so far from the polished, accomplished man he had once been, that I had to force myself to picture the old William.

What I recalled was not an emaciated Rip van Winkle, but a strong lean man who three years before had come to my hangout in the forest by a wide bend of the Don. It was summer. I had a garden. I was a happy bum. Until William Sterling had blown apart my simple world with his problems with Matt West. "The last time you talked to me was the day of the flood, William. I warned you to get out. I was nearly drowned myself."

"Matt doesn't know and somebody has to tell him —" he interrupted, shooting me a beseeching glance. Again I noticed the odd light in his intense eyes. It occurred to me that he was on some strong medication. Judging from his spectral appearance, I could only think he meant he had a disease of which Matt was ignorant.

"You have AIDS, William?" I asked uncomfortably. "Is that why you pretended you were dead?"

Surprisingly, he smiled. "Really, Ellis, you are still so conventional, so without imagination. No. I do not have AIDS. Or HIV either," he declared archly. It was his old tone, the patronizing one he and Stow had perfected when we were in law school, the tone they'd employed to keep a poor Italian boy like me in my place. Until I learned to use the tone myself.

"Then what is it that Matt doesn't know?"

The gaunt wreck of a man struggled to answer. The arrogance he had briefly displayed deserted him. He fought for words; I fought the urge to get away. I wanted to be kind. I knew what it was like to have to beg for the barest necessities. When I'd been homeless, I prided myself on my independence. But there were nights so cold I cried for shelter, and mornings so bleak that I sought company even among those who shunned me. I didn't know what William wanted, but I did know how it felt to be desperate.

"Do you need money for a place to stay? Is that why you've sought me out?" I asked. I reached into my pocket and pulled out my wallet.

I thought I was being charitable, but a look of consternation flashed onto William's face. He shook his head slowly from side to side not only in denial of my offer but as if in astonishment that I had made it at all. And then, in his hopeless stumbling way, he left me and loped off down the street. This time, I lost sight of him before I even made it to the corner.

I was so shaken that I had to sit down on the nearest available seat, which turned out to be the curb of College Street, and collect my wits before I could go home and to bed where I tossed and turned all night. I had a strange dream. I was in Blane Office Tower. I was waiting for Jeffrey in his office. "Here he is," the receptionist said. A blue door opened. My son stepped out. He *was* Jeffrey. But he looked just like ravaged William Sterling.

It wasn't until I woke up that I realized what William wanted. He wanted me to tell Matt that he was still alive. Why in heaven's name couldn't he tell Matt himself?

Over the next couple of days, I conducted my own Charington Simm film festival. I rented videos of all his films and studied them meticulously, leaving my room only twice to get food.

Simm had a grandiose vision not only of the world, but of film itself. His works were complex and gigantic, often sweeping sagas that spanned generations and continents. It was easy to see where the money went. And less easy, as Sammy Lito had pointed out, to see where it came from. For Simm's vision, huge as it was, was an artistic vision, not a popular one. There was a time when I enjoyed intellectual films but that enjoyment had not survived my days on the skids. Like most people who had no money, I never went to the movies unless they were showing free at some shelter or community center. And in those surroundings, whatever wasn't thrilling was loudly booed off the screen. Watching the slick, cheap comedies and the fast, mindless action films, I soon developed critical faculties both less subtle and more articulate than those I'd had before my downfall. "If it doesn't move, kill it," was the attitude of the viewers with whom I'd come to sympathize entirely.

So Simm was far too ponderous, serious, slow, in short, too "artsy" for me.

But he did have one thing going for him. His daughter. I had no reason to disbelieve Matt when he'd told me that Carrie had spent a lot of time on the street, but she had also spent a lot of time working with her father. It seemed to me that there were rather large numbers of very young, very beautiful girls in Simm's films, but Carrie was a standout among them. She appeared in almost every one of his films, beginning with one in which she was a babe in arms.

By the time she was three or four, Carrie Simm was already an actress. I watched in wonderment as she portrayed a nineteenth-century waif abandoned on a transAtlantic voyage, a parentless girl growing up with criminal brothers in the bayous of Cajun Louisiana, a young teen running whisky for a ruthless mother during

Prohibition. Sometimes she played a central role in the story, sometimes a tiny cameo. Sometimes she spoke. Often she didn't. But she was always there, as if she were her father's muse, his talisman, the ace up his sleeve. I found myself playing her scenes over and over, studying every nuance the way I'd studied the police composite of the shooting. What was it about this girl that captured and held you until you lost track of how long you'd been frozen on a single frame?

I was asking myself that question for the hundredth time as I rewatched a video of the film Simm had made immediately prior to the one premiered at the film festival. I heard a knock, but I ignored it. I didn't want to be interrupted. But the knock sounded again, this time accompanied by Tootie yelling through the closed door, "Are you dead in there, Mr. Portal, or what? You didn't come out in thirty hours."

I froze the video and opened the door. Tootie was standing with one hand on the door frame and the other on her hip. The hand on the frame held a small white envelope. "A letter came for you," she said, flicking the envelope in my face. "I hope it's not like an emergency or something. If it is you're dead meat because I been trying to give it to you since yesterday. You're getting as deaf as the other geez types."

I took the letter and opened the door wider as if to invite her in. She swept past me and plunked herself down on the chair in front of the monitor. The film was frozen on a street scene with no actors visible. Tootie glanced away. "I don't exactly need to talk to you," she said, "but I wouldn't mind."

"Is it more news about the house?"

She shook her head sadly. "There's not going to be

any more news. Tomorrow I have to sign the papers. They're going to take it."

"Did they name a price?"

"Yeah. An okay amount of money if money's all I want, which it's not hardly. I want another house and the city won't give me enough for anything decent. The payments on this house were finished by my grandmother. But if I could learn about mortgages, then maybe I could get another good house. Do you think you could tell me about that stuff?"

I was about to answer that I'd be happy to help, when my eyes fell on the address of the letter she'd handed me.

"Hey, what's the matter? You look pale or something. Who's that letter from, anyway?"

"It's from up north, from Moosonee."

"Like from your friend, Queenie?"

"Yes."

"Well, so? How come you look so shocked?"

"I guess it's because I didn't expect to get a letter from her. I didn't realize her skills had reached the point where . . ." I heard a little gasp. I looked over to Tootie just in time to catch her staring at the television screen. She must have clicked the remote because the film was active again. Tootie was staring at Carrie Simm as if she were looking not at an image but at the girl in the flesh. I recognized her expression as the same one that must have been on my face when I'd seen William Sterling.

It was as if she were facing the risen dead.

CHAPTER FOUR

Dear Your Honor,

I guess you're real surprised to get a letter from me, but don't get me wrong, I'm not doing the writing all alone, not yet. I'm sitting by the Moose River watching the snow fall and the tide come in from James Bay and I'm thinking how different it is up here from down there where you and I had so many adventures together. I said "you and me" but my friend fixed it. She's another student at the nursing college. She's from Atiswapiskat, a settlement two hundred miles north of here. She's helping me right. Write! She just showed me explanation points. Exclamation. She's fixing most of the mistakes in my talking, too. So if I don't sound like me, that's why.

Queenie "sounded" exactly like herself in the letter, exactly the way she'd sounded in all the conversations we'd had the previous winter when I'd pretended to be a Court Services Officer so that she and I could trap a killer who was preying on desperate court "groupies". Matt had worked on that case, too. And earlier, on the sad and useless task of keeping Moonstar Johnson alive. Queenie,

Matt and I knew a lot about each other, but after the disturbing run-in with William and the unexpected arrival of this quite articulate letter from Queenie, I wondered what we *didn't* know.

As I read and reread Queenie's words, I could hear her voice, but it was a one-sided conversation. I couldn't say to her, "Tootie knows something about Carrie Simm, maybe even knows where she is, but clams up every time I so much as look at her." "Clams up" was Queenie's term, but it suited me, too. Reticence was part of her culture. Not only the culture of the Cree, but the culture of the street, which made it part of my culture, too. But if I was going to find Carrie Simm, I was going to have to do a lot of talking and I was going to have to start now. My job with the police was as good an excuse as any to avoid dealing with my other problems, chief among them the anxious feeling that sooner or later Jeffrey and I were going to have to come face to face.

Northlight-Estelle occupied a renovated factory complex on King Street near Dufferin, not far from Lake Ontario about a mile southwest of the main downtown intersection of Yonge-Bloor. A less grandiose man than Charington Simm might have chosen this location for his production company out of efficiency; it was accessible to communication and transportation services. It was central enough to be convenient but far enough from busy Yonge Street to avoid some of the horrendous traffic congestion that infested most of the city core.

But I doubt Simm even thought of these features. The minute I saw the place, I knew what had appealed to him. In the last quarter of the nineteenth century, Toronto had been a sister city to London and counted itself among the grand urban outposts of Queen Victoria's empire. In that era a prosperous industrialist would have been seen by his workers as the local embodiment of the Queen's power. He would have been perceived as little less than a prince.

Northlight-Estelle looked princely. Five six-story brick buildings, separated by narrow walkways, ranged around a central cobblestone courtyard with an ornate cast-iron fountain in the middle. Perhaps when they were new, the bricks had been red and fresh-looking, but now they were stained reddish gray-brown first by the smoke from the old industries and the old city, then by the pollution of the new. The way graying dignifies a man, the aging of these stately buildings seemed to render them worthy of profound respect, the same sort of respect Simm considered *his* due.

It was noon on a brilliant day, but the wind was cold and I hurried through the open iron gate that led into the complex. A shining brass plaque beside the main door read, "Director's Suite". It wasn't until I was standing in a small marble foyer with several tall wooden doors opening off it that it occurred to me that the complex seemed deserted.

I had expected to pass security and had planned on using a technique that had served me many times in the past, the fictitious appointment. I would ask for the woman Sammy Lito had said was Simm's second-in-command and partner, Linda Stalton. By the time her secretary checked the appointment, I would have figured out a way to force myself into the inner offices. But this proved unnecessary. One of the huge wooden doors was wide open.

Behind the nineteenth-century door was a modern

office twelve feet square. A second door, ajar, flanked a small desk that held the usual tools of the receptionist-secretary: a compact, multi-line telephone system, a fax machine, a computer, a radio tuned to a classical music station and playing almost inaudibly. A sloppy pile of unopened mail slid down toward a finely crafted leather portfolio crammed with small yellow "phone message" slips. There was a cup of coffee beside the phone. I could see steam rising from its surface.

Whatever other furniture had been in the office was gone, except for a cheap metal folding chair behind the desk. A tidy double row of mover's boxes leaned against the wall in front of the desk.

I walked over to see if the boxes were labeled, hoping for a clue to the disposal of the late director/producer's holdings, when I caught sight of a broad wooden arch at the end of a short wide hallway outside the door. Taking a step down the hall, I peered through the arch into an adjoining room.

The space was sixty feet long, an expanse of polished oak floor and exposed, sandblasted brick. Crystal chandeliers on golden chains glittered in the mid-September sun that spilled from the leaded panes of a wall of windows two stories high. Each window was crowned with a fan-shaped crest of stained glass depicting a step in the process of manufacturing a carriage.

This had to be Charington Simm's office. Despite the nineteenth-century architecture, the room was wall to wall with black leather couches and armchairs, stainless steel tables and lamps, black bookcases. Movie poster portraits of beautiful youthful film stars, including Carrie, and framed certificates of industry awards occupied all the wall space. On a shelf above a massive black

58

marble desk sat the most valuable and exotic objects in the room, three Golden Award statuettes.

In this office, too, mover's boxes sat in neat rows against the wall. All were sealed, but on the desk sat a partially filled box with the lid up. I peered in. The box held messy bundles of correspondence, most of it on the letterhead of "fisbec", FSBEC, the Far Sun Bank of Eastern Commerce. I gingerly poked the bundles, the way you poke an animal to make it move. The piles slid over. A small white square caught my eye. An envelope. On the front, written in a strong, deliberate yet feminine hand was the single word "Daddy".

I lifted the envelope. A slight scent clung to it, some girlish floral. It felt empty. I turned it over and saw that to the point of the back flap clung a sticker about two inches long and an inch and a half high. The sticker sported a pink-and-white border made up of several different renderings of the word "Love". In the center of this frame was a black-and-white photo of the faces of three boys pressed cheek to cheek.

I recognized this type of sticker. In my habitual wanderings, I sometimes idled time away in shopping malls, where I had seen a machine that produced such stickers when a couple of toonies, two-dollar coins, were inserted. Teenagers and younger children crowded around the machine trying to jam multiple faces into the picture without distorting the shot.

I dug for my glasses. When I put them on, the slightly blurry image resolved sharply into three *female* faces. Carrie Simm's perfect high-boned cheeks squeezed against the white rounded cheeks of Tootie Beets. Beside Tootie's was a feline, almost sinister visage, narrow, sly and knowing.

"Oh, I'm sorry. I would have had that one packed, too, only I didn't expect you until two. Here, let me get at it and then you can take them all away."

Startled, I dropped the envelope back into the box. Standing in the doorway was a twenty-year-old with a stunning figure and a good set of teeth. The archetypal director's secretary and would-be actress. Somebody had told this kid that peppy friendliness was a virtue. She kept up a cheery monologue while she reached into the box, juggled the packets of papers until they were evenly distributed, then pulled out one of the hidden drawers in the marble desk and bundled more letters with elastic bands from a supply on her slender wrist.

"It's so sad, that's what it is," she bubbled, "tragic. I guess lots of people are going to be out of work now that he's dead. I can't tell you how many girls got their start here. Some of them even got to work abroad — you know, in various foreign countries. I've only worked here a couple of months and already Mr. Simm had me in mind for an upcoming foreign production. Of course that'll never get off the ground now. Though I have to say, you can't walk down the street in Toronto without bumping into a movie production. I guess I'll just try for another assistant's job." She slapped the lid on the box, yanked a length of packing tape across it and sealed it shut. "Mr. Simm was a nice boss and a real artist, too. You can bet a lot of people are going to miss him." She drew a breath and smiled a Hollywood North smile. "Except for the person who shot him, of course."

Linda Stalton, Executive Producer, and Simm's second-in-command, was not nearly as forthcoming as his receptionist, although she didn't refuse to see me when the receptionist informed her that "one of the liquidators" needed a word. She stood jamming papers into a shredder, pulling her surgically perfected face into a tight frown but not raising her eyes as I entered. "Don't give me any grief about files," she offered gratuitously. "These are personal and nothing the court would be interested in."

I had been a criminal judge, not civil, so I wasn't fully familiar with bankruptcy law. Nevertheless, I was pretty certain that the court would be "interested" in any papers pertaining to Simm's business.

"If the firm is bankrupt," I ventured, "the court would need everything that reveals the state of Charington Simm's affairs."

"Is that so?" Her voice wavered with some barely controlled strong emotion. Some combination, I guessed, of rage and grief. "And just what is there left to *reveal*? Charington Simm was a bastard in a bastard's business. He threw away his own money and he threw away anybody else's he could get his hands on. Anyway, what's it to you?" She frowned again as if she were annoyed that I wasn't wearing a trucker's uniform.

She shoved an especially thick sheaf of paper into the shredder. The machine balked and spit back a shower of confetti, spraying the cool Ms. Stalton as though she were an autumn bride. "He's lucky somebody put a bullet in his head. Saved him the trouble of doing it himself when this big house of cards comes tumbling down." She gestured vaguely as if to take in the whole of Northlight-Estelle. The thought of that Victorian solidity being swept away seemed impossible, which is probably what old Queen Victoria had thought about *her* empire.

Clearly, Linda Stalton was out of control. I recalled

61

Sammy's comment about it being unlikely to find her and the ex-Mrs. Simm in the same room. Envy, jealousy, rage. If I were one of the homicide detectives, which, I reminded myself, I was *not*, I would have checked out that angle. But wasn't this the sort of inquiry Matt had specifically instructed me to avoid?

So what?

I plucked out of my sleeve the questionable, but only, ace I had. "Sammy Lito sent me," I said.

The hand above the shredder paused for a fraction of a second, the only warning I had of an abrupt and complete change of attitude on the part of the Executive Producer. The frowns became smiles. The bitter, brittle, defensive voice cooed, "Well, that explains it."

"Explains what?" I choked, stepping back, for the woman suddenly seemed uncomfortably close.

"Well, you don't exactly look or sound like a moving-van driver, do you?"

I almost expected her to bat her unnaturally long, thick eyelashes at me. What was this flirtation? Nervously, I looked toward the door.

"You're right," she said, catching the direction of my glance. "This isn't the time or the place." She took a few steps toward an antique rolltop desk. She opened a little door and pulled out a metallic object that glinted in the light from the windows. I flinched when she flipped open a gold business-card holder.

"What did you think it was," she laughed, "a gun?"

"No, I . . ."

She pulled out a card and scribbled an address on the back. "Here." She handed it to me, and after a moment's embarrassing hesitation, I realized I had no choice but to take it.

"We can talk tonight at my home. Come around seven. I'll be waiting."

"Talk? Talk about Charington Simm, you mean?" I sputtered, palming the card.

She frowned, then quickly smiled. "What else would we have to talk about?" She tried to hide the irritability that had evidently returned, but she couldn't fake pleasantness for long. I didn't know what the lady's problem was, but I made up my mind to accept her invitation. Either I was a more fearless detective than I had hoped or else I was a life-risking fool.

"Wow! You got a date or something? You look cool!"

Tootie was lounging on the bottom step of her front porch when I walked out at half-past six, as nervous as if I *did* have a date. "What are you doing out here?" I asked, stepping over her.

"I'm taking one last look at my trees. I bet those developer animals are going to chop 'em all down even with autumn leaves on 'em and everything." She squinted up at me, "You're not half bad for a relic. Who's the lucky broad?"

"This isn't pleasure, it's business," I retorted.

"'If your pleasure isn't business and your business isn't pleasure,'" Tootie chanted, "'then you're not in the Life.' I heard a hooker say that once. You think it's true, Mr. Portal?"

"Sometimes business *is* pleasure, Tootie," I answered. "But I have a very strong premonition that tonight is not one of those times."

How right I was.

Half an hour later, I stood on Linda Stalton's flagstone patio and took a deep breath before I worked up the courage to press the brass doorbell of a very small house on a very exclusive stretch of Highland Avenue in Rosedale. From behind the door I heard the melodious cascade of an expensive set of chimes, so I expected a maid to open the door. I was taken aback when Linda Stalton answered herself. I could see at once that seduction was not what she had in mind. She wore the same clothes I'd seen her in earlier, a red suit with silver jewelry, all edges and angles. "Good," she said. "You're here."

She pointed to a doorway and I preceded her into a sparsely furnished living room. The modest decor puzzled me. She held a top position in a large production company and should have been drawing a hefty paycheck.

"Can I get you something? Wine? Water?"she asked. Her tone was rushed, perfunctory. She nodded curtly when I chose water.

She left me standing there while she went off to attend to the drinks. I still couldn't guess what our meeting was intended to accomplish, but I hoped it would include some information about Simm's business dealings if I could keep the discussion impersonal.

I heard her heels click down the hall and she reappeared with a tray that held two bottles of water and two glasses. She put the tray down on a small table, then handed me a bottle and a glass. Her hands were unsteady. I hadn't noticed that when she'd been stuffing the shredder. She sat in one of the stark room's two simple chairs. I sat in the other. "I've admired Charington Simm's work for a long time," I lied. If I feared any resurgence of the passionate denunciations of earlier in the day, I needn't have worried.

"Yes," she said, "he made some wonderful films." She took a sip of water, "But that's not all he worked on."

"Yes, I understand he's been remarkably supportive of young talent."

Linda Stalton stared at me as if I were a complete idiot. "You *did* say you came because of Sammy, didn't you, Portal?

"What?"

She stood and as she did, I was sure I saw her stumble and hit her leg on the edge of the chair. But she gave no indication that she felt pain or was thinking about anything except the intense words she spat at me. "Look, let's quit wasting all this time. Sammy said you're looking for a business to invest in."

I'd given up film investing about the same time as my wife had figured out that my film friends were also my cocaine suppliers. I wasn't about to tell Ms. Stalton *that*. "I'm not interested in financing films, I'm sorry if Sammy gave you that impression. I'm interested in Simm, what kind of artist he was, what kind of man."

"Forget that," she said, jerking her glass to her lips and gulping her water. "Sammy says you're an ex-judge with a record. He says . . ."

I pushed away a gut feeling that I better get out of there. But anything that had to do with Charington had to do with Carrie and I wasn't going to back down before I'd even got started. As if she realized there was a chance I'd bolt before she got what she seemed to be after, Linda Stalton sat down and slowed down. "You're correct," she said. "Investing in films can be dangerous. Charington was a genius. But his vision was too big for his budget. Always. Some of his films were made with as little as five percent of his own capital. He made a major feature every

65

two years. There was no way he could keep up with his bankers and backers. They've closed in like turkey vultures now that he's dead. They would have picked him clean even alive. He's lucky he went when he did."

Suddenly, it occurred to me why her decor was so modest. I took the chance of pressing her even harder.

"Simm convinced his employees to be backers, too, didn't he?"

"Don't be ridiculous," was her only comment on that theory, but she kept her eyes on mine. I got the uncomfortable feeling she was appraising me and finding me inadequate for her plans. Any moment, I felt I would be bade goodbye. So I was amazed when her taut features registered a conspiratorial look and she asked, "Does the term 'chipping' mean anything to you?"

The question was so unexpected that I had to search my memory. "It means using heroin in small enough doses to convince yourself you're not addicted," I ventured.

"It's a business like any other business," she replied. Now it was my turn to stare at the utterer of such an idiotic statement. Until it dawned on me that she was actually making perfect sense. "Are you telling me that Simm was involved in drugs? That he was an addict?" As soon as I said it, I saw I didn't have it quite right. "No," I amended, "a trafficker. Simm was a trafficker — that's how he raised the ninety-five percent. That's the other thing he worked on!"

"Chipping isn't addiction," Stalton defended. "All you need is a little to get by on. Charington looked after his people. He made a big point of shooting his films in order. He'd start on page one of the script and shoot until he was on the last page. Let me tell you, that results in some major sitting around. Talent gets restless. They're not going to work for a director who keeps them in their trailers all day, day after day. So we provided. And they were grateful. Chipping is very relaxing; it's the most amazing feeling when you first get started."

I didn't need any euphoric descriptions of drug abuse. "If you've been 'chipping' as you call it for the many years you've worked for Simm, I'd say you're a complete addict by now."

She squared her shoulders and stared me down. "From what Sammy tells me, you're no stranger to drugs yourself. A man who judged criminals and was one has got a lot of contacts. And the tax people are sniffing around you, too. So it must be clear to you that you need, and can get, a high, fast return on your cash. When Charington died, part of his business was left hanging. You're in a position to pick up on that. That's all I'm saying."

She was being suitably vague, but I got the gist. I'm a little past outraged indignation, but I was insulted. It's a cliché of the drug world that there's a hierarchy of the hooked, and hooked on heroin is at the top of bad. I knew many a cokehead whose only claim to self-respect was that he'd never done horse. It was an excuse I'd used myself.

"I made a mistake in coming here," I said. "And you made a mistake in asking me to come. I'm not going to become a heroin dealer — not to you or any other of Charington Simm's druggies."

"You've made a number of mistakes yourself, *Judge* Portal," she sneered. "And you're making another one now. If you're not willing to follow the rules, you'd better stay out of Charington Simm's game. Think about that."

With cool command, she heel-clicked across the

uncarpeted room and showed me the door. It was a good performance, just as if she wasn't desperate for a fix and furious that she hadn't been able to score one off me.

I had to stand outside her house and do a little more deep breathing before I could make my way over the bridge between her street and the poorer neighborhood of the Sherbourne subway station. I didn't know why I was so upset. Maybe it was because I was a recovering addict myself, along with a lot of other recovering bad habits. I felt sorry for Linda Stalton. Like a number of Charington Simm's "people", she'd lost more than one life support when he died. Even though a drug dealer was a good thing to lose, you still felt the pain, *literally* felt the pain.

I decided the anxiety that gripped me was also due to an understanding of my own vulnerability. Word seemed to be getting around that I had money and was willing to invest it. It was not particularly reassuring to realize that Carrie Simm's father had been dealing drugs to his associates. That would connect him to suppliers who were, as his friend Sammy Lito pointed out, nobody as old-fashioned as the Mafia.

I thought about the fear I'd sensed in Lito at the film gala. Who else was he afraid of? He had obviously become some sort of a hanger-on in Simm's crowd. He seemed to know all the players: Simm's widow, the suave Chinese whom I'd seen with her. Carrie had been part of this crowd, too. Clearly Sammy was involved in Simm's drug dealing. Were they all?

The last thing I wanted was the first thing I got when I reached home.

"I understand you're looking for a new place to live."

"My living arrangements are a private matter, Stow,"
I said, pressing the speaker button on the phone and
stretching out on my bed. I felt bone tired from the day's
sordid revelations.

"Sit up, Ellis. I can't converse with a man who is
supine."

Startled, I popped up and perched on the edge of
the bed with my bare feet on the floor. "How did you
know . . . ?"

"One of my former partners is the judge who has
signed the city's expropriation orders for the entire block
where you live." Before I could tell him that wasn't the
question, he added, "The human voice changes drastically with changes in bodily position. I'm surprised you
never had a case that depended on evidence of that
nature."

Well, excuse me, Perry Mason.

"I called to tell you that I've changed my own living
arrangements, Ellis. I'm somewhat embarrassed to be
speaking to you about this because I'm aware that I was
rude to you at the time of Harpur's death last December."

"You accused me of killing her, Stow."

"You suffered a loss, too, Ellis, but I could only bear to
be mindful of my own. I can't say I've made much
progress in putting her loss behind me, as it were. So I
decided it might help to sell the house and buy a condominium on the Toronto waterfront. It's absolutely lovely.
Overlooks the harbor and the lake beyond."

"Congratulations, Stow. I wish you happiness."

Ignoring my sarcasm, he continued, "Ellis, you could
buy in the same building. There are no units left for buy-
ers without sponsors, but I can . . ."

"No, thanks."

"No" was not a word with which John Stoughton-Melville was fully familiar. "You'd have a large suite, completely serviced: housekeeper, cook. But more importantly, the investment opportunity is absolutely unparalleled. If you invested three million right now, I guarantee you would be looking at five million in less than two years' time."

"I'm not interested, Stow."

"I can certainly arrange a bridging loan if the tax people are getting anxious."

I wasn't about to point out that I'd rather sleep under a bush, which I was, after all, particularly good at, than waste my money providing luxury accommodations for myself. I am no hero but I've learned an old truth, which is that no honest man rests until all honest men rest. "Thank you very much, Stow," I said as politely as I could, "but I've already made other arrangements."

"A proud man never knows who his friends are," Stow said with a softness that was menace, disappointment or both.

"Yeah, Stow. I guess he's lucky that way."

He laughed. Nothing is more angering than to have a man laugh at your insults, especially if the laugh is genuine, almost jolly. It irritated me that Stow had an exceptionally merry laugh for such a serious, almost frightening personage. "If you change your mind, Ellis, don't hesitate to contact my office."

Over the course of the next few days, I had ample occasion to regret my rash dismissal of Stow's interest in my predicament. If there is anything as depressing as being evicted in Toronto, it has to be the torture of looking for a home under duress. Some people *become* homeless because they can't stand the process. I was lucky now. I could use Matt West as a job reference. I had a bank account. I had an accountant who could vouch for my present financial stability. I even had Tootie's offer of a recommendation. But nothing saved me from the exhausting and sometimes humiliating little dramas played out by me and prospective landlords and landladies all across the city.

"It has a lovely view for a basement," I was told as curtains were swept back to expose a window three inches above the asphalt of a driveway.

"The greenhouse has been completely renovated since the drug dealers were ousted in June," another landlord helpfully informed me just as I was about to tell him I'd take the top floor of a beautiful century-old home on a quiet street overlooking a park. I could just imagine who strolled there at night.

"At two thousand a month, I admit it's a little steep for one room, but still, you can't get much closer to Yonge and Bloor."

I still had absolutely no intention of buying in Stow's "vertical mansion," or even his neighborhood, but it occurred to me that his condo must be empty most of the time, since he actually lived in Ottawa. Perhaps I could stay in one of his rooms for a week or two until I could investigate suitable alternatives to the totally unsuitable homes I was being shown.

When I broke down and called Stow, he amazed me by expressing delight at the prospect of my acting as a glorified houseboy, though of course he didn't put it that way. I found his magnanimity suspicious, especially when he said, "I'll send one of my people to pick you up." I declined. I took public transit for old times' sake, the old times in which I had cared so much about

Stow's opinion of me that I lost track of my opinion of myself.

I had no trouble finding the building. It occupied a slim spit of land extending out into the harbor at the bottom of the city. When I had worked for the city two years before on a project to revegetate the Don River valley after the great flood, I had heard of a proposal to turn this abandoned industrial site into a harbor park. The proposal, I was told, was the brainchild of a brilliant young urban designer who wanted to recreate the harbor the way it had been before the arrival of white men. I was supposed to meet the designer but I'd been too occupied with my own work in the valley. Later I learned his project had been defeated by a narrow vote in city council. Instead, the land was sold. The grain elevators that had once sat on the site had been razed but in their place, I now saw, rose an incongruous monument to another age and clime. Instead of concrete towers in which grain had been stored awaiting shipment across waterways frozen for a third of the year, I saw glowing in the autumn sun, a stone palace fit for a Mediterranean king. It was an elegant rectangle of peach-colored marble comprised of row upon row of arches framed by fluted pillars. At the very top, an ornate frieze of laurel wreaths circling medallions was supported at each corner of the building by a larger-than-life marble statue of a woman staring across Lake Ontario to the country beyond the blue waters. Despite the rich classical folds of the garments of these colossal goddesses, that far country was not Greece or Rome. It was Niagara Falls and Rochester, New York.

I was checking my pocket for a streetcar token to get me out of the neighborhood when I was startled by the approach of a liveried doorman who informed me that the young man was waiting for me.

What young man? I felt a chill breeze off the water, a reminder of the coming of winter. The hobo's memento mori. I followed the doorman.

We crossed a lobby of dark green, highly polished, silver-veined stone and stepped into a small elevator that carried us soundlessly upward. When the elevator door slid open, I found myself face to face with my son.

I think both of us gasped, but I'm not sure. My first thought was not about Jeffrey at all. It was about Stow and his underhanded, manipulative control. "Son," I said, "Jeffrey, what did Stow tell you?" I'm sure I stammered.

"He told me to be here if I wanted to see my father." Jeffrey sounded cool and composed.

I wanted to embrace him. I wanted to apologize. I wanted to tell him how much I regretted all the wrong things I'd thought and done and been. I wanted to promise that if he would just forgive me, I would never be proud, stupid or confused again.

Of course I did nothing of the sort. This was not my excitable Italian father with his peasant's ideas on the expression of emotion. This was I, Ellis Portal, a man of the law and the streets. All I did was stand there and gape at the lean, handsome person who seemed to be studying me.

The years between twenty-one and twenty-nine had turned Jeffrey from a boy to a man, but they had erased none of his boyish good looks. The smooth blonde hair, the icy blue eyes — his mother's eyes — only cool instead of warm, the slim build that hinted of unexpected strength. "You look great, son. My God, you look so great!" Despite myself, I took a step toward him.

He extended his hand. I thought he was embarrassed by the emotion I was trying so hard to hide and wanted to calm me down with a business-like handshake. "Easy, Dad," he said, and I realized he had extended his hand because he thought I was about to fall. The thought struck me as funny. I began to laugh.

"Are you all right?"my son asked. He looked alarmed. There was no doubt in my mind that he knew how things had gone for me since I'd broken off contact with him. His sister, Ellen, would have told him every-thing because I asked her to. Jeffrey might well think I *was* a crazy old man. Actually, at the moment, I felt that way. I couldn't even think of an answer to this simple question even though I had planned for years what I would say if I ever saw him again.

Smoothly he stepped into the breach of my muteness. "Stow said you're looking for a place. I'll show you around. FSBEC has a stake in this, so it's as good an investment as you'll find."

He sounded like a recording, as if Stow had told him what to say to save face in case the efforts at forcing a rec-onciliation failed. "FSBEC?" I asked. The Far Sun Bank of Eastern Commerce of whom Charington Simm had been a client. "Jeffrey, I shouldn't have come here. I'm not really interested in living in such a grand place as this."

"This place is like a nightmare, isn't it?" Jeffrey said, and for the first time in what may have been a decade, I saw my boy grin. "It's so absurd. They've designed this building in such a way that every door in the place is invisible when it's closed. Like something in a bad mys-tery novel. I'm glad you don't want to live here. It's the first good thing I've heard about you since I reached the age of majority."

Stunned by his blunt statement, I didn't know whether to laugh or cry. I smiled. Jeffrey smiled, too. "Come on," he said, "let me show you around. I promised Stow I'd keep you here for a quarter of an hour. He loves the place so much that he thinks you'll be sold, too."

I felt so euphoric at this unexpected meeting, this undreamed of rapport, that I didn't even think to ask why Stow was so eager to get me involved in this project. But I felt a stab of jealousy when we began to tour the apartment. Why was my son so close to Stow that he had intimate access to Stow's apartment?

I decided to be happy first and ask questions later, which turned out to be wise. The old silence descended between my son and me and we said little as Jeffrey led me through Stow's palace: the mahogany-panelled billiard room, the fifty-foot long dining room done completely in white marble, the master bed suite with its own swimming pool, whirlpool bath, sauna and gymnasium.

It wasn't until we reached the stone balcony with its waist-high balustrade that we regained the comfort we'd briefly achieved. In companionable silence we gazed out at the sapphire waters of the lake. The two big corner goddesses stared down on us with maternal expectation. I studied the distance between them. "Why this apartment occupies the whole width of the building!" I observed.

Jeffrey shook his head. The sun skittered in his hair. "Stow is ecstatic about this building and when I'm out here, I can see why." He gestured toward the expanse of Lake Ontario as if to say that even a Great Lake was not too large an item for Stow to appropriate to his own use. Slight as the gesture was, it showed both disgust at Stow's greed and admiration for the man's vision. Jeffrey had the easy grace of Stow, the confident stance, the reticent manner, as though he would never waste a word. He could have been Stow's son. Maybe, I thought, he should have been.

"The view is magnificent," I responded, my eyes scanning the scene, coming to rest on the shifting bands of azure and turquoise where the inner harbor joined the deep indigo of the outer harbor and the lake.

In answer, Jeffrey merely nodded. Then he shot me a sidewise glance. In his cool eyes was a flicker of a question, a flash of warning or rebuke.

I stepped away from him and sought the comforting sight of the steady horizon. From some distant beach not visible to me, a vee of geese took the wind, rose into the clear sky, undulating with a rhythm that mimicked the waves. "If I said I was sorry for everything, Jeffrey, would it make any difference?"

He smiled again, softly, ironically, I thought, but he didn't answer. Instead he asked, "What should I say? Should I tell Stow that you're going to live here for a while?"

"Jeffrey," I answered, daring to move closer, to lay my hand on the fine silk of his suit, "why don't you tell Stow to dynamite this monster into a heap of rubble and let Lake Ontario wash it away piece by pretentious piece?"

The geese caught an outward breeze, adjusted their orientation, then disappeared over the water. Nothing stopped them in their southbound flight. Not even the sound of a crazy old man and his son laughing into the wind.

CHAPTER FIVE

I asked Jeffrey for nothing and I offered nothing. We parted without promising to see each other again, but I knew we would. I awoke the next morning feeling euphoric and nostalgic. I decided on the spur of the moment to investigate the building Jeffrey's mother and I had lived in as a young married couple. I dressed quickly and dashed downstairs. Tootie was in the living room packing. We nodded to each other before I bolted out the door and hailed a cab. A persistent, cool drizzle dampened the city as I sped north, then east along Eglinton to the residential neighborhoods bordering a deep and familiar ravine of the Don River.

On a side street a little past the intersection of Eglinton Avenue and the ravine, I got out of the cab and on foot cut through a deserted parking lot behind a low-rise apartment building. I stopped dead in astonishment at the wreck before my eyes, an abandoned red brick low-rise. The exterior was dark with grime and whole sections of brick had fallen away, revealing cinder block beneath.

Across the front of the building, rusted iron balcony

railings curled beneath broken windows. At the front entrance to the building, a splintered glass door stood permanently ajar as if the ghosts of former tenants still came and went with impatient energy. Cast-iron letters above the door had once proudly spelled out the name "The Suburban", but now all but the first and the last letters had rusted away. The sun had set indeed.

Late in the summer of 1968, when every other young person in the city seemed to be a hippie, Jeffrey's mother and I asserted our solidarity with the establishment by moving into the most conservative, middle-class building we could afford. We stood at our living room window and gazed at the view. Beneath us, a paved parking lot, wide enough for two rows of cars, gave on to a forested slope that descended toward a broad bend in the Don River. In the middle of this bend, a boulder rose twenty feet above small white rapids like a guardian of the valley and the waters. Beyond the river lay a meadow, beyond that an old apple orchard and farther still, a steep cliff that dropped precipitously to a gorge cut into the northernmost portion of the ravine. The building seemed an absolute heaven for young marrieds. Breathless from the stairs, the view and the excitement of being newlyweds, we had unrolled our new carpet and made love on it. How sad that the intervening decades had done even more damage to the marriage than to the derelict apartments.

Now I made my way along the side of the building that led to the rear parking lot. I wasn't surprised to see patches of green where grass and weeds had triumphed over asphalt. The rear walls also sported crumbling concrete balconies. Since they faced north over the ravine, the balconies had once been a spectacular place to spend the warm days of summer. Involuntarily, my eye sought the balcony of 417. A frayed and faded blue umbrella mounted on a dingy enamel table drooped in the mist.

At the north end of the parking lot, a row of ramshackle garages gave way to a muddy path into the ravine. I had taken the path countless times in the past, and I negotiated it with confidence now, despite the slipperiness of rain combined with autumn leaves. I was soon soaked to the skin but that was nothing to me. One of the things I'd learned as a homeless person was that if I ignored rain I soon forgot that it was raining at all, except for freezing rain, which is another story altogether.

By the time Jeffrey was born, his mother and I had moved from the Suburban, but I used to bring him back to this ravine to teach him about nature. His pudgy, little-boy hand clinging to mine, we'd stand on the lip of the ravine watching hawks soar over the river and the old meadow. Once a red fox came down to the water to drink and Jeffrey said, "Daddy, do animals like the city better or the country?"

"That depends on whether you are a rat or a cow," I had answered. Of course it was the wrong thing to say to a five year old. I could see Jeffrey struggling to understand what I meant. I kneeled in the soft grass so my eyes would be level with his. "Jeffrey," I said, "I think every animal, every creature, is happiest where he feels he is supposed to be."

The rain ceased as I followed the path into the restored wood that was once a meadow. I was already beginning to pick up the muffled roar of the rapids, and a walk of a few minutes brought me to the bank of the river. On this dull day, the water above the rapids was a deep green, turning white where it encountered the base of the big boulder before rushing several miles down-stream to Lake Ontario. The name of the ravine was Wig-more and near this spot by the river, perhaps driven by the same nostalgia that was driving me now, I had built my summer encampment when I became homeless.

I followed the river now, searching for remnants of my former home. Though the flood three years earlier had scoured the valley, it had been quirky in its rise. Parts of this ravine had been spared.

But I found nothing of the garden I had once tended, a garden of plants stolen from the gardens of others. There was nothing left of any of the succession of huts I had constructed of scraps of metal, cardboard and plastic. The jugs in which I'd stored my water, the plastic boxes in which I had kept my books, the holes I had dug for hid-ing objects had disappeared. Nature had swept its green hand over my habitation and wiped it away.

I turned from the site and prepared to cross the flat central forest of maple, spruce, oak and ash toward the remaining trees of the ancient apple orchard and the cliff at the northern extreme of the ravine. As I moved, my eye caught the glint of gold on the ground, some object partly obscured by a fallen red leaf.

Immediately, I thought of the golden ring worn by Matt West. If Matt was still wearing it, didn't that mean that he still cared for William, still mourned him? Sooner or later, I was going to have to tell Matt that William was not dead after all.

I bent down to retrieve the bit of gold, but it was noth-ing but a piece of foil from a cigarette pack. I shoved it into my pocket and walked on. I found the northern cliff so eroded that I risked plunging over by standing at its edge and peering hundreds of feet down to where the river, fast flowing because of the autumn rain, made a wide and gracious bend.

I began to descend with eagerness to revisit the scene of my life as a "bush person". Despite my genuine remorse for the errors that had led me to homelessness, I sometimes missed the freedom of that life, the anonymity, the lack of harassment from landlords, taxmen, and "friends". As I scaled down the slick cliff, I realized to my dismay that I was nowhere near as supple as I'd been when I'd been living rough. After much grabbing of tree branches and brush, I managed to make my way to the foot of the cliff. Here the erosion was much less dramatic and the familiar features of the area nearly unchanged from the days when I had made my winter home here. The river bend in the forest had provided enough shelter in summer, but once winter gripped the city, I needed more. Unlike Queenie and her pals downtown, I refused the indignity of stretching out under a piece of plastic strategically tented over a warm subway grate. Being claustrophobic, I dismissed even the idea of sleeping in one of the underground heating pipes that criss-cross the city. A man I knew had been cooked to death in one.

In a cave by this bend of the river, I had not felt claustrophobic but enclosed, embraced by the wall the river had made to protect itself. On this autumn day, I paused to reflect, the street people were probably already lining up to score sleeping bags from the free stores, already vying for the eight-foot squares of Styrofoam discarded by furniture outlets, or else steeling themselves for a winter's incarceration in the shelters. But not the bush men I had been. We had other ways of surviving winter. I had my cave.

81

Nothing had changed the perfection of the spot, a rock carve-out about ten feet deep and thirty feet wide, opening onto a pebbled beach and the water's edge. Even in winter, this water seldom froze, but because it was polluted, I could not drink or wash in it and had to use laboriously melted snow.

Across the river from this site another cliff rose hundreds of feet toward a crown of red oak and dark green blue spruce at the top. On a still winter day, one could build a fire on the beach and sit looking at the trees and the sky and forget entirely about the piercing cold and the great pulsing city only blocks away.

But today my cave showed no trace of habitation and no matter how congenial and sheltering this spot had once been to me, it struck me as shameful now. A man who looks backward cannot walk forward, Queenie used to tell me. I couldn't live with Stow, or in the Suburban or in a hole in a wall, either. I had to get serious about my future.

That afternoon, I found Tootie hard at work in the kitchen. She wore a tight black skirt about ten inches long, white stockings and knee-high, leg-hugging platform boots in some glittery material that sparkled when she moved. A ruffled pink-and-white striped apron tied around her neck and waist with large pink bows completed the ensemble.

"Everybody but you and me found someplace to live," she reported. "Those two student guys got rooms at the university. That old fossil — older than you, anyway — he went back to live with one of his kids. Even Elizabeth got a place. This social worker dyke came for her from a battered women's hostel." She pronounced it "hostīle", but I didn't correct her because I was sure she'd mispronounced it on purpose. "I don't know where the other two went," she continued, "but all their stuff was outta here this morning, except for this crap."

With both hands, she scooped cutlery from a drainboard by the sink, held it over an open cardboard box and let it fall with a loud clatter. As they fell, I could see that no two pieces were alike.

"I guess everything came from Good Neighbor Helps thrift shop," I commented.

"Yeah, right. And there's where it's going back to." Tootie waved her hand in a gesture that seemed intended for the entire house. "Furniture included. I'm leaving this place like I came. With zip minus zero. Nothing."

"But this was your grandmother's house, Tootie."

"Yeah," she said sadly. "When I was little and I used to sneak here to get away from my so-called parents, this house was full of great stuff. Books and statues and paintings of forests. But, like I told you a long time ago, when my grandmother left me this house, I had to go to court to keep it and while I was waiting for the judge to make up his mind, my parents sold everything in the place."

She picked up a colorful stack of mismatched plates and carefully laid them in a box into which she also shoved the crushed classified section of the *Toronto Daily World*. I saw several advertisements circled in red.

"Are you looking for a job, Tootie?"

"Get real. I never had a job in my whole life. Somebody else circled those ads. Renting this house was my best and only business. Now I'm s.o.l."

She turned away and pulled a few towels from a rack, dropping them into a laundry basket on the floor. I wondered whether she was hiding tears because her voice was hoarse when she said, "Running this house was the only good way I ever made money."

"The city and the developer will settle with you soon," I tried to reassure her, even though I felt I had nothing to offer. Not even advice about mortgages. The last conventional home I'd owned had been paid for in cash.

Tootie shrugged. "Where are *you* going to live?"I asked.

I held a cupboard door open for her as she took down a few coffee mugs, examining each, then tossing them into a big plastic garbage bag. "I got an offer from some friends," she said. Something about her tone was uncharacteristically evasive, almost sly. I couldn't decide whether she was inviting me to question her further or warning me not to.

"Tootie," I ventured, "do you hate your parents for how they treated you?"

She tossed a few more mugs into the bag. Both of us winced when they crashed. "I used to," she said, "All the time drinking and fighting and cheating. Plus never home." She shook her head in disbelief. "But now, Mr. Portal, I don't hate nobody. Not even pushers or pimps or social workers or the Children's Aid or nobody."

I helped her twist the garbage bag closed and stood aside as she shook open a fresh one. "Why, Tootie? Why did you stop hating?"

"Because I been sa-a-a-a-ved." She shook her hands and rolled her eyes. I thought it a rude and mocking display, but I couldn't be sure exactly who or what she was making fun of. I helped her take down more mugs and dishes. For a while we worked in silence. Then she volunteered, "I really meant it about not hating nobody, Mr. Portal. What about you?"

"You mean have I been saved? Maybe I have, Tootie. I almost thought so yesterday. I talked to my son for the first time in eight years."

"Holy sh —" She caught herself. "Is that why you wanted to know about me and my parents? Like in case your kid hates you?"

I studied her pale face with its dark, dramatic features. I didn't know how any parent could reject a girl so wise. But then I had managed to reject a son as patient, as unmarred by bitterness as Jeffrey had seemed. "I guess so, Tootie. Parents do terrible things to their children."

"So what did you do, exactly. Beat him or what?"

"I deserted him."

"When he was a baby?" Tootie's dark eyes registered such disgust that I hastened to set her straight.

"Good heavens, no. Jeffrey is twenty-nine years old!"

She seemed to be doing a mental calculation. Finally she said, "What's the big deal? He was already old when you took off. He probably didn't even notice you were gone." Maybe she was right. It had never occurred to me that what I considered reprehensible might have been merely annoying — or even somewhat of a relief — to Jeffrey.

"Hey, lose the long face. I'm only kidding, Mr. Portal. I'm sure your son missed you. I'll miss you a whole lot, myself."

"Tootie," I said, as if it were a natural follow-up to her kind comment, "Does Carrie miss *her* father?"

It was a risky question. With rough, abrupt motions,

Tootie tore open the cupboard under the sink and began shooting cans and bottles of household cleansers onto the floor behind her. She squatted, digging deeper and deeper until I feared she was going to disappear like a mouse behind the plumbing. I toyed with the idea of leaving her, when she emerged to ask me, "Mr. Portal, you're asking questions. I got a question for you." Her tone was belligerent.

"What, Tootie?"

"If I got in trouble, bad trouble, would you help me out?"

"Why, Tootie, of course I would. But what do you mean? Do you mean the house? Or do you mean something else?" I had be careful, to say as little as possible or she'd clam up.

"Well, yeah, sure, I'm in trouble about the house but that's just, like, a temporary thing that maybe I can figure out. You said so yourself." She stared down at her hands. Despite her labor in the kitchen, her nails were long, dark red and shiny. "But I mean what if a person did something that landed them up in jail? Could a judge who was their friend get them out?"

Despite all I'd been through, I felt the old words spring instantly to my lips. "Our laws are fair, Tootie. Justice doesn't depend on friends." She shot me a look of contempt, as though I'd told her exactly what she had expected to hear from a fossil like me. "But," I added before she could say anything, "I was in jail and I had a friend who is now a judge and he got me out. If you tell me what you're afraid might 'land you up in jail', I'll tell you about what my friend did for me."

"Tell me anyway," Tootie replied.

I hardly knew where to begin. After a few moments' thought, I said, "Tootie, like your parents, I've been a fighter and a drinker and a cheater, too. I cheated on my wife and my family and even on my friends. When I was young, before I married, I fell in love with a brilliant, red-headed lawyer. Her name was Harpur Blane. She was not in love with me, though she teased me mercilessly. When the time came, she married one of my best friends, John Stoughton-Melville. Maybe you've heard the name?"

Tootie wrinkled her white brow and pursed her red lips. "Like, I should have, but . . ."

"He's a Justice of the Supreme Court of Canada."

"Wow! You really did hang with big shots, didn't you?"

"Yes."

"And that's how you became a judge yourself?"

I laughed. "It wasn't quite as simple as that, Tootie. No, the way I came to be a judge was that as the years went by, I worked longer and harder until working was all I did. After a while, my family learned how to get along without me. And then I turned to other women. And when those women were unfaithful to me, I turned to drinking for company, and I even tried drugs."

"You were a *judge* on drugs?" I glanced at her, expecting disapprobation or at least disappointment. Instead, her black eyes were fixed on me in undisguised admiration. "Wow, a person like you must really know stuff about life and all that!"

A street urchin like Tootie knew a thing or two about life, herself. So what kind of trouble was she in that she needed additional knowledge from the likes of me? I remembered the three faces on the sticker photo and I wondered if I could get her to open up about the cat-like third face beside hers and Carrie Simm's. "I was extremely foolish taking a risk like that, and extremely lucky that I never got caught. But sooner or later, my world was bound to fall apart. A smart girl like you must have figured out that something went wrong for me."

"No," Tootie laughed sarcastically, "I thought you liked living in a rooming house better than Rosedale." She leaned against the kitchen counter, her white arms crossed in front of her, and said softly, "So what *did* happen? I mean on account of the drugs and cheating on your wife?"

"One evening when I was coming out of a bar, I saw Harpur walking past. When she ignored me, I thought it was a snub. I saw her from time to time, but no matter how many years passed, I never got used to the idea that she hadn't considered me good enough to marry; she was much too ambitious. Anyway, I don't remember exactly what happened, but I ended up being charged with assault. They said I tried to choke her. I would have been charged with attempted murder if her husband hadn't helped me out."

Anybody else would have stepped away from a man admitting assault. Tootie didn't budge. I admired her for that, but I felt a stab of fear that my story would turn her off, lower me in her opinion. "Mr. Portal," she said, "are you telling me that you attacked this guy's wife and he helped you get out of trouble?" She seemed amazed.

"Yes, Tootie. That's the kind of man he is." *Can be.* "I know that's surprising, but . . ."

"It's what the Ferryman would want him to do."

"What?"

"Forgive. Live and let live. You know . . ."

I *didn't* know. I waited for her to say something more about the Ferryman. "So that's when you went to jail?"

"Yes. For a very short time."

"A judge in jail! Bummer," she said. I sensed concern in her tone and I was touched.

"I survived."

"But I guess that, like, said 'bye-bye' to being a judge?"

"Not exactly," I answered. "Judges are appointed for life and to remove one requires a hearing and other procedures. In my case, strings were pulled. I ended up on sick leave, but only after I had spent six months in Parke-Manning."

"The loony bin?"

I smiled. "The mental health center."

It seemed to me that we talked for a long time because the afternoon light faded and evening fell with that sweet coziness that overtakes a house on an autumn evening, even, I was surprised to note, a house scheduled for demolition. Tootie listened with such rapt attention that I went on to tell her about my life in the street and finally about my going to the valley and my camps by the river. She asked for specific locations, the smallest details.

"Sometimes I been homeless myself," she told me. "Like if I got kicked out of a squat by the cops. You know what I hated about it the very worsest?"

"What, Tootie?"

"Being dirty. Yuchh . . . I used to sneak into people's swimming pools in the middle of the night."

"Me, too. Except I preferred public fountains. I forgot all about the law against trespass. Like a lot of laws, that one means one thing to a judge and quite another to a bum."

"A dirty bum," Tootie said. "A dirty bum with a dirty bum!"

We both laughed, an old miscreant the mentor to a young one. But I soon became serious again. "Tootie, if you're worried about being homeless again, I don't think . . ."

"It's not me. It's somebody else." She moved away from the counter, picked up a cardboard box and marked it "hazard waste". She plunked the cleansers into it, then crossed the room, opened a narrow closet door, pulled out a broom. As she swept, she mused, "You know, if I won the lottery, I'd build a big house with three times as many rooms as here. And for people who couldn't pay all the rent, I'd make bunks in the basement. I don't want nobody to live outside. I never slept outside in winter. No way."

"You can though," I said. And I proceeded to explain how I had made myself comfortable all winter long. She seemed to hang on my every word and, flattered by the close attention of an impressionable, even if worldly-wise, young woman, I became expansive. "My cave was quite warm, really. I insulated it with plastic and card-board. I carefully made a fire to keep the walls dry, heat the place and cook. Ventilation is important. You can't make a fire until you've established efficient crosswise airflow."

"What did you eat out there?"she asked.

I told her how to look for the yellow flower of the Jerusalem artichoke that blooms late in summer. "It isn't an artichoke and it's not from Jerusalem," I pointed out. "But its roots are tubers. Do you know what those are?"

"Like potatoes or something?"

"Right. I used to roast them on an open fire. But you must not harvest them until after the first frost. On a nice October night, you can sit in your cave, eat your tuber and feel that you are king of your house," I enthused.

"I prefer my *real* house," she answered sharply and began tearing down the house rules posted all over the kitchen. *No cooking before 6 A.M. Or after 11 P.M.* She yanked a sign off the refrigerator. *If you didn't buy it, don't eat it.* She scrunched it into a ball, shot it toward the garbage bag, then picked it up when it landed on the floor.

"So, you'll go live with friends," I said innocently. "Like who?"

"I don't talk about my friends," she answered defiantly. "That's dangerous."

"Why?" I didn't expect her to answer. I reached down and held the trash bag shut while she strangled the top of it with a twister.

"Because your enemies can wring your friends' necks." She pushed my hand away when I tried to help her lug the bags closer to the back door. "If they don't shoot back first," she added, straightening her young body and rubbing her hands together.

"Are you saying you have friends who own guns?" I asked in alarm.

Tootie crossed back toward the floor near the counter where she'd left the box. "Mr. Portal," she said, sending me a stern glare, "you been on the street. I been on the street. Most people out there hate guns. But not everybody. Could we, like, talk about something else?" She dragged the box over near the bags, opened the door and pulled them out. A draft of crisp air blew into the kitchen and with it came an orange tabby cat. I'd never seen the

91

beast before. I thought one of the house rules was *No pets allowed.*

Tootie took a white china bowl out of a box destined for the Good Neighbor Helps store. She filled it with milk and whispered, "Here Star, here Starry-Cat." The tabby drank and Tootie watched until the milk was all lapped up. Then she filled the bowl again. "The reason I liked running this house," she finally said, "was so I didn't have to live alone. When I was with my parents, it was like being on a desert island. Nobody to talk to. Maybe your kid thought that about you."

"Probably."

"Well don't worry, Mr. Portal. He'll be okay. The day I ran away for good, I got lucky. Most girls, they run into a pimp at the bus station or one of the malls. There's real mean guys out there. Some of them even take girls away and make them sex slaves. I won't lie to you. I talked to Carrie Simm once or twice. She told me there's this guy from Belgium or someplace." I waited for her to finish her thought but she just shrugged.

"Did *you* manage to stay away from pimps?"

"Yeah. It was summer. I was fourteen. I was sitting on this milk crate outside the Eaton Centre mall, around the back, off Yonge Street. I was a little scared. I already ran away a lot of times by then, but always to my grand- mother. This house," she said, glancing at the dismantled kitchen. "Only my parents always hauled me home. So I finally decided *screw them.* Like I said, I was scared, but happy, too. The first time in my life I felt free. Free and afraid. Weird, right?"

I thought about the winter nights I had spent in my cave beside the river. Sometimes I could hear coyotes calling from the cliff across the water to other coyotes above my head. And just outside the entrance to the cave, I could hear the wind whistle like a hungry animal on my scent. And as the streams caught in the cliff expanded as they froze harder and harder, all around me echoed the cracking of rock.

At such times, a sense of absolute aloneness, of understanding that no one on the face of the earth knew where I was would choke me. I waited for the terror of my complete isolation to engulf me. Often it did. But sometimes, too, I was infused with such a sensation of liberating peace that I cried tears of joy. "Yes," I answered. "Weird and true."

"Anyway," Tootie continued, "this do-gooder broad comes up and starts talking to me about how I could go home again if I wanted to. She says, 'You don't want to end up in the catacombs, do you?' I didn't know what she meant, but I heard this other voice go, 'You get away from her. She's my sister and if anybody's going to take her home, it's me.' One: I don't have a sister and two: I never saw this person in my life. She had a real deep voice and I was sure at first it was a man, probably a pimp. But it was actually the Lynx."

Tootie shot me a wary glance. "I guess a person who's been a judge has seen hookers and them a lot of times. I never been one. Not really. But I don't know about the Lynx. Maybe you even had the Lynx in court. She's been around."

I saw my chance and I took it. "Why do you call her 'Lynx'? Does she resemble a cat?"

Tootie made her red-tipped fingers into claws, scratched the air and growled. "I'll always owe Lynx big-time because she saved me from the pimps and from those people that want to send a girl back to parents worse than jail."

"So this girl you call Lynx, she took you in?"

"Not hardly. There wasn't exactly a place to take me in *to*. But she did show me how to find places for sleeping and how to get food without any money. She told me I didn't ever need to turn a trick as long she was my friend. And she was right. And if I can, I'm gonna do the same for my friends."

Tootie was so adamant on the issue of friends, I wondered if Carrie was another girl Lynx was protecting, or claiming to protect. A couple of the worst pimps I'd ever encountered had been female. I threw the book at them.

As if caught up in her reverie, Tootie went on. "Best of all, with the Lynx as my friend, I got to meet other girls, girls who hung together in the malls and the parks. It's six or seven years now."

"Tootie," I dared to ask, "were they a gang, these girls?"

"What *is* a gang, anyhow?"was Tootie's rejoinder. "People make such a freakin' big deal out of every little lousy thing. We were just friends being friendly. Same as anybody. It's not like we beat on people or cut them. No way. Even those spider tattoos? Just a joke. Sometimes on the street a cool thing happens and everybody picks up on it. One day we heard you could get tattoos that looked like these black widows we saw in this John Wayne movie. To gross people out seemed like a good idea at the time."

I listened carefully to all this, but I wasn't buying it. Matt West knew Carrie from the street. She was no little fun-loving kid who got bug tattoos just to scare adults.

Neither was this Lynx person. I only needed to remember her picture to speculate that she was probably a nasty piece of work.

As if Tootie suddenly realized what I was thinking, she stopped abruptly. "Actually," she said, "I got a lot of work to do here. And you got to empty out your room. Where are you going to keep all that stuff? You haven't even got a . . . ."

"Is Carrie Simm with your friend Lynx? Is that why she's still missing? Where are they, Tootie? Do you know? Because if you do and you're hiding that information from the police, you could be obstructing justice. And that *could* 'land up' a person in jail."

If it was possible for Tootie's white face to grow paler, it did. I felt like a threatening old fool. She seemed to sway for an instant. But she surprised me. Visibly, she rallied. "Look, Mr. Portal," she said, "I think I already said I don't talk about my friends. I think you better pack up the crap in your room. Time is, like, running out."

If I felt bad then, I felt even worse when I got to my room and found a stack of empty boxes with my name carefully marked on each one — Tootie's way of being helpful, the same combination of kindness and control that I'd come to expect.

For one moment, I considered just filling a small shopping bag, leaving my phone, my computer and everything else and heading back to the ravine. I laid out on my bed the only objects I thought of saving: my reading glasses, Queenie's letter, my bank books and my black silk judge's robe with its red sash. But if a twenty-year-old girl who had lived by her wits from the time she was fourteen had enough self-respect to conclude her affairs honorably, so did I.

I stayed up most of the night and cleared my room, packing everything but a few necessary items. I left my clock radio beside the bed and set it for the morning, determined to get an early start on apartment hunting. I was ready to move to my new home.

If I could find one.

CHAPTER SIX

When I awoke my room was freezing. I pulled the blanket to my chin and sank farther into the warm depression of the old mattress. A new bed was not one of the things I'd spent my restored wealth on. To sleep on a mattress at all still seemed a luxury.

As well as being cold, the house was completely quiet. All the sounds I'd become used to in nearly a year of living with Tootie and her other tenants — voices, hacking smoker's cough, radios blaring rock music, running showers, ticking clock down the hall — had been silenced. Nothing. And in the perverse way of the human, all that I had so bitterly complained about, I suddenly and mightily missed.

I glanced over to see the time. The digital display on my bedside clock radio was blank. I checked the plug and found it firmly inserted in the wall.

Cursing the cold, I sat up, drew the blanket around my shoulders and put my feet on the icy floor. Tootie was a careful manager of her household but she'd never been a skimper on heat.

I'd left my clothes on the room's single chair, and as I

hopped across the room to retrieve them, my eye fell on my phone. The display screen was black.

I lifted the receiver. No dial tone. No static. No huff of my own breath amplified.

As if needing one last proof to convince me of the obvious, I hobbled over to the doorway and flipped the light switch. Nothing.

I grabbed the door and jerked it open. "Tootie!" I yelled.

The name echoed in the empty house. "Tootie?" I repeated softly and uselessly.

Every room of the house except my room and the kitchen was completely empty. In the kitchen stood the boxes Tootie had been working on the night before. Everything was packed, including the few utensils that had belonged to me. Even the orange tabby's white china dish had disappeared.

I noticed that the back door was slightly ajar. I opened it and peered into the narrow alley that ran beside the house. The garbage bags we'd put there the night before were gone. So were the recycling boxes, blue for paper, gray for metal and glass. The flaps of the "hazard waste" box waved in the wind.

I closed the door and locked it. Then I unlocked it again. Maybe some homeless person would discover the house and use it until it was demolished. And welcome to it.

On the first floor, the dining room that Tootie had always used as a combination office and library was tidy. The long table at which I'd seen her working on her budgets was bare, the chairs neatly placed around it. Opposite the dining room was the little front parlor where residents sat only when some guest with highly important business held them captive in one of the grim leather chairs. It was here that I had signed the divorce papers that had turned me from a bum into a wealthy man.

Taped to the front door was a handwritten note.

Mr. Portal

I'm sorry to have to leave so sudden, but last night late I got a call that my friends could get me a ride to their place first thing today. The Good Neighbor Helps truck is coming at 1:00. I'm sorry about the electricity and phone but the city has to turn them off when I leave. Don't worry about finding a place. Somebody is always watching out for you. Like me and my friends say:

$$T$$
$$F \quad M \quad W$$
$$B$$
$$T$$

The Ferryman will be there.
Love, your Landlady (EX)

I sank onto the bottom step of stairs, dropped the note to the floor and cradled my head in my hands. I had driven her away. Just as, sooner or later, I'd drive Jeffrey away again. In fact, except for those few moments of rapport with my son on the grandiose balcony of Stow's apartment, I'd antagonized every person I'd dealt with in the last couple of weeks. I hadn't reported back to Matt about the case — or about seeing William, either. I had treated Sammy Lito as though he were a powerless worm. I had confronted Linda Stalton and accused her of being a junkie. I had even taken on Stow, though, come to think of it, that was nothing new. And now I'd frightened Tootie and robbed myself of any chance of getting more information from her, let alone any chance of helping her before she ran to her questionable friends. Who were these pals who showed up in the middle of the night, anyway?

I shivered and it wasn't from the cold. If I wanted information from Tootie, other people probably did, too. I wasn't the only one who'd seen that sticker with the three faces. Presumably, Charington Simm had seen it and so had the long-legged girl who was packing up his office. I picked up Tootie's note. I couldn't remember whether I'd ever seen her handwriting.

I had got too close to Tootie, asked her too many questions, pressed her too hard. Despite what the note said, she might actually have been afraid to be alone in the house with me any longer. If that was the case, what exactly was I getting close to? If I were right and Tootie had access to Carrie Simm, was she in danger? Charington Simm's killer had not yet been apprehended. The killer's motive went unexplained. Could that killer be after Carrie, willing to dispose of Carrie's friends to get to her?

I studied the note. Who was this "Ferryman" Tootie kept talking about? There was no surer way to lure a person — young or old — than with vague promises of salvation through self-improvement. That was the obsession of the times. What did Tootie mean when she invoked the name of this character, as if he, whoever he was, could help *me*? I regretted having told Tootie about my brief and stupid foray into drug use. I hoped she didn't think I needed a dealer. On the other hand, if the Ferryman were some sort of cult figure, he could hardly lead a girl gang and at the same time offer solace to men well past their prime.

I read and reread Tootie's words, but they offered no

clue to anything except the immediate necessity to do something about my belongings. For one wild moment, I thought of calling Jeffrey for help, but I felt immediate embarrassment at the idea. The last thing I wanted him to think was that I was now some sort of a tiresome, old-man burden to be shouldered. Nor did I wish to disturb my daughter, Ellen. I even desperately thought of Stow and his million-dollar condo. Then I remembered what Tootie had said about coming to this house empty-handed.

So I packed one plastic bag after all, left all my expensive technology in boxes on the floor, walked down the stairs and out the unlocked front door in time to see the Good Neighbor Helps truck turn the corner and head up the street.

My stomach was gurgling, churning and hurting as I walked up the long, low cascade of steps that led under a canopy and up to the front door of 40 College Street. I told myself I was hungry, but my real problem was that I was petrified to tell Matt that his life partner wasn't as late as we all thought. I had no idea how I was going to break the news, but if I didn't, I wouldn't be able to tell Matt about Tootie, either. I decided the best way would be to try and find out what Matt knew.

I attempted to study him surreptitiously by standing in total silence in his open doorway, but even without raising his eyes, he knew I was there. "Corelli's been nosing around to find out whether you're coming in on a regular basis and I didn't have the balls to tell her you'd fallen off the face of the earth," he said by way of greeting. He sounded the way he always sounded. Not happy. Not unhappy.

"Hi, Matt," I said with forced nonchalance. "How have you been? Have you received any interesting news lately?"

He looked at me as if I were an alien. "What's the matter with you, Portal?"he asked in that deep cop voice they use while casually wrapping their fingers around the handle of a baton.

"Just hungry, I guess." I strolled over and selected a doughnut, a Tim Horton special: vanilla cream icing with multicolored sprinkles and a thick, sugary strawberry filling with just the right edge of tartness. I bit into it too fast, sending a red stream shooting down the front of my only shirt. I put it down. I didn't feel like eating anyway.

A slight flicker of a smile crossed Matt's face but no sign of unaccustomed joy. I tried to force myself to just *ask* about William, but when I opened my mouth, the words that came out were, "Tootie Beets has disappeared."

Matt let me babble on. "We weren't supposed to have to vacate her house for another week, but she took off in the middle of last night. She didn't even say goodbye, except for this note."

Matt took the paper from my hand and dropped it on his desk. His expression was almost patronizing. "Look, Portal, we all could use a brush-up in basic street smarts now and then. What I mean is, you get too emotionally involved with these street kids, you end up hurting yourself."

"I'm not emotionally involved," I countered. "And Tootie Beets pulled herself off the street. I'm afraid for her."

Matt didn't reply. I could see he was studying the bottom of Tootie's note with its cross-shaped cryptogram about the Ferryman.

"She goes on about that character," I offered. "I have no idea who he is."

Matt leaned back in his chair. He held his arms in some way that made them visible only up to the wrist. Beneath the short sleeves of his police shirt, powerful muscles rippled his brown skin. I found the office a little chilly myself. It was late in the year to be wearing short sleeves. Looking at those muscles, I felt afraid of Matt. He was the one in charge of the search for Carrie, not me. I got the feeling I'd best not forget that fact.

"Leave this Ferryman thing to me," Matt said. "But don't get yourself bent out of shape over it. Tootie takes care of Tootie. She puts out that she's arrow-straight right now, but she was a regular little terror when I used to run after her and her pals with the Youth Bureau. I always took her for a ringleader, but a couple of times, I could see that sometimes she's easily led, you understand?"

"Yes, Matt," I answered. "In fact, that's exactly what concerns me. Tootie *does* know Carrie Simm, just as you suggested."

Matt looked interested for the first time. "What have you got?"

"Last night Tootie opened up. She admitted talking to Carrie. She said something about a Belgian man, some sort of evil pimp. I got the impression that both Tootie and Carrie are depending on a third party, a girl with the street name of Lynx, to protect them against the Belgian."

Matt stood. One hand appeared to be in his pocket. The other poured coffee into a blue mug with four silver letters NYPD. He came back around his desk, lowered himself into his chair. I couldn't tell whether I was wasting his time. He took a long draft of the brew. "Keep talking, Portal," he said.

103

"I haven't been idle during the past couple of weeks. I know you said to stay away from the Charington Simm homicide case, but I did a little checking around anyway. Simm died bankrupt. His production company, Northlight-Estelle, is being liquidated. But apparently, Simm had another concern going on the side. His business partner, Linda Stalton, revealed to me that he was a dealer — probably even a trafficker — in heroin." I was pretty proud of this bit of sleuthing.

"I'm not sure you can trust information from a junkie who's grieving the loss of her dealer, her business partner and her one-time lover," Matt said, as if nothing I was telling him was news. Miffed, I sank into my chair. It occurred to me I could shock him by telling him something that really *was* news, but I controlled myself. As if he could read my thoughts, some of them, anyway, he continued, "Let's not get touchy, Ellis. I'm listening to what you're saying." He lifted his coffee mug and the motion caused a little breeze that threatened to blow Tootie's note off the desk. Without a second's hesitation, Matt nailed the paper with his stump. I tried to hide my shock. Matt gave me a straight stare. "Go on," he said calmly.

"The day that I was at Northlight-Estelle, I spent a few minutes alone in Simm's office. I saw an envelope from a letter his daughter had written him. On the envelope was one of those stickers the young people like so much. This one had a photo on it and in the photo were Carrie Simm and Tootie Beets. With them was a feline-looking person who could only be this Lynx."

"A recent photo?" Now he was interested again.

"It could have been taken yesterday. But there's still more. The week after Simm died, I lied my way into the closing ceremonies of the film festival. Simm's widow was there. I mean his ex-wife. She was in the company of an extremely well-dressed man — Vietnamese, Korean, maybe Chinese. Anyway, Sammy Lito, my contact at the festival wouldn't tell me a thing about this man. I was in such a hurry to get away from Linda Stalton that I didn't think to ask her about him, but she has to know him because she knows everybody else in the crowd of Simm's people at the gala. There must be a connection . . ."

"Assuming the man's a heroin contact because he's Chinese? Come on, Portal. I never figured you for a racist."

Great. I'm a racist who's embarrassed by handicapped people and afraid of black guys with big muscles. Not to mention the William mess. I felt like going home. Until I remembered that I was without one. Again. I steeled myself and continued. "Hear me out. Simm was a man who always needed a lot of money. His films were big budget. Even a hundred million goes fast when you're filming epics. Where did that money come from? If he was dealing heroin, where did the stuff come from? One way or another, I've spent a lot of time in court. It's not racist to say that the Far East has been deeply involved in heroin since the British established the opium trade a hundred and sixty years ago over the protests of the Chinese."

Matt leaned forward. He wasn't taking the trouble to hide his handless arm anymore. "Even if Simm *was* a dealer and this so-called Chinese man was his source, what's that got to do with Carrie Simm — or with Tootie Beets, for that matter?"

"Look at that note. The Ferryman will be there. He's always there when you need him. Doesn't that sound like drugs to you?"

105

"Yeah, along with cults, rock star fan clubs and ancient Greek myths," Matt answered. A thought struck him. "Do you recall seeing the Chinese man in the DVD of Simm's shooting?"

"I can't remember."

He opened a drawer and took out a disc in its lidless plastic sleeve and handed it to me. "I'm knocking off early today. I'm going out of town for the evening and if I don't get on my way, I'll never get clear of the city. I know you've got some hi-tech at home. Why don't you take this and have a good look at it."

"I can't." At the sight of the shiny disk, it suddenly hit me what delights I had so blithely abandoned.

"Why not?"

"Tootie had to empty the house, so I left all my belongings except these." I pointed to my plastic bag. "The Good Neighbor Helps thrift store sent a truck to the house to cart everything away."

Matt shot me a look of exasperation. "You're a hopeless case, Portal, you know that? Did you at least put your name on the boxes?"

As I nodded, he lifted the phone, put the handset down on the desk, then punched a series of numbers on the phone base. "Donations headed for neighborhood thrift stores are processed at a central warehouse before they're distributed around the city," he said. "Maybe I can catch your things."

I gave him Tootie's address and the approximate time I'd seen the truck. Thank God Tootie had put my name on those boxes. I felt the sting of realizing I might never see her again. Maybe I *was* too involved. Maybe I should just forget her. And Carrie Simm, too. I wasn't doing a stellar job of discovering any clues to their whereabouts. I'd been sound asleep when Tootie had run off. The most amateur sleuth in the most jejeune mystery novel would have heard her departure and tailed her. And if I was hopelessly bungling my dealings with the children of other men, how could I hope to straighten matters out with my own. *Maybe I ought to do Jeffrey a favor and forget about him, too, while I'm at it.*

"So where do you plan to sleep tonight?" Matt asked, breaking into my self-pitying thoughts. He had the good grace to keep his eyes off me as I struggled to think of an answer to this question. I was touched. Maybe he thought I'd say the "Y" or the main men's shelter with its hundreds of beds. Those days were gone.

"There's a Bed-and-Breakfast in Yorkville, not far from here," I finally answered. "Today's Friday, but I don't think I'll have trouble getting a room if . . ."

Matt glanced at his watch. "I'm screwed with the traffic already," he observed. "I might as well wait until after rush hour. Why don't I drive you over to the B & B?" He gave the situation a little more thought. "As a matter of fact, I wouldn't mind some company on this trip out to the country tonight. Why don't you come along? We can talk about that other matter."

"What other matter?" I asked in alarm.

"The matter you're trying so hard to pretend you don't know," he answered.

We waited out the rush hour in Matt's house in the charming restored Victorian neighborhood called "Cabbagetown". His house was distinctive, a brick facade enlivened by window boxes, painted shutters, pastel gingerbread woodwork and stained glass. A tiny front garden behind a fence of wrought iron and white pickets burst with the late-blooming flowers of September, especially mums in rusty oranges and muted purples. Dark green ferns, shadowed with late afternoon sun, filled the hollows with dappled light. Matt squeaked open an iron gate and led me up a short flagstone path to a red door that he unlocked to reveal a hallway stacked with boxes — my boxes.

"How did you get my things here in less than two hours?" I asked in amazement.

"I'm a cop,"he answered, as if it were the most important thing he could say about himself.

I took a quick glance around. Like the other late-Victorian houses in Cabbagetown, this one was far grander than the Irish immigrant shack it had replaced more than a hundred years before. Those early immigrants whose diet had given this part of town its name were gone, but the name remained. In Matt's living room, old brick had been exposed, wide oak-planked floors restored. On tables, shelves and the wide windowsills, smooth, polished soapstone sculptures of whales, manatees and Inuit hunters glowed in the sunlight. I realized with a start that I had seen some of them before — long before. William had begun his art collection when we were young lawyers. I felt profoundly uneasy, trapped almost. Was William here? Was he going to pop out from behind the oil-rubbed pine furniture and yell boo? I tried to reassure myself.

But no one came to welcome Matt home and he didn't call out a greeting, either. He asked me to sit and wait while he changed his clothes. I wasn't sure why he wanted me along on his drive. I dug in one of my boxes for a fresh shirt and quickly changed. I could hear Matt moving around upstairs.

Like a mouse who can tell exactly where the cat is, I began to sneak around the first floor of Matt's house. He had a number of ingenious devices intended to compensate for the loss of the use of his hand. A pedal on the floor opened the fridge, for example, and there were knee-high buttons near the doors so he could open them with his leg if he were carrying something. But these clues didn't tell me anything about William. On Matt's fridge, a number of snapshots, lined up under round magnets that bore the seal of the Toronto police, stared out into the kitchen like mugshots in a police photo lineup. The people in these pictures were black, white, Asian. There were far more photos of men than of women, but otherwise, the pictures weren't much different from those belonging to any family. One shot of two handsome men in tuxedos with white rose boutonnieres gave me a tug of guilt and regret. It was Matt and William a decade earlier.

I left the kitchen and moved through the dining room. On a table in the corner was a phone with a fairly elaborate control panel attached to two large speakers. I went over to examine them. My eye caught a carved wooden object like a hand-crafted napkin holder. It was stuffed with letters, all bearing the wildly colored floral stamps that tropical countries print specifically because they know collectors expect them. I was about to squeeze one of these letters out of the holder to learn its origin, when I realized it had been a few minutes since I'd heard any sound upstairs. I peered into the hallway. I gasped at what could only be a hallucination.

Against the backdrop of my tower of boxes, stood an exceptionally tall, strong, one-handed, black, middle-aged male in full Scottish regalia. A splash of white lace erupted at his dark throat. A black jacket in fine wool sat smoothly on his wide shoulders, narrowed to reveal his trim waist. A kilt in the boldly patterned but subtly colored Red Ross tartan of the Toronto Police Service brushed his knees. Smart white spats, accented with a flash of ribbon in the same tartan hugged his muscular calves. A long-haired white sporran with black and silver tassels was suspended on a chain from his hips. The handle of a ceremonial dagger protruded from the top of his stocking. Despite the skirt, the lace and the shaggy purse, Matt looked as formidable as Robert the Bruce.

"For generations the Scots have been the backbone of the Metropolitan Toronto Police Service," Matt declared as if he were giving evidence in court, "and I'm not ashamed to say that my late father — born in Glasgow — was one of them."

"But —"

"He married a Jamaican nurse he met on an overnight shift."

At the risk of once again being accused of political incorrectness, I decided to act as if I found nothing unusual in any of this. "Okay," was all I could say in response. Then it occurred to me to add. "Does this — uh — get-up have something to do with our drive?"

"Highland games in Kirkconnell." Matt said. "Come on. We're late."

Matt's timing was good and we did manage to get out of the city and onto the 400 highway without getting snarled in the thick Friday exodus. In an hour we were in the fertile farmland northwest of the city. The trees downtown were still green, with only a touch or two of red, but here the maples and oaks shone orange and gold. We passed towns and villages, many of which advertised

110

weekend "Fall Fairs", a favorite September and October pastime in rural Ontario.

All the while we traveled, I kept thinking of how to tell Matt about William. Even though I hadn't heard from him again, I couldn't put our encounter out of my mind. But every time I tried to broach the topic, the conversation veered in a different direction.

"The reason I asked you along," he began, "is to have a chance to talk to you away from Headquarters."

"About something personal?" I asked gingerly.

Matt took his eyes off the road for a split second to meet my gaze. "No." Could he tell I was relieved?

"Corelli goes on and on about how hot she is for community liaison and public cooperation," he continued, "but the fact of the matter is, she doesn't understand that in order for lay involvement in police work to be more than window dressing, we've got to share a lot more information than she'd be comfortable with."

I wasn't sure whether I should be flattered or suspicious at being the invitee to this private little tête-à-tête. He was driving his own car, an unassuming Saturn rather than a screaming cruiser, but in my life on the street, I'd been picked up a few times and I was starting to remember what it felt like. "Why would you want to tell me things in your car that you couldn't tell me at the office?"

Matt burst out laughing. "I thought we agreed this wasn't going to be personal, Ellis."

I felt so embarrassed I wanted to jump out of the car and join the cows munching grass in the fields beside the road. But Matt went back to business.

"Ellis," he said, "I want you to tell me everything you know about that Asian you mentioned."

I wished I could tell Matt something startling — or at least helpful — but I couldn't. "I already told you, Matt. I saw him at the gala. He was very well turned out. Beautifully cut suit, expensive-looking but not a designer I've ever seen before. I think that means he doesn't buy his clothes in Europe or North America."

"Good," Matt said.

Since this was the first word I could remember him utter in praise of my work, I felt confident to continue. "The man was perfectly at ease at the gala. No sense of his being an interloper or wanna-be. You get that at these film events, but not from him. He seemed to know Charington Simm's wife."

"Did you observe them talking?" Matt asked.

I realized that I hadn't actually seen the Asian speaking to anyone. "No, Matt," I reported. "And that's it. That's all I know about him. Except that when I asked Sammy Lito who he was, Sammy said he didn't know."

"Sammy would say he didn't know his own name if that suited his purposes," Matt said. He glanced out the window and studied a string of signs at the edge of the highway. "Not far now," he observed. "So," he went on, "the next thing you hear is that both Tootie and Carrie are afraid of a Belgian guy." Matt's voice was slightly patronizing as if he were showing off for a trainee.

"What are you talking about?"

"You really helped me out this morning, Portal," Matt said. "Before you told me about the conversation with Tootie, I had nothing but a hunch to connect her and through her, Carrie Simm, to Harmensz van Rijn."

What the hell was he talking about? "I'm lost, Matt."

"We're almost there," he responded.

"I'm not talking about this drive . . ."

"Me either," Matt answered. "Harmensz van Rijn is our Asian."

"That's some name for a Chinese."

"Tootie may think he's Belgian, but by birth and citizenship, he's Dutch. Ethnically, he's Hakka. Ever hear of them?" He didn't give me time to answer. I would have had to say no, anyway. "There's a sizeable Chinese population in the Netherlands and a good proportion of them are Hakka," Matt explained. "They go way back, these people. Some claim they're the original inhabitants of China, the indigenous people. But they were driven out of their own territories generations ago. Even in China, they're known as 'the guest people'. Regrettably, they're also known as first-class crooks. But dabbling in the international heroin trade is only a pastime of some Hakka, what guys like van Rijn do in their spare time."

I was beginning to get it. "And what this character does full time has something to do with Carrie's disappearance, something worse than heroin dealing or homicide? I can't imagine."

"At the moment, I can't imagine, either," Matt said. "I've handled a lot of missing kid cases in my time. This one stinks. Where's the tearful mother on the nightly news begging for her kid's return? Where's the touching portrait nailed up on lampposts? Everybody except Charington Simm gave up on this girl a long time ago. And I think he would have given up on her, too, if there wasn't any further way he could use her to make money.

"So there are many who wanted him dead," I observed with the acumen of Jessica Fletcher.

"I told you before, Portal. Charington is not my problem. Carrie is." He hesitated. "And that's why I need you to go deeper."

"What do you mean deeper?" I didn't like the sound of this.

"You're going to have to find Tootie Beets. There's no other way. And when you find her, then you're going to have to get her to take you to Carrie."

I felt totally out of my element. "Why can't you do this, yourself, Matt? Why can't you use your Solomon cover again?"

Without taking his eye off the highway, he raised his right wrist.

"You can do this, Portal. You're not a bum anymore. You pulled us out of the fire twice before, solving cases nobody else would bother with. Forget Solomon. I need you to go undercover with your hobo routine."

"How am I supposed to do that?" I thought about my age, my weight, which was beginning to show the effects of all those Tim Hortons treats, and my creaking bones. "If I start questioning street kids," I said, "they're going to warn each other that some old guy is poking his nose around. I'm afraid my interrogation of Tootie is what caused her to disappear."

"All the more reason for you to stay with me on this one." Turning the car effortlessly with his single hand, Matt exited onto a winding dirt road. The car didn't lose speed as he tore along, sending stones spitting up through the open window.

"You're with me, Portal. You're on the payroll. It's a done deal."

We turned off the dirt road and onto a grassy field lit by floodlights. Even before Matt shut down the ignition, I could hear the unmistakable skirl of bagpipes. He smiled. "You're going to experience a little police culture," he said, "a bit of cop color."

We got out of the car and I followed him into a tent full of about fifty men similarly dressed. They'd been at the beer for a few hours to judge by the hearty camaraderie and the noise of their laughter, augmented by the squeak of the pipes.

A one-handed man can't be a piper, even if, like his father, he'd once been a champion. He can't, like his Jamaican uncle, be a drummer, either. But he can be a drum major and Matt made an imposing one as he led the massed pipes and drums of the United Scottish-Canadian Highland Police Band out onto the field where five hundred officers stood to salute the flag to open the Kirkconnell Highland Games.

There were a lot of men out there, but I caught Matt's eye a couple of times and the second time he gave me a great big grin, as though he'd known all along I'd end up doing exactly what he wanted me to do. Typical cop.

CHAPTER SEVEN

We left the grounds at midnight, with the white stars thick in the moonless sky and our breath visible in the cold autumn air. We walked to the car in silence, but I knew the hour had come, the hour at which lovers reveal their secrets and friends discuss their faults. In the moment in which I chose to tell Matt what I knew, the only sound was the steady hum of his tires on the empty road. "Matt," I said, "I've seen William Sterling. He's alive."

I braced myself. I wouldn't have been surprised if Matt had run off the road. The reaction I was least prepared for was what took place. Matt remained silent. He kept his eyes on the road. He steered the car skillfully with his left hand and his right forearm. He set his gaze on the highway before us and he said simply, "I know."

"He contacted you? I knew it! I knew he would figure out that was the only way." I stopped, afraid my immense relief was unseemly. I was so happy to have the self-imposed burden of this revelation off my shoulders that I didn't see how grim he was.

"I've known William was alive, his condition and his whereabouts since shortly after the flood," he said, with repressed fury. "Friends wrote to me about him. He himself never saw fit to contact me. Not in three years." Matt clenched his square jaw in an effort to control himself.

Great. Here I am in the middle of the night, in the middle of nowhere, stuck in a car with a man who's going to tell me about his love life. "Look, Matt," I said with a stupid little laugh I couldn't prevent. "I suppose I could be angry, too, since William was a friend of mine, but just so long as you know — we, um, we don't have to discuss it or anything. I just wanted to make sure . . ."

"He probably thinks I found somebody else," Matt said.

"I don't know." I glanced outside. It was pitch dark out there. It never got that dark in the city, even in the valley.

"Well, I *did* find somebody else."

I don't want to know this. "Really," I said. "Anybody I know?"

"Yeah," Matt answered to my intense discomfort. "It's somebody you know, all right. But you can stop squirming over there, Portal. The man I found is me. When William disappeared and I became 'physically challenged'" — he spat the words out with contempt — "I finally had the courage to face who and what I am. I found myself."

"Good," I said inanely.

"If William's got in touch with you lately, as I assume he has," Matt said, breaking into my thoughts, "he wants something. What is it?"

This question and the tone in which it was asked

made me a little angry and for the first time since his "death", I felt a stab of tenderness, call it loyalty, for William. He had been my friend long before he'd fallen for this hotshot hunk, Matt West. "He didn't ask anything of me, Matt. Not even money, though he looked pretty ragged. Well," I hastened to add, "not his clothes, just his face."

"He has spells. When he almost drowned, he was oxygen-deprived. It caused periodic bouts of amnesia. Since he's back in Canada, he can get drugs to control it. He can live a normal life."

"You seem to know a lot about this," I ventured.

Matt didn't answer right away. He'd been through a lot in the past three years, the loss of his hand, the disappearance of his lover, and now his unexplained reappearance. He'd picked up his life and moved on. William, it seemed, had not been as strong. A decade older, he had been a mentor to Matt, but no one had been a mentor to William.

"Portal," Matt said softly, "the day after I lost my hand, the day I woke up without it, you know what I thought about first — the very first question that came into my mind? It wasn't 'Is William going to still want me?' No. The first thing I thought of was 'Is the police force still going to want me?'" Automatically, he stiffened and sat up straighter.

"If William calls you again, Portal, you tell him two things. You tell the coward to talk to me in person."

"Okay, Matt," I said quickly. "And the other thing?"

"Tell him to get a damned haircut."

"How do you know how his hair . . ."

"Just *tell* him."

We drove for a good hour without another word until Matt, mercifully, began to talk about our work again. As we neared the city, he said, "I've got a lot of respect for you, Portal. I've always known that you put yourself on the line at Second Chance."

Second Chance had been a seemingly respectable hostel in Toronto for pregnant teenage girls. Beneath its benign exterior it had also been the center of a bizarre medical scheme on the dark edge between legality and illegality. The girls were being used to furnish fetal tissue for experimental therapy. We had put a stop to that but I'd lost track of the place in the succeeding three years.

"Has Second Chance closed down?" I asked.

"Yes and no," Matt answered. "The board of directors disbanded and the corporation dissolved after selling the building. But a few of the board members moved over to Queen Street and started a new facility for female young offenders on parole and girls at risk of coming into conflict with the law. It's a good thing, too, because when Second Chance closed, there wasn't one other facility specifically for female YOs in the city. The kids call it 'Juvenile Hall', sort of a street joke. The real name is Fry Hall, after Elizabeth Fry, the prison reformer."

"I doubt that Tootie Beets would go near a place like that," I said.

"No," Matt agreed. "For one thing, "Tootie's nineteen or twenty and most of the girls at Fry Hall are under sixteen. Some are mothers already at fourteen." He paused. "Carrie is fifteen."

"Was Carrie Simm pregnant? Is that why she disappeared?" The thought of a pregnant fifteen-year-old losing her beloved parent, her emotional support, was sad. But it was only slightly worse than what had happened to my own children, having their father go from public acclaim to public disgrace. With a start I realized that Jeffrey might be trying to reach me. But how would he know where I was? I could go to his office and leave my number. Was that too bold? Too obvious?

"No," Matt said, drawing me back. "No chance of pregnancy."

I didn't like the finality in his deep voice. "How can you be so certain?"

Matt stared at the approaching lights of the city. "Because she was sterilized."

"Sterilized!" I repeated. "At fifteen?"

"The trouble with asking questions, Portal, is that you don't get to pick your answers. Yes, she was sterilized. Charington Simm was careless in some ways and very careful in others." Matt eased into the outside lane, guiding his vehicle with the effortless touch of his single powerful hand. "Carrie was pay dirt to her father when she was working and a big liability when she wasn't. In order to maximize her worth and minimize the trouble she was capable of causing, he had her surgically altered."

"How do you know this?"

"I'm Solomon the Wise, my man. I know."

No wonder Matt had referred to Simm as a prick. No wonder Linda Stalton called him a bastard. No wonder, either, that Carrie's mother had divorced him. I felt enraged, but then I remembered the facts I'd known before I worked on the Second Chance case. In the old days of involuntary sterilization of young women in Toronto, some victims never knew of the procedure. It was not impossible to run across old women from poor families who had born illegitimate children, then married, only to discover to their shock that they could bear no legitimate children because they had been "fixed" during the delivery of their first child.

"If I'm going to look for Tootie," I said, "I'm going to have to check out some of the catacombs. You told me about them and Tootie did, too. Right before she disappeared we had a little chat about our previous living arrangements. I told her I lived in the Don River Valley and she told me that she'd lived with street kids who kept her out of the catacombs."

"They're nowhere and everywhere," Matt answered as we exited the 401, the major east-west arterial north of the city, nearly empty now at 2 A.M. We slid onto the silent streets of downtown. "It's a generic term, like 'squat'. In fact the kids use it to mean practically any squat, illegal living space, that's below street level. A catacomb could be one of the ghost subway stations, like the one beneath Queen Street. Or it could be a big disused sewer or heating pipe. Commonly, it's an underground garage in an empty building. A catacomb is the most dangerous type of squat in the city, but I guess the idea has a certain romantic charm because we are constantly moving street kids out of them. It's like trying to keep a raccoon out of the attic. The more holes you plug, the more openings the little bastards find. Just once in my life, I'd like to find one kid who actually does what he or she is told."

Jeffrey. Jeffrey always did what he was told. Does he now do whatever Stow tells him? I pushed away the idea of Stow manipulating my son. He didn't work for Stow, did he? And even if he did, Jeffrey was a man, now, not a boy.

"I don't know about this idea of going back on the

street, Matt. Even as homeless people, the young live in their own world. In four or five years of living on the street and in the valley, I hardly ever encountered them, though I know there are thousands."

Matt agreed. "One of the things that breaks my heart about street kids is that they waste such imagination, such ingenuity staying away from adults. When I was working the Youth Bureau, I couldn't believe their tactics. I had poor kids camping out in the basement of rich kids, sometimes for months, without the host parents ever catching on. A kid would take his supper down to the basement rec room pretending to eat in front of the TV, and then give the food to some other kid living behind the furnace."

"I'm sure they camp out in and near the ravines, too," I added. "There are a number of old apartment buildings that back right onto the river valley in different parts of the city. But as I said, I'm too slow to run up and down ravine walls chasing teenagers."

"You never know," Matt answered. "Kids live in deserted grain elevators down by the harbor, in empty factories, in houses scheduled for demolition just like Tootie's. A squat can burn down, incinerating a teenager who's fallen asleep while stoned or even a kid who's simply built a fire for warmth or light. They're in empty schools, stores, hospitals. You don't have to be faster, Ellis, just smarter. And don't worry about Corelli," he hastily put in. "I'll tell her you're engaging in outreach among housing-challenged youth. She'll go for that. And, as I said, I've been okayed to memo the paymaster."

I thought about the taxman.

"And we won't send you out there alone, either," he

said. I didn't have time to ask what that meant. We had arrived at my new home. All I had time to say was, "Okay."

It took me a day or so to set up temporary quarters in the B & B on Hazelton Avenue. I hadn't told Matt, but I'd only been able to get a good room on short notice by calling in a favor. A couple of years before, I'd renewed my acquaintance with the owner, Margaret Ducharme. Now a dignified businesswoman in her early forties, in the old days she had appeared before me. I didn't remember her at first, but she said that I'd been lenient with her on a procuring charge and that my treatment had allowed her to chart a new path. If the location of her B & B was any indication, I calculated that Ms. Ducharme's new path was lucrative, indeed. Hazelton was alive with decorators and collectors popping into and out of Sotheby's and the Chinese antique store, the window of which displayed an exquisite screen of a slender, long-legged stork contemplating a lotus flower. A gray-and-white clapboard church, converted into a ladies' club buzzed with well-dressed matrons coming to lunch or arriving for painting and drawing classes. Chez Ducharme, with its iron gate, its gabled roof and its garden of firs, commanded a choice spot near the corner of Berryman Street. When I was a boy, I knew a lad who lived on Berryman, who could only attend school between January and June because he received only one pair of shoes a year — in the Christmas box handed out to poor families by the *Toronto Daily World*.

Years of life in the criminal courts had made me wary of dramatic rehabilitation and I feared that several of the guests in Ducharme's B & B were something other than tourists in Canada to see the fall colors, but I didn't ask any questions and neither did she. She allowed me to plug my phone into one of her lines, gave me a room with a private bath, and programmed a key card to let me in any time of day or night. Considering the "undercover" mission I was about to undertake, I thought it only fair to warn her that my personal appearance was about to degenerate, but she said that I'd fit right in with some of the arty types that were her customers.

In the meantime, I felt I needed to let Jeffrey know where I was. I didn't allow myself to observe that this had never seemed necessary before. I simply set out for Blane Tower determined to leave my phone number and address with the receptionist, hoping I'd again run into my son "by accident".

I didn't have far to go. The northeast corner of Yonge and Bloor adjoins the Yorkville neighborhood. As I turned the corner, I saw something I'd not noticed the last time I'd visited Blane Tower, which was that it wasn't "Blane Tower" anymore. This was not surprising, given that Stow had packed up his office three years before when he'd accepted the appointment to the Supreme Court. What *was* surprising was the name on the discreet brass sign on the corner of the building. FSBEC. The bank seemed to be everywhere. Either Stow had sold Blane Tower to FSBEC or the bank was his tenant.

The last time I'd been there, I'd also not checked the building directory because I already knew that Jeffrey's firm occupied Stow's old legal office. But now I strolled over to the desk of the concierge. Two uniformed men sat behind a ten-foot slab of polished gray marble tilted at a forty-five degree angle. Neither man offered to help me find what I was looking for, which was good. It gave me time to study the business names on the slab.

Jeffrey's firm was called "Urban Edge". I had no idea what that meant, but it sounded young. Except for a few other firms with equally catchy names, all the floors were taken up by divisions of FSBEC.

Feeling a twinge of nervous anticipation, I waited for the elevator. I couldn't help but remember that the last elevator ride had put me face to face with my boy. A soft chime rang. The elevator door opened. I rode. A soft chime rang. The elevator door opened.

But this time, there was no one on the other side of the door. Not even the receptionist, though she'd left a yellow sticky that read, "I'll return in five minutes." How many times had I told my secretary *never* to do that? Now I had no idea how long I would have to wait to see Jeffrey.

Who was I kidding? He might not even be there and if he was, he might be too busy to see me, just as he had been the last time. I didn't want to talk to that American lawyer of his. I peeked over the counter and spied the pad of yellow stickies. Carefully, I composed a pithy note, writing it in as tiny a script as I could manage and saying how much I'd enjoyed running into Jeffrey and how I hoped we could get together soon. I added my address and phone number. I stuck the note on the inside of the counter, level with the receptionist's eye.

Satisfied, I turned to leave.

Then I changed my mind, tossed the note in the garbage, wrote another. "Jeffrey, call your father. 416-555-1234."

Really, I was acting like an abashed, eager lover. Or

was I? What did I know about lovers? I hadn't had one in eight years.

Second Chance hostel for girls had been in an old Victorian mansion on a residential street not far from "The Track", where hookers and respectable homeowners had carried out internecine turf wars over used condoms in front-yard flower beds.

Fry Hall was in a much more sensible location, a refurbished storefront on busy Queen Street East with several floors over the store and a large detached garage in the rear, reached by a drive between the store and its next-door neighbor. In the drive was parked a brand-new Windstar. On the side of the vehicle, someone had professionally stencilled a five-foot logo of a big pink angel flying out from behind silver prison bars. It reminded me simultaneously of corrections and cosmetics.

I hadn't forgotten the conversation with Matt a few days earlier, in which we'd agreed that it would be unlikely to find Tootie Beets or Carrie Simm near Fry Hall. But I wanted to check it out anyway.

Innocuous from the front, the store had been converted into a studio or workshop. I could see one or two young women with their heads bent as if working or studying. The upper windows had closed blinds. The lower windows and doors had bars, but, I suspected, intended to keep people out, not in. There didn't seem much to learn from "Juvenile Hall".

I turned to walk back along Queen toward the nearby subway station when I noticed a group of three girls coming up the drive from the garage at the rear.

They laughed and talked in the unmistakable staccato of the young and the street. As they got nearer, I expected the usual barrage of profanity, but instead, their speech seemed demure. This gentility did not extend to their appearance, for even I, who have seen plenty, have seldom seen tougher-looking girls. An impulsive jolt of curiosity compelled me to crouch behind the front corner of the van and spy on them.

One, a black-skinned youth much darker than Matt, had her head shaved except for a long tuft of hair at the top that stuck out in a ponytail unnaturally stiff, unnaturally straight, and unnaturally bright red. The second girl, Caucasian, had short spiked blue hair the color of veins in anatomical blood-circulation charts. Despite the briskness of the autumn afternoon, these two wore sleeveless vests. The long, lanky, third sweetheart sported a biker jacket studded with chrome. They all had skin-tight jeans and black boots so big and heavy that I couldn't understand how they walked at all, let alone with their liquid gait.

The October sun glinted off their ferocious piercings — rings and studs through their eyebrows, nostrils, ears, lips, knuckles and, I was sure, in many places not presently visible.

I couldn't really catch their conversation, except to note that it was animated, as if they discussed an event they had just shared, something enlivening or inspiring. They seemed to be all talking at the same time. In a moment of eagerness, I leaned forward too quickly and hit my head on one of the van's side mirrors. It hurt, but I did not cry out. Nonetheless, tiny as the sound of the impact was, the girls immediately ceased talking, the way birds in the wood simultaneously cease their chatter the instant they sense a human presence. They looked around mutely, and I saw one of them flash a rapid hand sign to the others. The two responded with a similar hand

127

sign. None of my past experience had taught me about the secret hand signals of the young people — except that they existed. The signal had to be a warning, however, and they all heeded. Without any further talk they ran off down Queen Street.

But even though I had not caught one word they'd said, even though I'd come nowhere near making a direct connection between the Hall and Carrie Simm, my afternoon's jaunt had not been in vain. Because as the girls had flashed hand signals, I'd noticed the muscled upper arm of the second girl. She had a tattoo. The same tattoo as on Tootie's farewell note. And the third girl? The third girl was the Lynx.

How to search the city for the haunts of homeless girls? At the public library at Yonge and Bloor, I fought for the next turn on the computer. On the web, I had no trouble learning how to get a room in a homeless shelter in Chicago. I found a site that purported to list every book in which homelessness had ever been mentioned, including novels, poetry collections and the Bible. I even found something I wished I'd thought of myself, a "Hints for the Homeless" web site, in which articulate homeless people shared tricks of the trade. I learned a fast new way to dry wet socks using two pieces of reflective material.

But I didn't find any site that gave me a clue to the whereabouts of Carrie Simm and Tootie.

My time was up and a particularly aggressive ten-year-old was threatening to call Security if I didn't vacate what the child insisted on calling "the public workstation". I went down to the library's newspaper section, intending to kill an hour before I went out into the streets for a lonely supper. When I'd lived at Tootie's, I'd never condescended to eat with the other inmates, I mean tenants, but I guess I must have sensed their presence then because I sensed their absence now.

It occurred to me to try to find the *Toronto Daily World* article about Jeffrey. I didn't know the date, but the helpful librarian quickly located it. My fingers trembled with anticipation as I turned the pages until I found myself staring at Jeffrey's picture. I felt so proud that I wanted to nudge the library patron beside me. Reading eagerly, I learned that it had been Jeffrey whose plan for the harbor had almost been accepted two years before. Which meant that I had missed seeing him then. Perhaps missed out on two years' reconciliation. It would have been good to have him see me when I was a city consultant. Well, now I was working for the police, wasn't I?

"You might be interested in this article, too," the librarian told me when I showed her the picture of my son. My eye fell on the headline, "City and Developers Join in Lucrative Housing Starts".

At first I read the article hoping to learn more about the fate of homeowners like Tootie, and while there were some examples of houses like hers that had been appropriated, most of the article was about the three types of grants offered to developers by the city. Developers could build luxury units for a small number of wealthy owners in neighborhoods like Tootie's if they also built new low-cost housing in poorer neighborhoods. Individuals with green space design credentials could tear down housing that had become derelict if they could prove that open land was more beneficial to the city than repairing the buildings. Under the third type of grant, a private individual could receive matching city funds to provide low-cost housing by renovating derelict property back to proper housing standards, under the label "step-up program". The city claimed that the grants balanced the need for more green space and higher income-producing properties for developers at the same time as addressing the needs of low-cost housing consumers.

At the bottom of the article was the address of a web page to learn about derelict properties that were eligible step-ups. Matt had been pretty specific about the types of structures the kids used as catacombs. I copied the web address, went back upstairs, waited until one minute past the hour and ousted the obnoxious ten-year-old from the workstation.

It took me half an hour to wend my way through a couple of sub-categories of proposed "step-ups". Some were public buildings vacated in government cutbacks, but most were private buildings that financially strapped owners were unloading. After careful study, I narrowed my search to six properties with underground garages in the downtown core. For security reasons, addresses were available only to qualified grant applicants, but each building was assigned a number.

Only one of the six was described as totally vacant. I clicked on its number and a detailed series of images grew visible on the screen. Behind stately window frames without glass, story upon story of them, was nothing but air. The structure loomed like a tall, well-dressed man with some dread mental disease.

"This downtown ghost has three completed levels of underground garages and twenty floors of uncompleted apartments," the caption read. "The residence was planned as the flagship of a series covering a city block, but construction was halted a decade ago when the planned apartments were found to be in contravention of a zoning bylaw calling for the retention of green space."

I hit the Print key and a grainy photo emerged along with a tiny stylized map, showing a square bound by Bloor, Yonge, Queen and the river. Something about the building in the picture rang a bell. I was sure I'd seen it. I'd spent so much time roaming the streets of Toronto that many buildings were familiar, but familiar like the faces of strangers without names. I knew this building but not its address. I studied the picture and the stories began to come back to me. This was the "Marble Widow". For years I'd heard tales about her, mostly contradictory. The place was a cesspool. It was clean. It was freezing in winter and stifling in summer. The air-conditioning and heating still operated because the owner didn't want what was standing to be ruined by extremes of heat and cold. It was dangerous. It was safe. It housed old geezers. It had a nursery for homeless babies. Crack addicts lived there. And a priest. And a former member of City Council. I recalled having once met the man. He was certifiably crazy but nobody had noticed until his term was nearly up. The Marble Widow seemed a perfect place for a squat.

But what street was the building on? In my mind, I traced countless journeys through the neighborhoods, but these mental wanderings were fruitless. And while I could picture the building clearly, a lone tower perched at the northwest corner of some city block, my mind couldn't move beyond that block to the nearest intersection.

The next day it occurred to me that I might be able to locate the Marble Widow if I could gain access to the building records at City Hall. I hit on passing myself off as a grant applicant.

At 8 A.M., I waited in Nathan Phillips Square in front of City Hall with my eye on the door and my phony story clear in my mind. Despite my early arrival, there were people ahead of me in line when the door opened. Outside, on the square, city workers were preparing the central fountain for its annual transformation into a skating rink. I wondered how many more seasons would go by before all that concrete would be replaced by trees in Jeffrey's award-winning plan.

Without warning, an image returned to me. Jeffrey and his sister, Ellen, and I had been skating one winter afternoon. Suddenly eight-year-old Jeffrey left the rink, sat down on a bench and began to weep. Ellen sat beside him, took his hand, and he stopped. But neither child would tell me what was going on. I took them home. I let it pass. Now, more than twenty years later, I felt the tears at the back of my own throat. How could I have been such a careless father? Neglect, as I had so often told criminals, is just as evil as malice.

Someone nudged me from behind. My turn at the counter had come. Beneath a sign reading "Permit Alley", a cheerful city employee stood before a stack of bound maps, blueprints and plans for building projects.

"I have a question concerning the zoning of a project proposed under the city's matching grants for step-up housing," I explained.

The young man asked, "What's the address of your property?"

"You know," I answered, assuming an air of confident nonchalance, "I've got two properties under consideration for the grant and I'm afraid I may have confused the two when I applied. One of them falls under a zoning bylaw concerning green space and I —"

"What are the addresses?"he repeated.

I gave him Tootie's old address. I thought if I had one legitimate grant applicant, I could fake my way into learning the address of the "second" application.

The young man smiled knowingly. I took this to mean I was doing well. He was taking me for the developer of Tootie's site.

I was wrong.

"It won't work." The man leaned across the counter and tapped his pen against the edge of one of the bound volumes. "This is a very generous grant program and there aren't that many eligible buildings downtown. The competition for funds is stiff. I don't know what you're trying to pull, but there's no way you're involved in the development of the address you just gave me. I know every contractor on that site."

"Okay," I said, backing off. "It's true. I'm not a contractor or a developer, either. I'm just trying to find the address of this building."

I pulled out the picture I'd printed.

His eyes widened and he shook his head. "Forget it. That building is already being developed. If you have a legitimate interest in the grants, you must file a legal application for a property you either own or have an option to buy. Otherwise, I most certainly cannot reveal zoning information or street addresses."

In my days on the street, a conversation like this would have ended with me telling the officious little prick that he was a stupid lackey who cared more about rules than about innocent people like Tootie who were being thrown out of their neighborhoods. I would have told him where he could put the city and its bedmates, the developers. In the old days, I would have ended up shouting and he would have ended up calling Security. I would have found myself escorted to the farthest corner of Nathan Phillips Square and dumped ignominiously in front of the courthouse where I'd sat as a judge.

But I'd outgrown my taste for shocking civil servants. "Sorry to bother you," I said and I turned to leave.

"Just a minute," the young man whispered. "If you're really interested, why not take an application form and see what you can do about finding a partner who's got a building? You might even be able to option one yourself. The option works just the way it does in the film business. All you need is five percent down and a letter of intent for the rest."

I didn't need to ask him how he knew about movie options. Who in Toronto didn't?

He disappeared for a moment, then reappeared with a file folder, out of which he took a single sheet of paper.

I accepted the paper. In my anger-management problem days I would have rolled it in a ball and shot it at his face. Instead, I folded it and put it in my pocket. "Thanks," I said, very politely.

I thought hard. I sketched a grid. I memorized the printout. South of Bloor, north of Queen, west of the river, east of Yonge. I made up my mind to walk every block of that area, between a hundred and a hundred fifty. At a block a minute, I should have done it in a couple of hours.

Five hours later, having tramped in what seemed like ever diminishing circles, I was walking through the south end of St. Michael's Ward, a gigantic high-rise, low-rent project, when I stopped to rest.

"The Ward" was poor when I'd been a law student doing volunteer work there and it was poor now. But it was far from depressing. Outside the old grammar school that had been there since before I was born, a chirping gaggle of bright-sweatered children ran and scrambled, fell and picked themselves up, laughing, rejoicing in the freedom of after-school on an autumn afternoon. Chinese, East Indian, Tamil, Ethiopian, Iranian. I recognized these ethnicities as I had once recognized the Italians and Irish, both now totally assimilated and living in fine houses like the ones my father had helped build. Someday these children too would move away from their government-subsidized apartments, would make a better home for themselves, would leave space here for new immigrants to fill. Canada is a cold country with a warm heart.

I walked the width of the project, a few city blocks, and crossed Jarvis Street, intending to grab a doughnut before heading for the subway. I needed a new plan. My research and wandering had led me nowhere. I didn't know where Carrie Simm was. I didn't know where Tootie was. I didn't know where to look. And worse, I was just too out of shape for all this. What I really wanted right then was to lie down.

I idly studied a wooden fence along the sidewalk. It rose eight feet, but from four feet down, it was painted with the wildly colorful art of young children. Some teacher had lettered a heading that said, "What I would do to make Earth a better planet." Beneath the phrase, the kids had painted their responses in words and pictures.

"Give a neat toy to every kid in the world," one child

had written, then illustrated the thought with an elaborate depiction of a structure made of interlocking building blocks. The shape of the building in the drawing was familiar. I stared at it for a minute. Then I stepped back and looked up. The eight-foot fence was surrounding the tower I'd been looking for all day.

I had found the Marble Widow.

CHAPTER EIGHT

I found four sturdy wooden fruit crates from the garbage bins behind the supermarket across the street and threw two over the fence for later. The other two helped me scale the fence, which was locked with a rusty padlock. I trespassed onto the wide drive that circled in front of the Marble Widow. I could imagine the sort of traffic the original builder had envisioned for this drive: BMWs and Mercedes. But because of the zoning bylaw halting construction, no traffic had ever graced this drive, which was now littered with empty beer bottles and pop cans and ragged remnants of plastic shopping bags.

I stood at the foot of the fence for a moment to get my bearings. The round monolith loomed above me. Its sheathing of dark red polished stone glowed like burnished porphyry in the soft autumn afternoon. But there any claim to beauty ended. Where the front entrance must have been intended, was nothing but a gaping fifteen-foot hole in the wall. I stepped through, my feet crunching bits of shattered glass and broken plastic. An eerie gray-brown light suffused the cavernous tower. Instinctively, I glanced twenty stories up. Failing daylight filtered through paneless western windows. The building had the feeling of a stopped film reel, motion stalled at some critical moment and never resumed. Up the middle, a core of electrical and plumbing installations rose. Decayed wire and warped tubing twisted in the air high over my head. A few steel girders, like the spokes of a wheel, poked out from this central core, but for the most part, the vast space was empty. In dark shadowed reaches at the very top, I sensed the lazy circling of winged creatures and realized I was in the presence of bats.

And, I soon saw, of rats, one of which eyed me from under a half-rotted denim shirt in a heap near my foot. I eyed it back. A rat can chew off your face if it's hungry and you're lying down drunk, but I wasn't and it couldn't. It turned and ran.

Walking close to the dimly lit wall, I felt for stairs down to the parking garages, though how such lower levels would be illuminated, I had no idea. Halfway around the tower, I found a dull gray iron door at the end of a hallway. Rust had eaten most of the paint and the door was propped open by a chunk of broken concrete. I leaned through and saw a rusted metal staircase.

My experience with underground garages was limited to the few times I'd fitfully slept in them. Most office and apartment buildings in Toronto are fully occupied and to sleep in the garage of one is to beg to be ejected, if not arrested. When I got to the bottom of the stairs of the Marble Widow, I was surprised to see that a system of grates provided light and ventilation from outside. I could see patches of daylight through these grates and realized I was now beneath the rear yard of the building.

The nearest grate allowed enough light to see the garage wall covered with intricate painting even more intensely colorful than the work decorating the fence outside. I myself had sent one or two people to jail for persistent defilement of public and private property, but my time on the street had changed my mind about a number of so-called "offenses" and graffiti was one of them. The daring, sophisticated work — signed or "tagged", as the street artists referred to their signatures — exploded on outdoor surfaces across the city, as skillful as the work I'd seen in galleries.

Stylized letters in an unknown alphabet spelled out words in a secret language. Each letter was as tall as I and formed in graceful outlines of shiny black enamel. In matte finish, the outlines were filled in with shades graduating seamlessly from deepest indigo to white. Peeking from within, above and beneath these letters were a host of full-color, humorous, highly distinctive faces with round cheeks, bulging eyes and grinning mouths. They reminded me of the stone faces carved a hundred years ago into the stone lintel over the main door of Old City Hall Courthouse. Those faces depicted living members of the municipal government of the time. I was sure the garage wall graffiti depicted the faces of the new government of the alleys, the underground and the street.

I breathed a silent prayer that gang members had deserted this site as completely as the developers had. Accordingly, I ventured away from the light, further into the garage. I stopped in my tracks when somewhere behind me, I heard a muffled cough, then shuffling steps headed in my direction.

Frightened, I fell into a crouch, rolled under the stairs

and threw my trembling hands over my head. When I lived in the ravine, I often saw a vicious young animal attack a lone old animal and torment it to death.

Cowering in the dark, I smelled something rank. Out of the deep shadows, a figure slouched toward me with an outstretched hand holding a bottle. I pulled deeper into the alcove beneath the stairs but I could smell the old familiar combination of stale sweat, dried urine, dust, tobacco smoke and tooth decay — the fragrance of life on the skids. It mixed with another old familiar smell: alcohol. I thought I was done with both those aromas.

"Hey, buddy, want a drink?" This unexpected invitation was accompanied by a sharp kick in my exposed ribs.

"I don't drink anymore. But thanks for the offer," I said with as much nonchalance as I could muster, unwinding myself from my cowardly curl. This was nothing but an old drunk and being an alumnus of that fraternity, I felt more pity than fear. In silhouette, my ragged host poured the offering down his own throat, shuddered dramatically, then ran his tongue around the top of the bottle. Not for the first time, I thanked God I was on the wagon.

"You got a wallet?"the man asked abruptly. Before I could answer, he swung the empty bottle. It hit the metal stairs with a spray of glass that showered my hair and face.

"Yeah," I said shakily, "I got a wallet."

"Reach in your pocket real slow, grab the wallet and give it here."

I did as he bid, fumbling with fear but not wanting to show it. "Keep the wallet, just let me out of here," I said.

I'd taken precautions. All I carried with me was a small amount of cash.

He yanked the wallet out of my hand. I could hear his fingers rifling it, extracting the few bills. He shoved it back at me, hitting me in the chest. "Get the hell out of here," he commanded.

I scrambled up the metal stairs, eager to get back onto the street. But when I reached the top, I noticed something I'd missed — another metal door. It looked rusted shut. I pushed with all my strength and it gave so suddenly that I lost my footing and fell forward into another cement-walled space, a fifty-foot space at ground level. Well-lit by floor-to-ceiling windows still with glass intact, in the middle of this space was a swimming pool, that amenity that graces most Toronto apartment buildings. The law says that swimming pools cannot be accessible to the public: they must be behind locked doors, walls or fences. Whoever owned this derelict hulk of a building was obviously aware of the law, that pool windows must be maintained even though the pool is empty. The old lawyer in me crept nearer to confirm my conclusions.

I nearly cried out in shock when, from the depths of the concrete pit, a dazed pair of blue eyes stared back at me. I've spent time sending people to mental hospitals and I've spent time in a mental hospital, myself. I recognize a mentally ill person when I see one.

And she apparently recognized me. "I know who you *are*," she screeched painfully. "I know who you *are*."

My first thought was that this waif's frantic recognition of me was based on courtroom experience. Perhaps I'd sentenced her. But then I realized that this child, with her gaunt face, skinny body, her head with its halo of pale brown spikes could not be more than thirteen. She would have been five years old when I left the bench.

She stood rigidly among small piles of belongings on the bottom of the empty pool — clothing, sleeping bags, boxes, folded newspapers. I couldn't tell whether the girl's stiff stance showed fury or fear. The thought that she feared me filled me with sorrow.

"Don't be afraid."

"Don't torment me, asshole!"she screamed, balling her bony hand into a fist and shaking it in the air. She wore a man's tattered gray business shirt. Its frayed cuffs flapped around her thin arms. "What the hell do you want from me? You can't take me. You can't tie me up. You already tried chains. I ran away. I'll run again."

"I'm not here to hurt you," I felt compelled to say, as I edged closer to the rim of the pool. The items on the pool floor were not randomly scattered, and the space looked as though it were roughly divided into sections. "Do you live here with other people?" I asked, trying to keep my voice low and bending to one knee to minimize the authoritarian effect.

She shook her spiky head with an exaggerated side-to-side jerk. "No. I live with women. Only women." She craned her neck like a baby bird looking up to an adult for sustenance. "Got anything to eat? I got chopsticks. You got Chinese?"

Touched, I answered, "No, but I can get you food." It occurred to me that I would have to go back to the B & B for money first, but that didn't matter. "I'll come back," I said.

"You're just screwing me around," she answered. Then she sank down onto a sleeping bag, staring straight ahead at some invisible object. I watched until her immobility gave way to silent, rhythmic rocking. For the first time, I heard the sound of the wind whistling in the vast ruined tower. The nights were cold now. There could be frost, even inside a building if it wasn't heated. "I'll come back tomorrow and bring you food and warm clothes and a blanket," I promised, but received no answer. So I stood and as I rose, something brushed my ankle. I jumped, reckoning that I was encountering a large relative of the rodent whose acquaintance I'd made earlier.

But I was wrong. Curling against me as if she knew me, was the orange tabby cat Tootie had called Star. It bounded onto the low windowsill and listlessly licked the edge of a familiar white china bowl.

I came back the next day, cautiously reconnoitering for a breach in the fence. Doing the fruit-box trick had left me winded. When I found a loose board, I went back to the supermarket across the street and stocked up on inexpensive luncheon meat, cheap cookies, potato chips and chocolate bars. I got six big bottles of diet cola. These things were not what I thought a teen *should* eat. They were what I thought a teen *would* eat.

I also bought three thick blankets for a couple of dollars each at a nearby thrift store and five long-sleeved tight-looking black T-shirts at a dollar mart. Finally, on a whim, I picked up a little packet of stickers, all of which showed cats. I got a small album to stick them in, too.

As I hauled these things across the street, a long-forgotten memory returned. Without my knowledge, Jeffrey had returned to the ravine behind the Suburban when he was eleven or twelve. His mother talked me out of punishing him for going so far from our downtown home without permission. She said Jeffrey was only following up on the interest in nature I'd instilled. She was right. When Jeffrey was thirteen, he won a prize at an international science fair for replicating an experiment tracing the migration of a single monarch butterfly from the campus of the University of Toronto to a small town in upper New York state. And other thirteen-year-olds made do with sticky pictures of cats.

Keeping out of the way of brazen rats and thieving drunks, I juggled my burdens through the metal door, peeking into the pool room to find neither the waif nor the "women" she claimed to live with. I lowered myself on the corroding ladder very gingerly and spread my parcels on the floor of the pool like Santa Claus come early. Before I left, I reached into my jacket pocket for the half-pint of milk I carried and emptied it into the white china bowl on the windowsill. As if Star had been watching me the whole time, the cat appeared out of nowhere and scampered up to the bowl. I've never been the sort of person to wish animals could talk, but suddenly I found myself speaking to this beast. "Where's my little friend, Tootie? Is she here? Can you tell me?" The cat looked at me as if she wished she could answer.

The B & B on Hazelton Avenue was a step up from Tootie's rooming house. Every morning the dining room table was set with lace, crystal, china and silver. The first morning, I stayed away from the other guests, eating instead at one of my usual coffee shops. But the second morning, I smelled something I'd not eaten since my decline and I just couldn't resist. Bennies. Not the pills but the brunch: Eggs Benedict. I also could not resist hot showers with French hand-milled soap and I had forgot how thick a bathtowel is when it doesn't come from a dollar store.

Three days passed while I indulged myself in luxury. I kept checking my phone to see whether Jeffrey had called. He hadn't. But William Sterling had. I told him what Matt had said.

"He's furious with me?" William repeated. "He knows I'm back and he's *furious*?"

I was beginning to feel used. "William," I commented, "you don't exactly sound surprised or upset. What's going on?"

"Don't you see? If Matt is angry, he's still involved. He has every reason to hate me, but he doesn't." William paused. I could almost hear his brain working. "All he needs is for someone to talk to him about this a little more. To point out . . ."

"No!"

"Ellis, don't be obstinate. It's a small favor to ask considering all we've been through."

"All *you've* put us through!"

"It's not necessary to be accusatory." His haughty tone didn't make me as angry as it once had. To my surprise, I found myself happy the old pest was alive and perhaps even well. He certainly sounded a lot better than he had when I'd seen him. "If you won't talk to Matt, Ellis, at least have the courtesy to talk to me. Meet me for dinner."

"I can't. I'm working."

"Where?" He sounded stunned, as if my having a job were as amazing as his return to life. "I've worked for the city, which you would know if you hadn't been dead," I told him.

"I suppose you consider yourself quite the comedian," he retorted. "In any case, I've got to see you. I'll call again." He hung up before it occurred to me to ask how he'd got my phone number.

Whether or not Matt was furious with William, he was going to be furious with me if I didn't come up with some clue to Carrie Simm's whereabouts soon. I went back to the Marble Widow.

Outside, I hunkered against the wall and braved the cool wind for a couple of hours, but my surveillance was in vain. Nobody showed up, not the waif, not even the cat. I came back the next day and the next, but it wasn't until the third day that I again saw the crazy girl. This time she was not alone.

"Let me go. Let me *go*!" I heard her screams before I saw her. From my hiding place I watched as the skinny little spike-haired raver crossed the windswept rear yard of the tower, dancing between two larger, more solid-looking young women, who held her by the arms. Behind the three of them walked a tall, lean, vaguely threatening figure. I drew closer to the wall, determined not to be caught spying. I had reason to fear I would be because the three girls escorting the troubled one were the same three I'd seen a few days earlier at Juvenile Hall. At first this seemed an impossible coincidence. But then I thought it over. The Lynx knew Tootie. Tootie's cat was here. But where was Tootie herself? And where was Carrie? I'd heard no one but the drunk in the first level of the basement. I knew from the description on the web site that there were three levels of parking. The thought of checking out the other two levels made me cringe. I wanted to avoid it at all cost.

146

My thoughts were interrupted by a piercing shriek from the little one.

"Shut your mouth, you little freak. You're really starting to piss me off," the Lynx responded. Her voice was as deep as a man's and I remembered how Tootie had once mistaken her for a male pimp. "If you don't cut the crap, you'll land back with the loony tunes. Is that what you want, for us to haul your skinny useless butt back to the Parke?"

The captive broke free and threw herself on the Lynx, circling her stick-like arms around the other's neck in a desperate plea for mercy. "Get off me," the tall one hissed, pushing the little one away. "I got enough to worry about without you acting crazy. Calm down or I'm calling somebody to come get you."

"No, no," the girl whined. "I'll be quiet, I will. And I'll never touch you again. I promise, Lynx."

"Take her inside," Lynx ordered and the other two complied, hooking their arms around the thin girl in a protective gesture of awkward tenderness.

Lynx leaned against the cold red marble, reached into her pocket and pulled out a cigarette, which she lit with a belligerent thrust of her thumb against a cheap plastic lighter. She was lost in thought. As I watched her still profile, her body balanced on one leg, the other bent at the knee with her foot behind her on the wall, I saw that she was strangely beautiful. Hunger is the eye of appetite. I could see her feline grace, the clean line of her strong jaw, the lean power of her long limbs. A narrow ridge of scar tissue, like a thick white thread, ran from the outer corner of her right eye to the top of her lip, a sure memento of a knife. But the scar only added to the power of her feline looks. She had short, sleek hair the color of pewter. I could not see her eyes but I imagined them gray and wary. Her stance exuded the animal confidence of a creature who has chosen to fight. Despite the compelling attraction, or perhaps because of it, I felt an intense urge to get away and I was relieved when, after a few sharp puffs, Lynx threw her cigarette down and went inside.

I began to despair of getting these girls to help me find Carrie or Tootie. It had been a month since Charington Simm had been shot dead, three weeks since Matt had first asked me for my help on the case. I spoke to Matt nearly every day and he was encouraging, telling me that an investigation, any investigation takes time and patience. I knew this as a judge, but as a man spying on teenage girls, I had a different notion of time. And I always got off the phone fast because I didn't want Matt to ask whether I'd seen William, which I had not.

Buoyed by Matt's support, I gradually inspected all three levels of the parking garage. I found it a little odd that he didn't consider it particularly dangerous for me to be exploring on my own, but I persevered cautiously. On the second level down, I found a couple of sleeping bags similar to the ones at the bottom of the swimming pool, but I knew that charities bought them in bulk to hand out to the homeless. Those bags were all over the city. I'd seen them stashed near the courthouse the previous winter. Aside from the sleeping bags, I found nothing and no one, not even the loser who had lifted my wallet.

I had to be careful not to attract the attention of the inhabitants of the swimming pool, but I also needed to keep a constant eye on them, hoping for clues. I discovered the pool had adjacent change rooms. Like nearly everywhere else in the building, there were no doors separating the two spaces, so I could sit on a cold tile ledge in the change room and hear activity in the pool. I could also see the girls once darkness fell. I felt compelled to be very cautious in my observations of the young women. The fact that they were children of the street, wise, tough and used to abuse, made my caution all the more necessary. And besides, I was afraid of them.

Once I realized that life in the pool had a sort of rhythm, I timed my arrival to coincide with the twilight hour in which the girls got out their flashlights, lanterns and candles. Then I could observe them for a couple of hours before they departed a little before 9 P.M., leaving the youngest behind. I didn't know where the girls showered, but unlike the drunk in the basement, they did not give off any rank odor. As far as I could tell, there was no water on the premises, except for a makeshift cistern in the rear yard formed where a piece of an abandoned concrete mold collected rain water. I could only assume the whole of the building's first floor served as a latrine. Yet, the girls spent a lot of time fussing with their odd hairstyles and taking turns putting on makeup at an improvised vanity table made from a triangle of broken mirror propped on top of a fruit box I'd left inside the fence.

They discussed winning the lottery, finding a better place to live, and their fears about surviving the coming winter. Many girls who live on the street survive by prostitution. But I heard no talk of johns, tricks or pimps. Most girls in their situation are drug users. But I heard nothing of scores, dealers, busts or stashes. This puzzled me. I decided they were so wily, so skilful in subterfuge, so sensitive to the value of secrecy that they only appeared to speak innocently. I wondered whether they might be using a code I couldn't decipher.

When the other three spoke to the troubled one, whom they called by a street name that sounded like "Legion", they often resorted to a singsong baby talk. In general, Legion was treated about the same as the orange tabby cat. The other girls petted her, teased her, laughed at her permanent confusion, egged her on. "Legion's chewing on her blanket again. What flavor is it, Legion? Chocolate? Can I have a taste? Yum yum. Here, have a taste of my boot. It's caramel. Hey, look you guys, Legion is eating my boot!"

But they watched over her, too. They had found the parcels I left. All four of them wore the black T-shirts. Someone had painted the words "front" and "back" on Legion's shirt. I took this to be more than a mean joke. In the mental hospital where I was once a patient, more than one inmate went into hysterics because a T-shirt wasn't put on the "right" way, even when both sides were identical.

In all their discussions, in their infrequent disagreements and in any matter that required factual information, they deferred to the lean, scarred, cat-like Lynx. She was clearly the oldest. After a few days of watching and listening, I learned the names of the others, too. The one with the vein-blue hair was "Scots" or "Scotty" because she occasionally affected a Scottish brogue. She seemed to be a buffer between Lynx and the other two girls. Once when Legion and "Shiv", the black girl with the stiff topknot, were fighting, Lynx gave them so much hell both Shiv and Legion began to cry. Scotty quieted them, then told Lynx that she'd been too nasty and that she had to back off. Lynx and Scotty were obviously father and mother, Legion and Shiv their difficult children. Like a lot of fathers, Lynx was absent more often than not at these family gatherings. And every night Scotty and Shiv would also disappear into the darkness.

On the fifth or sixth night of lurking in the change room, I finally overheard a substantive conversation, though I wasn't sure what to make of it. The four girls were eating popcorn from big bagfuls you can find in the garbage at movie theaters after midnight. I heard Shiv say, "The Ferryman lookin' out for us. He give us blankets. Now we don't gotta bring them big sleepin' bags on the subway when we get outta here." She took a mouthful of popcorn, chewed it thoroughy. "They out there freezin' they skinny butts someplace right this minute, while we here eatin' like a pig."

"Shut up about them," Lynx snapped. "I don't want us to talk about them."

"Who's gonna hear?" Scotty asked. She moved closer to Shiv almost as though she was afraid Lynx might hit the black girl.

"We have to be extra careful," Lynx warned. "People come around. Who really gave the stuff to Legion, huh?"

"People maybe be lookin' for wood to make a fire," Shiv persisted. "I wish we could get ourselfs a fire. Then we could hang here all winter. We could make fires out of all kinds of shit. Steal wood and have a shitload of fires!"

"No stealing and no swearing," Scotty admonished.

"Fire!" Legion yelled. "Fire. Fire. Fire!" She hopped up and began to stomp out flames.

"Ain't no fire here, fool," Shiv said. "That's my exac' point."

"Cut this crap right now," the Lynx snarled. "No fire except on candles. And if you want to know how come, just look at her." She nodded toward Legion who was now in a frenzy of stomping, twirling and arm flailing. "Get her to chill before she kills herself."

From where I hid, I could see Scotty patiently put aside her bag of popcorn, approach Legion and take the girl's waving hands in her own. I couldn't hear her words, but the younger girl ceased her gyrating, and for a few minutes all four girls sat silently munching their meager supper.

"Carrie hate winter. She like a flower or somethin'. She can't never stand no cold," Shiv started again.

At the sound of that name, I inched closer. The walls of the pool flickered with the uncertain light from half a dozen candles as I peered cautiously down. The girl named Lynx stood abruptly, bounded across the space that separated her from Shiv and raised her hand to strike. But her blow did not reach its target, for Scotty was there first, her hand staying Lynx's in midair.

Though I could clearly see this encounter, I couldn't be sure I heard correctly when Scotty said, "Lynx, you got to stop being so bossy. And so mad. You said yourself that Carrie is going to be safe, that we'll get her away — to New York or Montreal. Remember? We gotta take trouble to the Ferryman. That's what he's there for."

"Even the Ferryman can't fix this," Lynx said dejectedly.

"The Ferryman can fix anything," Legion said. And her voice was as lucid as the others.

I *had* to find a way to talk to these girls but I couldn't just climb down into the pool and say, "How do you do?" "Undercover" or not, I felt ashamed to be spying. I had just about made up my mind to tell Matt that I was quitting when I got the break I needed. I found a go-between, what Matt would call, a "handler", in the shape of Star the cat.

Using the second of the fruit crates, I made a little feeding and watering station for her behind the makeshift cistern in the yard. It didn't take too long for the over-curious Shiv to discover it and toward the end of the week, I found a scrap of paper underneath the cat's dish. On it, in labored print was written, "Stare thanx yu." A little drawing of a paw served as a signature. I knew Shiv had left the note because I saw her. The next day, I came earlier than usual and waited outside the back door. When she showed up, I eased myself out of the doorway and risked a "Hi!"

Shiv was a sweet-faced kid and I felt shame when she jumped and a look of fear flashed across her features. Fear was soon replaced by her irrepressible interest in her world. "You gotta be a buddy a' that dirty ol' geez down the basement. Personally I don' mind havin' men come 'round, case there's some kind emergency." She pronounced the word with such care that I almost laughed at how she conquered its four syllables. "I'm gonna catch hell from Lynx for talkin' with ya. Lynx you got to listen to or you out. Only we can't stay here anyways because it's getting so f-in' cold at night. We could stay if we had a fire. I can build a f-in' fire. Wood and some good gasoline to —"

I could see why Lynx lost patience. When my children had been young, I tried to encourage them to question all they experienced, but sometimes their questions and comments came so fast and often they gave me a headache. And I had seen witnesses in court, too, who ran off at the mouth. If controlled, such a witness provided valuable testimony. If uncontrolled, they wore judges and juries down. I had to find a way to get Shiv to tell me *only* what I needed to know. Was the Carrie I'd heard mentioned Carrie Simm? If so, where was she hiding? Was Tootie Beets with her? I thought about Tootie and her writing. All the notices she always posted. The newsletter she printed for her tenants. The note she'd left me. It was a long shot, but . . .

"I knowed you right away for the guy who feed Star, 'cause"

"Shiv," I interrupted, "did Tootie teach you how to write?"

She seemed to ignore me, making a kissing sound as Star bounced toward us out of the afternoon shadows. Shiv stroked her coat, which was clean and thick. "Tootie, she help me some. Mostly I learn at school before I run. Some girls read 'n write at the hall."

"The hall?"

"Yeah. You could go in the day and learn stuff and at night you could sorta work there and get money for it. And if you help all night, watchin' girls when they sleep and that, you get extra money and some food to take home. You gotta be fourteen or else you too young. Sometimes they's criminal girls sleep there, but that don't matter 'cause they got like guards. When all the girls is asleep you get to read. I can figure out plenty of words."

"Does Tootie go there?"

"I don' know." Shiv hesitated. Star rolled over and presented her belly. "Legion don't go, that's for sure. She can't be let out too much. Sometime she hide and we can't find her. But mostly she afraid of the other side of the fence and don't never go near the street. Me, I go to the hall most every day and night. Scotty and Lynx, they used to go one night and don't go one night 'cause they use to take turns bein' guards downstairs."

"You mean they work as guards at the hall?" I was slightly confused.

"No," she said, "they guard Carrie. Before."

I tried to hide my eagerness. "Before? Before what?"

The girl shrugged her shoulders. Beneath her hand the cat squirmed and raised its back.

"Did Tootie take Carrie someplace, Shiv?"

She shrugged again. She wasn't easy to pump despite her love of words. She'd lived by her wits for a long time. "Beats me," she answered. She stopped stroking Star who scampered away. "Shiv," I persisted, "it's nice to have somebody to talk to. If I come back with extra food for Star, will you tell me more about Tootie and Carrie?"

"Are you a sex maniac who humps 'em and dumps 'em?"she asked.

"No."

"Then how come you keep comin' by?"

"You've seen me?"

"Yeah. Sure. But I jus' figgered you were buds with that sicko downstairs. He always talkin' bout scorin' whiskey and jumpin' broads. He make me wanna puke. But you ain't like him, right?" She looked up at me so trustingly that I felt intensely uncomfortable about pacts with the underage. Just watching them, I had already engaged in behavior construed as criminal in the upscale neighborhood I went back to each night.

But this was the street and the alliances formed on the street are like alliances formed among obscure nations. They may not make sense to the powerful; in fact, they may seem foolish and evil. But, hinged to survival, they have an innocence all their own.

"Shiv," I repeated, "if I come here again tomorrow with the cat's food, will you tell me where Carrie is?"

"Could do," she answered dismissively. "Here cat, here lady, here Starry," she called, and left me standing alone in the cold wind.

CHAPTER NINE

I felt confident I was getting close to some answers and the confidence made me careless. I decided I had earned a night off. At "home", I took a long shower, cut my hair and trimmed my beard. There wasn't much to the beard, but grooming provided an aura of distinction, I thought, as I stared at the olive-skinned, gray-haired man in the mirror.

As a law student, I had sometimes been coaxed into the coffee houses of '60s Yorkville, listening to folk songs and dreaming of freedom. The area gradually grew more and more fashionable. By the time I ascended to the bench, dinner at the Park Plaza Hotel had become an acceptable way to impress colleagues. When I achieved the status of bum, I avoided Yorkville with the same diligence I avoided churches, shelters and social workers.

But now I was free, having to live up to none of my previous standards. I strolled along Cumberland Street, peering into the tobacconist and catching a whiff of treasured cigars from Cuba, Honduras and Dominica. I eschewed the humble pleasures of the Pilot Tavern and headed instead for Yorkville Avenue and the Urban Inn with its sidewalk umbrellas, and wrought-iron fenced patio where white-aproned waiters snapped tablecloths smartly before laying them over round tables. A painted wooden dinghy that served as an oyster bar was out of service. Why not? Wasn't it October with an "r" in it?

This evening I would not be dining alone. Just as I had prepared to step out of the B & B, the phone rang. "Ellis, thank goodness I've caught you. We need to talk. Is this a good time?"

"Not exactly. I was just about to go out, William." I felt resentment at being interrupted on my evening "off". But I also felt the stirring of the same uneasiness I'd felt trapped in the car with Matt.

"Out to dinner? Marvelous. Where will you be? I'll meet you."

I hesitated, uncertain. Remembering how William had looked the night I'd seen him outside the window of the College Street cafe, I could imagine the impression he'd make in a respectable restaurant. Nonetheless, I told him where I was headed and asked him to meet me there. "By the way, William," I added, "how did you get my phone number?"

There was a short silence. "Why, Ellis," he finally said, "I got it from directory assistance. Wherever else would I get it?"

It was too cold, I decided, to eat outside. As I stood in line waiting for a table inside to come free, I kept my eye half on the efficient, friendly waiter clearing places and half on the door. When a lean man with well-cut gray-brown hair, a slim coat in gray-beige cashmere, gray wool trousers and expensive beige leather loafers stepped into the restaurant, I could see that he was about my own age. What I did not see at first was that he was William Sterling.

It wasn't quite a month since I'd last seen William. The drugs Matt mentioned, along with a return to his usual impeccable grooming, had worked wonders.

"Ellis," he said, removing a leather glove and extending his hand, "thank you for agreeing to meet. I see our table is ready." He nodded toward a waiter standing in front of us.

William preceded me and I studied his back as we followed the waiter to our table. William was in pretty good shape for a man who'd come back from the dead. He had nothing of the physical prowess of Matt West, but he carried himself with natural dignity. His hands were relaxed at his sides and I noticed he wore no jewelry. His golden ring, the one that matched mine, was now in Matt's possession. A volunteer had found it in the valley after the flood, and its recovery was taken as proof that William had drowned. When Stow had given his closest friends the rings, we had pledged our loyalty to each other. The promise had not included fidelity beyond the grave.

Neither William nor I seemed capable of beginning the awkward conversation we were evidently there to conduct. We busied ourselves with the mechanics of preparing to dine, but it was an efficient restaurant and we couldn't hide behind the menus for long. The waiter was soon back to take our order. Somewhat to my relief, William broke the silence in his well-modulated voice, accented with speech patterns that reminded me of his lineage of well-educated, well-bred, well-heeled people. "I apologize for the obvious discomfort I've caused you by my desperate appearance a month ago."

"I was more than a *little* surprised, William," I said cautiously, "and discomfort is hardly the word when viewing the living dead."

His laugh was brittle. "It's amazing what trouble a man gets into when he has to prove he hasn't died."

"William, please. Where have you been, for God's sake? Why did you pretend to have drowned, then pop up like a floater?"

"There were times over the past three years when I was convinced everyone would be better off if my body *had* turned up as bloated debris in the river," William said as if my impatience hadn't penetrated.

"Get on with it," I said testily. His eyes met mine for an instant, then skittered away to survey our fellow diners. "Ellis," he said, returning his gaze as if to impress on me the genuineness of his pain, "you're a man who's been through a lot himself. The last time we spoke in the valley, you were a transient living in a box. I understand that your circumstances have improved considerably. I congratulate you. I hope you'll forgive me the impertinence of thinking that your troubles would render you exceptionally capable of understanding the difficulties of others."

As a put down, the statement was so elegant I could only nod as in a chess game when one's opponent makes an especially skilful move. "Go ahead, I'm listening," I encouraged.

"Yes." He took a deep breath. "You will recall that the day we talked at your hut in the valley, I was near hysteria. As Stow's lawyer at Second Chance, I not only knew about the unorthodox medical procedures going on there, I facilitated them."

I shook my head. "Forget it, William. Second Chance is gone now. Stow's reputation remains untarnished. And any benefit Harpur reaped from the experiments is irrelevant. She's dead."

He flinched, and not for the first time in a long life of inconsiderate behavior, I regretted my bluntness, even though I suspected it was my own grief over Harpur's untimely death speaking. "I'm sorry," I hastened to say, "I assumed you knew."

"No. But I do know about Matt. That's he's healthy in spite of his dreadful injury. That he remains in our house. That he's doing well at work." Again his eyes roved away from my face. "That he hasn't found someone else."

I forced myself to be patient. If I could spend a whole week waiting to hear one word about Carrie, I could wait for William to get to his point. The arrival of the waiter with our soup, a thick broth robust with garlic and herbs, distracted us only momentarily. I scarfed mine down, but William didn't touch his. Obviously eating was the least important thing on his mind. "What happened in the flood?" I prompted. "How were you rescued? Where did you end up?"

He picked up his spoon, but put it down without using it. He began again, "By the time I found your hut, I had been pursuing you for a while because I was desperate and you were the only person who could give me the help I needed. Matt had disappeared. I already knew about his hand." He winced, and I did, too. "I didn't know whether his work had taken him deep undercover or . . ."

He hesitated, played with the silverware some more. I did not interrupt. "I figured then that if Matt were still alive, it was my duty to find him and your connections on the street would help."

"William," I pointed out, "don't you know Matt's in the same position right now? He knows you're alive. Don't you think he feels the same compulsion to locate you? Why are you playing this cat-and-mouse game?

161

"Let me finish," he said miserably. "That day you said you might help me, but you warned a storm was coming. Of course you could not have been more correct. I tried to get out of the valley, but I drastically underestimated the conditions." He shuddered at the memory. It wasn't a pleasant recollection for me, either. I'd nearly drowned myself. He went on, "I found myself on a path that suddenly erupted with water. I tried to cross it but I lost my balance and I felt myself being swept away. Finally, I went under. The next thing I knew, I was in an emergency mobile medical unit. Nobody knew my name. Everything on me, even most of my clothes, had been torn away."

Nothing about William's story surprised me so far. I knew the river. I knew the violence of the storm. I had spent a year of my life repairing only a fraction of the damage it had done to the ravines. I also knew about the quirky mercies of nature. "Go on with your story. Surely the mere lack of identification was not enough to cause you to abandon your life?" *Or to enable you to disappear,* I might have added.

He studied the crowded restaurant. I realized he was as much a lawyer as he'd ever been, stalling for time, mentally searching for the version of his story most likely to be accepted by a judge. "When I was first rescued," he said, "I didn't know who or where I was. Eventually, I began to have longer and longer periods of lucidity. When I realized all that had happened, I felt that my life as I had known it was over." His gaze met mine for a brief moment, then slid away. "In the world in which we live, Matt and I, it's still sometimes necessary to barter for the keeping of secrets. I had kept the secrets of others. Now I found a few helpful people to keep my secret. I fled. There were hundreds of people missing in that storm. Some are *still* missing over three years later, their families mired in the legal difficulties of having a relative who is neither dead nor alive."

He paused again. "Ellis," he went on, "having escaped death, I realized I could have a new start. I knew you *would* honor your promise to me to find Matt and that if he needed help, you would find a way to provide that help."

"You put a lot of trust in a bum, William." He smiled, a little arrogantly, I thought. As if he'd known something about me I hadn't known. "I had to go to Stow himself," I continued. "It was the only way to learn that Matt was okay. Matt's a strong man. Last year I had the privilege of working with him on a serial killer case. I can certainly understand your, uh, respect for him."

"You can call it respect if you want to. I prefer to call it something stronger," William answered. I was afraid our waiter might have overheard this conversation. He was gazing at William with unwaiterly fondness. I cleared my throat and the man swung a huge plate with a small trout on it onto the table in front of me, narrowly missing my nose.

"You fled," I remarked, flaking the tender fish away from the skin. "Where did you go?"

"Costa Rica. Matt and I had friends. They were shocked to hear what had happened to me and to Matt. They helped me heal. They found out that Matt was alive and had returned to work. They begged me to get in touch with him. They said he was in mourning, that I was torturing him. But I couldn't seem to write, or telephone, or . . ." He stared down at his own trout as if it were just another dead fish.

"This is all very touching, William, but it's not the whole story, is it? You couldn't get the horrible example of me out of your mind, right? I was a grim reminder of what can happen to a lawyer who falls afoul of the law."

"Oh, Ellis, not that! I'm not as concerned with that as I am about personal matters . . ."

"What could be so personal that you can't reveal it to a man who was your partner for more than a decade?"

He stared at me as though I were an idiot. It reminded me of the old days when we'd been students and I'd feared that Stow and the others had allowed me into their clique just to have somebody to kick around. "Well, William?"

"Ellis, I don't think you understand. I blame myself for Matt's mutilation. If I had not got involved in Second Chance, he would still be whole."

"William," I said with a gentleness I wasn't sure he deserved, "Matt is still *whole*. You don't have to worry about that." Suddenly the waiter was there again and now his eyes were on me with a leering twinkle. "Put the damn salad down," I commanded him.

"Matt knows I'm back, but he's proud. And he's angry. I need an advocate," William said desperately. "I need you to tell Matt how sorry I am. That I ran away like a coward. You're working with him again. I know that."

I wrecked my first career by allowing my personal life to interfere with my professional life. I was not eager to allow *somebody else's* personal life to interfere with my work now. To get between Matt and William would be insane. "How do you know I'm working with Matt?"

"Mutual friends keep me posted," William answered.

"Then why can't they help the two of you get your matters straightened out? I'm, uh, a little out of my league, here." But William looked so bereft, I took the risk of adding, "I think Matt wants you to call him yourself."

"How do you know that? Did he tell you?" Just my one sentence changed his entire demeanor. His excitement was palpable. I kept my mouth shut. "Please, Ellis, if you could just hint at my remorse to Matt, that's all I ask. And if you help me," he added, "maybe I can do something for you."

"Like what?" I poked my salad, but I, too, had lost interest in the arugula and cress dressed with blue cheese and slivered pear.

"Real estate. I hear you're looking for a place to live. Or investments. Your will . . ."

I already had a will. It left everything to Ellen and Jeffrey. I wasn't about to change that, although an image came to me of the four girls eating popcorn out of the trash. If William wondered where I'd suddenly got the money for arugula and real estate, he didn't inquire. Everyone seemed to know so much about me.

"You can still practice law?" I asked.

"Of course," William answered.

I got an idea. "Maybe you *could* do something for me," I told him. "A few weeks ago, it came to my attention the city is offering grants to renovate derelict housing stock. If the applicant has an option to buy a building, he becomes eligible for matching funds. For example, a buyer of a run-down building for two and a half million, can get an additional two and a half from the city to bring the building back up to standards."

165

William looked puzzled. "You're asking me to find you a derelict apartment building?"

"No. I already have one in mind. It's called the Suburban, or it was when I lived in it."

"You know, Ellis, memory is a funny thing, especially when you're our age. I can't remember what was going on in my life two months ago, but I do remember that building. When you and your wife had just married, you used to invite me there for dinner. She was getting pretty good as a cook. It was always Italian food, I recall. And you were always apologizing for it."

The memory of the old days still had the power to sting me. I had been in a headlong rush to end that part of our lives, to move us to better neighborhoods, more acceptable cuisines. Thinking about the past was a waste of time. But part of me longed to recapture it.

"I could use some information about that building. Find out who owns it and whether they'd sell. Get the grant application and see if The Suburban fits the criteria. I want to look into low-cost housing. Perhaps give a few people a decent roof over their heads.

This little speech was as much a surprise to me as it was to William, but as I spoke it, I realized how right it was. William seemed to agree. "Why, Ellis," he observed, "you're starting to sound like your old self: friend of the underdog, champion of the little guy, helper of those who refuse to help themselves. A less wise little brother of the Lord."

"Yes, William, and you're starting to sound like your old self: an arrogant son of a bitch."

"Good," he smiled. "Maybe we can all get back on track after all." He handed me a crisp business card. "I'll look into things for you."

"What's this?" I asked, looking at the unfamiliar address on the card.

"It's where I'm staying until I can go home," William said.

"By the way," I added, "you might check whether some sort of financial trustee is required to sign the grant application. If so, perhaps you can recommend some-one — if you're up to speed. I don't feel comfortable using my personal bank."

He nodded. "Maybe even Stow," he said softly.

"No, not Stow," I answered emphatically. "I'd rather have that megalithic monster FSBEC co-sign than ask Stow for a favor."

"FSBEC *is* Stow."

My head was reeling when William and I said good night. I cut through a mall not far from the Marlene Dietrich window. This building was where film festival organizers usually rented temporary office space during the event. Walking along a colonnade of shops and offices, deserted at 9 P.M., I saw a pile of familiar-looking moving boxes, the same kind I'd seen at Charington Simm's Northlight-Estelle. On a whim, I decided to take a cab, and within twenty minutes, I was outside Charington Simm's folly.

At night the place was positively creepy. No guard was at the gate and the pale spotlights did nothing to dispel the nineteenth-century gloom that settled over the old factory once the sun had set. At once I noticed a light on the third floor of the main building. Secure in my new role as a spy, I crept along the edge of the cobble-stone central courtyard and positioned myself opposite the lighted window. The blonde beauty I'd met packing boxes a few weeks earlier wasn't packing now; she was arguing, or at least carrying on a spirited discussion with someone. She shook her head, shrugged her shoulders. Then, the light in the room was suddenly extinguished.

I made my way to the main entrance of the building, hugging the wall to prevent the motion detectors from setting off the security lights, and my instincts were right. At night, most women exit a building onto the most well-lit street and the blonde was no exception. Neither was Linda Stalton, who followed her out. The two of them were still arguing. I watched as the two women crossed King Street and entered a coffee shop on the north side.

Keeping distance between us, I crossed, too. It's hard to hide in a coffee shop. Through the windows, I could see two men waited for Linda Stalton. Sammy Lito, in the same clothes I'd seen him in the night of the Film Festival, stood up eagerly. The fourth person remained seated. As I had observed before, this man was completely self-possessed and such men are not given to displays of eagerness. I hunched in the shadows of the street and watched Harmensz van Rijn extend his hand to the blonde girl. She accepted the handshake with deference.

Though I well know that criminal activity often goes on in some of the coffee shops of Toronto, I could not imagine this meeting to be anything but innocuous. They were all just too visible. Lito got everybody a drink. They sipped. They chatted. I started to get bored and cold. Then I noticed a long, gray limousine parked in the shadows of an alley that ran beside the coffee shop. This did not strike me as extraordinary, since even teenagers sometimes hire limos for special events. Still, I thought I'd take a look.

Van Rijn got there first. The young blonde was with him. In the partial light that filtered back from the coffee shop window, I could see her puzzled expression. She looked ready for some fun, but a little doubtful, too. I'd seen that look on Tootie's face a number of times. "Cool car, but you're a stranger," I heard the blonde say.

Van Rijn didn't answer. Since I'd never heard him speak, perhaps he was mute. He gestured toward the open back door of the limo. I wondered why he had opened it himself instead of waiting for the driver to do it. When the blonde hesitated, I saw van Rijn pull his hand out from his jacket pocket. Something metallic glinted in the low light.

I thought it was very presumptuous to bribe a much younger woman with jewelry so early in their relationship. Clearly he was slipping a bracelet on her wrist.

She didn't, I noticed, say thank you. She seemed speechless, too. Then I heard a small, nearly inaudible click. A person with a certain history recognizes that sound without having to think about it. Handcuffs.

A limo moves slowly but not as slowly as a fifty-eight-year-old man. I chased it for about half a block, when I puffed to a stop, did a one-eighty and headed back to the coffee shop. Lito and Stalton were gone. And Matt wasn't at headquarters, either. I called him every ten minutes for two hours before he answered.

"Slow down, Portal. Easy man," Matt said as I described what I'd seen. "You have to leave this to me. I can't have a civilian running around after suspects. It looks bad," he warned in his smooth, deep voice.

"A girl is abducted and you're worried about how things *look*! Give me a break, Matt." I was beginning to sound like an outraged citizen.

"I'm going to tell you one more time, Portal. This is a police matter. I appreciate the tip but I'm instructing you to *back off*. Do you read me?"

I was too stunned to answer. I was beginning to get the feeling I was missing something here.

"Ellis?"

"Sure, Matt, sure. I'll just leave everything up to you. Does that include Carrie Simm? Because if it does, it's a damn shame. I'm almost there. One more day. That's all I need. Tomorrow one of the swimming pool kids is going to tell me where Carrie is. I'm sure of it."

"Good. Good work," Matt said, sounding less like a would-be Chief of Police and more like himself. "You keep on the Carrie angle and leave everything else alone."

"Like the Simm homicide?" I couldn't help asking. "What's happening there? What I saw tonight has to relate to that. Simm and van Rijn might have . . ."

"The matter is still under investigation. There hasn't been an arrest yet," Matt cut in. He sounded like a public service announcement.

"No kidding," I answered. I wondered why I was bothering with this at all. I seemed to be going through a lot of trouble for Detective Sergeant West with very little thanks. I decided not to mention my dinner with William.

"Portal, don't get bent out of shape on this. I repeat. Stick to the Carrie angle. Please. I need you on that. Take my word for it." I heard him sigh as if he were very tired.

"Get a good night's sleep, then come in tomorrow and I'll look at everything you've got, okay?"

I felt mollified. A little. "Okay," I said. "It's just that I'm getting sick of witnessing kids being jerked around."

"There are a lot of things in this world I have been unable to stop," he answered wearily. Was he talking about crime, abuse, or love?

CHAPTER TEN

I had horrid dreams all night. Harmensz van Rijn was pursuing Queenie. Tootie and I flew from one end of the city to the other trying to rescue her but I was hampered by something weighing me down. I lifted my arm and saw that Carrie Simm, in a blood-splattered white dress, was handcuffed to my wrist. I woke up screaming, the way I used to in my first days on the street inside a urine-soaked doorway or the underside of a bridge. Confused, I called out for Queenie. Unlike the old days, she was nowhere to be seen.

I dressed and went down to breakfast, avoiding conversation with other B & B guests while I rehearsed my impending meeting with Matt. I wanted to review all the details about the girls at Fry Hall: how I'd seen them again at the deserted swimming pool and observed them in secret, trying to find some clue about Tootie and Carrie. I wanted to ask him about Lynx, reminding him that she appeared in the sticker photo with the other two girls. And I wanted to reveal my fragile deal with Shiv and the girl's offhand agreement to tell me where Carrie Simm was.

I stood by the lace-curtained window looking out on the leaves turning along Hazelton Avenue and planning my report when a dark blue Jeep Cherokee pulled up and parked. Out of it stepped my son.

Amazed, delighted, but feeling a twinge of apprehension, too, I ran to the door. "Good morning, Dad," he said, as if he showed up on my doorstep every day.

He declined an offer of coffee, which left me wondering what I should do next. Awkwardly, I gestured toward a little alcove with two overstuffed floral chairs. "Seat?" Jeffrey declined that, too. He was boyishly casual in jeans and a white sweatshirt with a tiny embroidered crest showing waves, a fish, a tree. I fought the urge to ask whether he was warm enough. Instead I said, "What are you doing here?"

Maybe the question was too abrupt or my tone too sharp. "Is it a problem?" he asked, his own voice turning edgy.

"Not at all, son!" I exclaimed, taking a tiny step toward him. Now I sounded too eager, too pushy. I stepped back. "What can I do for you?"

I saw him glance behind me before he answered. I flattered myself that he cared about my living arrangements. Perhaps he was just relieved that I didn't live in a box anymore. "You have everything you need here, Dad?" he asked.

"For the time being," I answered, embarrassed. "As you know, I'm looking for something more permanent."

He ran his long, slender fingers through his straight, thick, dark gold hair. His mother's hair. His mother's gesture. "Yeah," he smiled, "which brings me . . . Stow asked me to show you another property."

I felt a flash of rage. "Are you a real estate agent for

Stow now?" I snapped, instantly ashamed and contrite that already I'd lost control.

But Jeffrey, who has shielded himself from my anger for a good part of his life, did not respond to that anger now. "Stow has to arms-length himself because of his position. I help him out from time to time. Since Harpur died, he has no close relatives."

You're my close relative, I wanted to protest, but this time, I controlled myself. "What did you have in mind?" I politely inquired.

Jeffrey nodded toward the door. "I thought that if you weren't busy, we could pop over for a few minutes now. That way you won't waste any of your day."

I asked myself whether he was being facetious, addressing me as if my day were as crammed with business as his. But one look at his calm, smiling face assured me that far from being rude, he was being considerate, and to a father who'd seldom taken *his* needs into consideration.

"I'll get my jacket," I said. As I bounded back down the stairs with the jacket in my hand, I felt a strange sense of elation, as if something old and lost had promised to become new and restored.

Jeffrey drove with surprising aggression for so quiet a man. Half a dozen left-hand turns in the face of oncoming rush hour traffic, a couple of gas-pedaled yellow lights and four rolling stop signs later, we turned onto the crowded, run-down streets of a familiar neighborhood. *Oh no!* "Jeffrey," I said as we pulled up at the curb of a dingy side street, "what is this? What are we doing *here*?" Above us, the red tower of the Marble Widow loomed ominously.

"It's okay, Dad. Don't be alarmed. We won't be here long. I just want you . . . I mean Stow wants you to have a glance at this. It's a redevelopment site. You wouldn't live here yourself, of course."

Was that comment his idea of a joke, a reference to my previous homelessness? He wasn't looking at me, how-ever, and it occurred to me that he didn't know about the present inhabitants. He was craning his neck, studying the upper edge where the color of the building's marble sheathing darkened into an intricate pattern visible even down on the ground. "You'll hurt your neck," I said, and Jeffrey laughed.

He had a key to the padlock on the gate. He opened it and we crunched our way over the litter in the front yard and slipped through the opening. I was full of questions but anxious to ask them in the right order and the right tone. It seemed imperative that Jeffrey not know I was already familiar with this site. I didn't want to reveal that I was aware of Stow's connection to the Far Sun Bank of Eastern Commerce, either. And I didn't want it known that I was thinking of renovating the Suburban. Most of all, I definitely did not want the swimming pool girls to see me, especially Shiv.

But I also did not want to shatter this delicate rapport, this unexpected moment I had been given to share with my son. I took a swift glance around the abandoned tower. It looked exactly the same as it had the first time I'd viewed it from this angle. Except it was colder. "Let's go, Jeffrey," I said. "I'm not really interested in this place. I don't know why Stow thinks . . ."

"Come on, Dad. Don't be afraid. I'm right here. Just look around. Think of the possibilities here. This is exactly the sort of neighborhood you'd be interested in."

"What?"

"You're reading me wrong on this, Dad." Jeffrey reached out and put a hand on my arm. "What I meant is, you always cared a lot about people who didn't get a fair shake. I remember you talking about cases in court and saying that we always had to bear in mind the imbalance between the power of the law and the powerlessness of ordinary people, the kind of people who live in neighborhoods like this."

He gestured toward the ruin before our eyes. Out of the shadows came a rustling sound. In a heap of garbage not far from us, a rat scurried about, creating little trash avalanches. Jeffrey looked, too, but he didn't flinch. He loved wild creatures. Maybe he thought *I* was one.

"Jeffrey," I said, moved by his recollections, "There's no way I would ever have the money."

"You have seed money," he said. It did not surprise me that he knew about the divorce settlement and the division of the family assets. Of course he did. What surprised me was his lack of greed.

"Wouldn't you rather that I invested the money safely and grew the estate so that you and Ellen could have a decent inheritance? After the tax department gets its cut, that is."

"Dad, investing in a property for redevelopment is a tax shelter. You'd end up with the government owing *you*." A look of gravity came over his handsome features. "Besides, I don't want to be in a position where I'm waiting to benefit from your death," he said.

"Any other son would have told me to drop dead a long time ago!"

Jeffrey didn't get my joke. "If I inherited money from

you or Mom, I would spend it improving the lives of the people of this city."

Out of nowhere came the unexpected sound of applause, two hands clapping. By reflex, I started for the exit. But I was stopped by a familiar slurred voice. "Nice speech, buddy. Ya wanna drink?"

I turned. Shambling toward Jeffrey, rank and resplendent in filthy gray rags, his feet bound in layers of plastic bags, came the boozer from the cellar.

"Run, Jeffrey! Get out of here! He's a violent thief — a robber!"

But my son just stood there, frozen and staring as the old man came closer. "Hey, take a picture. What are you starin' at, anyway? You got a wallet?"

"Jeffrey, come *on*." I pulled at the sleeve of his sweatshirt, which seemed almost to glow in the sordid surroundings. The way he was gaping at the grimy geezer, Jeffrey could only be thinking one thing: that that was how *I* had looked and sounded and smelled. His father, the champion of people from neighborhoods like this.

I yanked him toward the space in the front wall of the building. I pushed him out into the sunlight. Behind me I heard the old tramp yelling, "Hey, assholes. What's your hurry?" Just as I got Jeffrey to the gate, I glanced back. The drunk was framed in the gaping hole. "Shiv says hello," he mocked. "Hump 'em and dump 'em!"

Jeffrey didn't say a word until we were parked back in front of the B & B. "Dad, don't be proud. You've got substantial capital. Invested properly, it can do some good. For the city and for us, too."

"Us? You mean you and FSBEC?"

177

Jeffrey looked out the window toward the corner of Berryman where a skinny old woman in a mink jacket was trying to untangle the leashes of her five cairn terriers. "I mean you and me," he said, without turning his head.

"No, son," I answered, "no deal between you and me that includes Stow."

"If you say so," Jeffrey replied with finality, just as he had as a little boy when ordered to do a task he couldn't see the wisdom of.

CHAPTER ELEVEN

I never made it to my meeting with Matt. I was so preoccupied with Jeffrey and our reunion that when the limousine pulled up beside me as I waited for the light to
change at Bloor, I hardly noticed. Its rear door sprang
open with such abruptness that I nearly ran into it. But no
one stepped out. Instead, I heard Sammy Lito's voice.
"Justice Portal, I guess you have to get in."

I recognized the small-time crook at about the same
time that I noticed he was twitching like a junkie running
on fumes. "There's a gun in here," he said, his voice
cracking.

"That's not funny, Sammy," I said.

"It wasn't supposed to be funny," he answered, and,
with a gesture surprisingly elegant for him, he moved his
hands slightly and I saw he was cradling a Glock like one
Matt had learned to shoot with his left hand. "You followed us. Now we're following you. Get in." Behind me
some dolt honked for the limo to get moving and set off a
cacophony. As if the impatient drivers motivated me and
not the Glock, I got in.

With deceptive grace, the limo eased into traffic and

continued south. I covertly studied Sammy to judge how likely he was to use the Glock, but in the dimness inside the car, it looked now like the little creep's hands were empty. He fiddled with a series of buttons on a panel on the door nearest him. I heard an ominous click and two frightening things happened simultaneously. Metal shutters snapped across the windows on either side of the car. A seatbelt flew out from somewhere behind me and pinned me without my touching it. I heard another click and realized the belt had locked.

It had been a while since I'd ridden in luxury limos and these were a couple of features I'd never seen before. "I can do without the mechanics, Lito," I said, but my bravado sounded unconvincing.

"Shut up, Your Honor, I gotta concentrate," Sammy replied. He pushed another button and soft light flooded the interior of the car. We seemed to be in a room about eight feet square illuminated by two lamps affixed to gold filigree brackets. Their shades were translucent jade, encased in more gold, intricately wrought and accented with black pearls. Lito, dressed in his usual black slacks and white shirt, sat opposite me in a black seat almost like an armchair. I saw that the belts strapping us to the seats were made of silk brocade with a delicate pattern of dragonflies and poppy blossoms. The Fu Manchu decor almost made me more nervous than Sammy, though it's always hard to remain calm in the presence of a gun held by an idiot.

I have read that a dog's sense of smell allows him to discriminate among odors even when many are presented to him at once. I had the same experience. I smelled Sammy's hair and his sweat and, separately, my own. From somewhere else, I caught just a whiff of some subtle mixture of jasmine and almond overlaying the bouquet of a costly cognac. And I smelled terror, the only scent whose source I couldn't pin down.

"What do you want, Sammy?" I forced myself to ask. I couldn't believe I had so misjudged him. He had to be far more powerful than I had guessed riding in such a custom limo.

"Well, like you know, Mr. Portal, it's not me who wants anything." He waved his hand as if to pull his gun out of the air. I flinched but no weapon materialized. Lito went on, "I won't lie to you, I'm not so good working on my own. I like some guidance. I liked working for Mr. Simm. I did a few little jobs for him. But the boss is dead, long live the boss sort of thing."

I didn't know what he was talking about. He was so jittery it was hard to capture his meaning, even though my life seemed to depend on it. For a moment I wondered whether he had hijacked the limo.

"What do you want with me?" I repeated. "What did you do with the gun?"

Confusion crossed his features as if he were trying to remember where he'd misplaced the Glock. "The boss has the gun, Mr. Portal. The boss has the gun." He shook his greasy head and his little ponytail flapped his shoulder like a dead herring.

"Van Rijn?" Beside my fear of the gun and the smells in the confined space, I was beginning to feel the panicky grip of claustrophobia. I struggled against the brocade seat belt, but that just made it tighter. "Let me out of here, Sammy." I gave the seat belt a yank.

"Don't move," Sammy hissed, and without warning, I felt pressure against the nape of my neck. An acrid odor of oil and burned powder from an uncleaned gun made me gag. I heard an intake of breath behind me and the Glock moved a fraction. Against my skin, it felt unexpectedly warm as if someone had been holding it close in a hot hand. This warmth, plus the disconcerting sensation of moving without being able to sense the speed or direction of the car, provided further inducement to nausea, but also, somehow, to a little burst of bravery. "You people better do whatever it is you intend to do with me because I'm about to lose my lunch all over this pretty car of yours."

I felt the gun move away, and I heard the soft rustle of fine fabric close to my ear. Van Rijn was suddenly sitting in a seat beside me. No seat belt snapped into place to trap *him*. I figured the gun was probably now pointed at Sammy because the lackey jerked into action. He clicked something again and a little mahogany cabinet I hadn't noticed slid open beside him. He reached in and took out a sealed bottle of commercial mineral water. From a shelf on the door of the cabinet, he selected a chilled crystal goblet and handed both to me, all the time keeping his eye on a spot over my left shoulder.

Remembering the bum in the Widow's basement, I contemplated smashing the crystal, grabbing the gunman and cutting his throat. Or I could have shaken the bubbly water and shot it in Sammy Lito's stupid face. But I know my limits. The almond/jasmine cologne and the five-hundred dollar cognac were out of my league. So was the Glock.

"Drink," van Rijn commanded. One word in perfectly unaccented English. I drained the bottle and handed it back to Sammy, along with the unused crystal goblet. My hands were shaking. So were Lito's. He managed to set the bottle down at his feet but it rolled away. When he bent down to retrieve it, the goblet slipped out of his hand and smashed against the edge of the cabinet.

At this display of ineptitude, van Rijn raised his other hand and pointed a slim black object at Lito's head. I squeezed my eyes shut, expecting to hear the blast of a shot. Over Sammy's head, a video screen suddenly sprang into life. It looked like a movie taken at a high-class strip joint.

"I have been told," van Rijn said, "that you are a man who appreciates the beauty of women."

I was so startled I just stared at him. In profile, Harmensz van Rijn, I couldn't help but notice, was a handsome man. I supposed he had to be if kidnapping young women was his day job. Suddenly angered, I lashed out. "I don't know what this is all about van Rijn, but if you're some sort of pimp, count me out."

"Justice Portal," he said in the silky tones of a bank president, "this matter is far more complicated than simple prostitution. Surely you've already realized that." He pointed the remote again and onto the screen flashed the still face of a stunning redhead. I'd never seen the girl before.

"Am I supposed to know this person?" I asked.

"Not unless you want to," van Rijn answered with a low chuckle. Above us, image after image began to flash on the screen, each beautiful face replaced by one even more beautiful. Sammy squirmed around trying to see, but one glance from van Rijn rendered him motionless, which for Lito meant twitching in place.

"What is this?" I demanded. One thing my life has taught me is that anger is stronger than fear. "Why are you showing me pictures of strangers?"

"Oh, you don't like strangers?"van Rijn asked.

"Allow me to accommodate you." He pointed the remote again and onto the screen came a motion clip of a lean young woman dressed in a short leather skirt and a lace vest, her back to the camera. She lifted the skirt to reveal garters holding up black fishnet stockings. The whole thing was so trite I almost laughed. Until the woman turned her head and I saw the Lynx in heavy makeup that hid both her scar and her beauty. "Get that off the screen, you pervert. I'm not a damn john!"

"Of course not," van Rijn said. "You're a man of business with three million dollars to invest. I can quadruple your money, ensure that you have a worry-free retirement."

"What?" I was beginning to feel as if the limo had driven onto another planet. "What are you talking about?"

Before he answered, van Rijn gestured toward the cabinet. Lito looked at him, puzzled. Instead of chiding Sammy the Loser, van Rijn made another gesture. This time Lito opened the cabinet and poured van Rijn a cognac, one with a bouquet so exquisite that for a moment, I mourned my long-ago evenings with a snifter coddled in my palms like a lover's face.

The voice of van Rijn brought me back to the limo, which seemed to be going in circles. "A generation ago," he said, "the government of China decided to stop overpopulation by imposing a strict policy of one child per family."

"What does that have to do with me?" I asked, although light was beginning to dawn.

"Like most experiments that neglect to factor in human nature," he said, "this one was doomed to failure. There are now millions of young Chinese men with no marriageable women to meet their needs."

Above us, the beautiful faces were still replacing each other on the screen. "And you meet that need with girls like that little blonde last night?" I asked.

"You sound very righteous, Judge Portal. No doubt you've already been to the police."

A jolt more effective than cognac shot through me. I frantically glanced around, trying to see the gun.

"Calm down, Judge. I didn't bring you here to shoot you. I brought you here to listen to a proposition." He stopped and laughed softly. "Wrong word. A proposal. A business proposal."

"Forget it. I am *not* interested in an area of the sex trade that would be better called slavery." I'm sure I sounded mortally offended.

"You better not yell, Your Honor," Lito piped up. Van Rijn silenced him with a frown. The lackey sank deeper into the ridiculous seat.

"Only a fool would take on a business partner who does not believe in the product," van Rijn said. "So no, Judge Portal, I do not want you involved in my trade. What I want is this."

With his remote, he stopped the parade of faces at the most beautiful face of all. The fine bones, the haunted eyes. The innocence. The knowledge. Carrie. Carrie Simm.

Was this photo more recent than the ones in the police DVD? I just couldn't tell. Suddenly, I thought I understood what van Rijn was after. The anger was running hot in me now, making me reckless. "Save your damn money, van Rijn. You want me to stay away from Carrie Simm. You know I'm close and you want me to back off. Fine. You look for her. You find her. You keep her. She's all yours. I'm glad to oblige. I'm sick and tired of the whole case anyway.

Just let me out of this car and I'll never go near anybody again who knows anything about Carrie. That good enough for you?"

"You don't get it," Sammy said. His voice was quivering.

"What?"

"You miss his point. The boss don't want you to stop looking for Carrie. He wants you to find her. He wants you to tell *him* first when you do."

"Why doesn't *he* look for her himself?"

"I intend to, Judge Portal," van Rijn answered.

I didn't get a chance to ask him what he meant. I heard another of those effective clicks I'd been hearing all through this little mystery tour. All at once the seat belt released me, the door opened and I found myself pushed out of the limo onto the sidewalk in front of my own temporary home.

I should have been more careful of my B & B hostess; the reformed madam. My being under her roof was information to be sold to the highest bidder, or the most desperate. Maybe Sammy Lito had used the information to stay close to his new "boss". Then I heard a shot like a truck backfiring, shattering the genteel silence of mid-morning Yorkville, and Sammy Lito slumped to the floor of the limo as the vehicle crawled away, just another big-money car in a big-money town.

The train to Cochrane left at sunset and I was on it. I cleared out of the B & B, after leaving two phone messages, one to William Sterling to tell him to call Matt West himself because I was going out of town. The other to tell Jeffrey that I would call him when and if I returned to Toronto. Later it occurred to me that the only sense either man would get out of my message was that I was hysterical when I called.

My next mission was to tell Matt about being kidnapped. Carrying a gym bag with a few possessions, I set out for headquarters, but before I had gone two blocks, I changed my mind. I wandered south past stores and restaurants until I found a coffee shop on the corner of Church, a place I used to frequent with Queenie. I sat down with a mug of coffee and stared out the window. On King Street, people walked aslant, like boats tacking into the gray leaf-strewn wind. I shivered, sipped, considered my position. That familiar, uncomfortable sensation, the gut feeling that the enemy was everywhere, gripped me. I had lost all sense of who knew what about me. My address, my money, my connections. Everyone was after me for something. How, for example, had I become so close to the police? I tried to reconstruct my recent conversations with Matt. What had he meant when he said that if I helped him, I wouldn't have to go it alone?

For the first time in eight years, I felt the same overwhelming sense of being trapped that I had felt before my breakdown. Where was my freedom? My privacy? My safety? Could I buy *that* back for three million dollars? I had done so once. The day I attacked Harpur Stoughton-Melville and became an outlaw. Maybe I needed to escape my life again.

But then I thought of the photos van Rijn had shown me. I thought of Carrie and of Tootie, whom I now despaired of ever seeing again. I felt grief. There was another freedom gone. The freedom of walking away from a person and never thinking of her again. Van Rijn was after Carrie. I didn't know whether Sammy was dead. It didn't really matter under the law. An inchoate offense. Intended. Begun. But not completed. The same as the offense itself. I now knew for sure that a killer was stalking Carrie, and anybody who might know where she was. I had to go to the Marble Widow and somehow warn the girls.

After I stowed my bag in a locker at Union Station, I took all but a couple of dollars from my wallet and locked the wallet up, too. I put the locker key in my pocket and took the subway five stops to Wellesley. From there it was a short walk to the Marble Widow, but I found myself running.

When I got to the fence, I had to rest before I squeezed through. My back hurt. I stooped over with my hands on my knees to ease the pain, but then I had to straighten again to grab lungfuls of air.

I was breathing in burned hair.

When I had been a judge, I'd been exceptionally attentive to olfactory signals. The slightest hint of alcohol on the breath of a witness altered the weight I would give to his testimony. I could detect jurors who were smokers. Since no one is allowed to smoke in the jury room, smokers are therefore more eager for trials to end quickly. And the faster a verdict is rendered, the more likely it is to be "not guilty". So some believe.

But living in the streets and in the ravine had honed my senses even more. I could smell my supper cowering behind a bush. I could smell disease and I avoided sleeping next to it, even outside. I could sometimes smell the difference between a real hooker and one who was a cop.

And now I smelled the results of a major fire. I braced my hand on the fence to ease through. My fingers came away covered with a thin film of powdered ash. Everything looked a shade grayer than its usual grime. Warily, I stepped into the building. Inside, the burned smell intensified. Singed rags, rats. I made my way toward the door to the pool.

By the time I reached the door, I could hardly breathe for the stench. In the little hallway, I saw an indistinguishable mass of partially burned material on the floor. When I carefully pushed the pile apart with my foot, I saw it was charred wooden slats. From beneath them poked a piece of smoky glass, the triangle of mirror the girls had used on their makeshift vanity table. I stepped through the hall and into the pool area.

All the windows of the pool room were gone, blasted into shards by the heat of the fire that had blazed and finally blackened the tile walls of the room and every inch of the pool itself. The effects of the household that had squatted at the bottom were unrecognizable: ashes, soot, oily black puddles of melted plastic. Even the metal ladder I'd used to lower myself the day I'd left my gifts was a warped pile of tubing at the pool's bottom.

Retching and choking, I stumbled outside. In the small yard behind the building, a thin skin of soot-covered ice floated on the cistern. I broke the ice, dipped my hand in the freezing, fetid water and splashed my face.

I staggered away from the cistern and nearly fell over an object I at first mistook for one of the sleeping bags from the pool.

I crouched down. My hands shook. My teeth chattered and the taste of vomit rose in my mouth again. I reached out and pushed aside a piece of blackened debris that covered the face of the little corpse.

She was dead but not burned. In fact, had her young

head and neck not been coated with gray ash, she might have been sleeping. On her side, her knees pulled up, her feet in their heavy black boots one atop the other, a girl with a thin face and spiky hair lay with her lips slightly parted. She wore a black T-shirt. On the front in white laundry marker was written, "Back".

"Legion! Goddamn it to hell!"

There was no one in this deserted ruin to hear my cry. Even the rats were gone. I sat on the ground beside the body, immobilized by a need to mourn this inconsequential child.

I prayed for her unstained soul, like the unbelieving hypocrite that I was. And then I gathered my wits and went back into the destroyed pool. At the shallow end, I eased myself over the edge. I carefully sifted through all the charred remains on the floor until I was satisfied no one else's body was there.

I walked a block to a public phone and dialed 911. I steadied my voice and forced myself to describe the pool, the yard and the location of the body. The dispatcher asked my name. I almost gave it, but then I caught myself. I hung up. I fled back to Union Station and retrieved my things. I had but one thought in my head. *Get out of town.*

CHAPTER TWELVE

Eastward long enough for daylight to fade, long enough to clear the acres of rail yards that sever the city from Lake Ontario. East by north east, turning as the Don River turns. North along the river. Then north until the end of steel.

North past old downtown factories, past Riverside Institute, out of which my friend Harpur Stoughton-Melville wandered into the river marsh, where we found her in her nightgown early in the winter in which she died.

North past golf courses, slick suburban high-rises, past Wigmore Ravine where I once lived in the cave at the river's bend.

Disappearing into the darkness of the north as day disappeared, swallowed into bedroom communities: Thornhill, Langstaff, Elgin Mills, Richmond Hill.

North past Lake Simcoe and into summer cottage country, the rocky reaches of lake shore and forest: Washago, Gravenhurst, Bracebridge, Huntsville.

North past the city of North Bay, seat of the Ministry of the Attorney General. North past midnight, passengers huddled on the faded tweed seats of vintage railway cars. Ontario Northland Rail.

Restless, swaying with the speeding train, I walked through the front cars. A few middle-aged couples discreetly slept upright, side by side, their heads nestled against the shoulders of their partners. If there were ever sleeping cars on this old run, there weren't anymore.

In the middle of the train, trappers and winter campers, their heavy padded coats in heaps at their feet, sprawled out of their seats and into the aisle, making it hard to pass.

The cars got older and shabbier as I moved farther back. In the very last cars, large families of native Canadian Indians, Ojibway and Cree, crowded together. Mothers and children curled in the same seat, their masses of black hair glowing as they spilled over the seat backs.

Watching these Natives, I couldn't help but remember all the times Queenie and I had slept together. Not as lovers. We'd never been that. But as derelicts and drunks. I'd been too immersed in my own misery to feel protective of her then. My middle-class manners had dictated that I give her the best spot in a desolate doorway or let her sleep on a park bench while I took the grass, but that was the extent of my concern. But then we'd dried out and after that, I'd been restored to the kind of wealth that allows — no, compels — a man to help others. She was the first person I thought of. Now as I sped toward her, I assumed my old friend would be happy to see me, an assumption often unwarranted in the life of the random traveler.

At dawn, the train pulled into its northern terminus, Cochrane, where five thousand souls lay fast asleep in the tidy little buildings that lined its compact and frigid streets.

I was still restless. It would be five hours before the departure of the "Little Bear", the local train that would take us another two hundred miles north to the Cree town of Moosonee. Thoughts spun in my head uselessly as I whiled away the time. I ended up thinking how good it would be to have somebody to tell my troubles to. Somebody safe. Somebody sane. Queenie.

The Little Bear proved to be more of a relic than the train that brought me to Cochrane. I watched the scraggly muskeg swamp roll for a hundred miles, marked at intervals by scrawny fir trees, some hundreds of years old, but no taller than me, with trunks no thicker than my leg.

When we reached Fraserdale, all roads ended and the map was nothing but empty white space, veined with a network of rivers.

All in all, it took almost twenty-four hours to get from Toronto to Moosonee, and the northern night came earlier. It was dark again when we pulled into town and the train doors slid open to eject me, a few tourists, some Indian families, and any trappers who'd not already departed into the bush. Within minutes, I was alone outside the one-room wooden train station. A few white flakes swirled in the cold air and for the first time I noticed a thin layer of snow.

I had made no reservations in my mad dash, but when a Cree Native who kept saying "The Lodge?" gestured toward an old but well-maintained van a few yards away, I got in. Painted on the van's side was a five-foot high representation of a mythical bird with outspread wings, the pinions ending in arrow points. Two middle-aged couples arranged themselves and their luggage, and we all settled in for another ride. Roughly forty-five seconds later, the announcement, "The Lodge!" took me by surprise but I followed the two couples into a rustic structure that, even on the edge of the Arctic, bore an uncanny similarity to the typical summer family resort. The same wood paneling, the same ancient television in the same lounge, the same faded print of two figures paddling across calm orange waters against the same setting sun.

I needn't have worried about lacking a reservation. We five were the only guests, and fighting off earnest offers of company at breakfast the next morning, I ate alone facing a window that looked out over the saltwater Moose River, which rose and fell with the tide.

All I knew about Queenie's position here was that she was studying at the College of the North in a special program for native Indian women who planned to become community health workers. I had paid for her books and fees. I wasn't sure where she lived and thought that Moosonee probably offered limited possibilities for out-of-towners. But maybe Queenie wouldn't be perceived as an out-of-towner. Maybe she'd be regarded as one who had finally come home. Whatever the case, Queenie had steadfastly refused all offers of financial help from me except for expenses directly related to school, so I assumed she must be staying with family or friends.

I was finishing my breakfast when I saw an animated group of Cree women on the road. I watched with interest as one woman, whose age I guessed at about forty, related to the others some narrative that held them enthralled. Her face was lit with happy energy. Her hands, though economical in their motion, seemed to illustrate her words vividly. Her hair, which despite the cold was not covered by scarf or hat, was straight and thick and darkly gleamed like pewter.

A good storyteller, the woman gave little away in her expression, which became more deadpan as her tale progressed. Only when she appeared to reach the punch line, at which her audience exploded into laughter inaudible to me, did she allow herself to laugh, revealing for the first time the gap where one of her front teeth was broken. And I realized I'd been watching a Queenie I had never known.

Hastily I threw on my jacket and bounded out the door. The women still stood in a small knot around Queenie, speaking softly. At my approach, however, they all fell silent and the disgrace of the interloper flooded through me.

"I'm sorry, I —"

"Your Honor! Oh, my goodness! How . . . ?" Queenie's voice, though husky, rang like crystal in the cold air. "What are you doin' up here?"

"I needed to talk to you," I answered absurdly, as if I'd just strolled over to our doughnut shop at Church and King instead of barreling twenty-four hours across forest and rocky shield, river, lake and muskeg.

She said a few words in Cree and the other women, nodding and waving, walked off, headed away from the river and toward a modern complex of buildings made of red brick and sporting a sign in the distinctive curved, dotted and triangular symbols, based in part on shorthand, that allowed the Cree to represent their unwritten language. I assumed the sign read "College of the North".

Glancing toward the buildings, I felt compelled to

say, "If you're on your way to class, Queenie, I'll wait. We can meet later. I have time. I mean, I don't want to interrupt you. I —" I couldn't say anything more. I just reached out and embraced her. In the cold breeze off the river, I could smell hints of salt and ice. I wanted Queenie to smell like she used to: woodsmoke and sweetgrass. I wanted her to smell like the clean autumn street on an evening after a day's hard rain. I wanted her to know she was my only friend. "*Kee way tin,*" I whispered. Her Cree name. It means "north wind" and she taught it to me after I helped her learn to read.

"*She wah nei lah way ow,*" she answered. *South wind.* The name she gave me the day I taught her what "long-winded" means. "You must be in a lot of trouble to come all this way," she said softly, pulling away.

"Two people I know died," I blurted, "one in a fire, the other shot right in front of me."

She put her hand on my sleeve in a spontaneous gesture of comfort and consolation. "I hope it wasn't somebody real close."

I thought about the contempt I'd had for Sammy Lito and the hopelessness of Legion's brief life. "I didn't know them well at all, Queenie, but maybe I cared more about them that I realized. Or maybe," I added truthfully, "I'm just frightened for myself."

"So you ran away up here? Why didn't you go to the police? Matt West would help you. He helped us before."

I shivered in the cold. Queenie's jacket didn't seem much thicker than the one I wore, but she didn't seem to mind the wind. Which amazed me. In the city she wore so many clothes you couldn't see her figure from September to July. Her face seemed almost unlined, too. "Being up here agrees with you, Queenie. It's only been two

196

months but already you look like you fit right in, the picture of health."

"You look a little pudgy, yourself, Your Honor. You need me to share doughnuts with. I guess bein' up here I live more healthy. Plus I got friends to help me at school. But . . ."

We turned from the river and began to make our way up the main street of town, a stretch of about three blocks on which there were buildings widely spaced: a tourist shop and restaurant, a few houses, a church, a squat brick building with more bars and grilles on the windows than a Church Street pawn shop.

"But?" I waited for Queenie to say she missed me. Instead, we stopped in front of the small church.

"You gotta come in here sometime," she said. "They got beautiful new stain glass windows with pictures of Indians and animals. Owls, rabbits, moose and that." She stopped and turned to face me, the cold wind from the wide river blowing her thick, straight hair back from her face. "But I miss you a lot. The reading you taught me is real good. The teacher said I can comprehend all my books. But writing? That's a real different story. Otherwise you could write to me and tell me your troubles and I could write back and save you comin' all the way up here." She glanced into my eyes, and reading something there, added, "Don't get me wrong. I'm glad you come. Came."

"I'm glad I came, too," I replied.

"But how do you figure I can help you?"

"I thought about that all the way up here, Queenie. The main problem is, I don't know who to trust."

"The woman and the snake," Queenie said knowingly. I thought she must be referring to an Indian legend.

"The Garden of Eden," she explained with an accusatory smile as if, like her, I should be reading the Bible every day. "Generally speaking, you trust a person who has a snake for a friend and you're gonna get bit. What I mean is, maybe you oughta keep better company. But don't worry, Your Honor. No snakes here. Not in town, anyway. I'm happy you trust me. I hope I can help."

We turned a corner and I realized we were headed away from the college. "What about your class?" I asked. "That's where you were headed, isn't it?"

"I was only goin' in early to help a couple of the girls with a assignment about alcoholism. Guess I know a thing or two about that," she added with a rueful smile.

"I suppose we both do," I responded.

"You see that buildin' over there — ?" She pointed down the street to the barred windows and the grille across the door. "That's the liquor store. And when you get inside, it's like it was all over Ontario twenty years ago. There ain't no booze on the shelves. You gotta fill in a form and give it with cash to the man behind the counter and he goes where the liquor is locked up and brings it back to you."

We gazed at the sturdy brick walls, the iron barriers. "Wouldn't have stopped me," I told Queenie.

"Nah, me either."

It was a reformed drunk's joke and we laughed together as we made our way through the little settlement. It was time for school and the streets were full of children, many of whom stared at me, knowing at once that I was an alien. I wondered if that's how a boy or girl from Moosonee felt on the streets of Toronto. "Where are we going?" I asked.

"My first class ain't — isn't — until noon and it's only

about 8:30 now. So we're going over to where I stay. You game for that?"

"I'd be grateful," I told her. She smiled and took my hand. Suddenly, Queenie became the leader and I the follower. I gave myself up to it and after a short, freezing stroll, we arrived at the edge of town. Beyond a few streets of neat frame houses, I could see only fields and straggly fir trees.

"These here are the generation houses," Queenie said, and though I didn't know what she meant, I noted the pride in her voice.

"Generation houses?"

"Yes. We call them that because the people who live here, the Cree, I mean, are the first generation to live in houses instead of in what you would call a teepee."

"You mean a tent? The Cree still live in tents?"

Queenie smiled the beautiful broken-toothed grin I missed so much. "Some of 'em live under picnic tables in the park at the corner of Jarvis and Carlton!" We laughed again. I had forgotten how good our mingled voices sounded.

"Lots of Moosonee Cree still spend most of the year in tents in the bush, hunting and trapping," she continued seriously, "but now they got notebook computers with software that keeps track of where they set their lines and the Internet to tell them how much people around the world are paying for skins and that."

"The world is changing."

"Yes and no," Queenie replied as she led me up the concrete steps of a simple green house completely unadorned and unlandscaped. The contrast between the bleakness here and the lush vegetation of Toronto's parks and ravines made me wonder if Queenie missed Toronto.

As if she read my thoughts, she said, "Not a lot grows easy and it isn't as pretty up here as in the city, but nobody's gotta sleep on a doorstep, neither."

I couldn't argue with that. Even with its simple furnishings, her house was palatial compared to the tiny cubicle in her city rooming house, where she'd cooked on a hot plate and awakened to the bells of St. Mike's cathedral calling the street people into the day.

I remembered waking in Tootie Beets's house. I felt that dreadful grief again. Queenie sensed it. She sat me down at a smoothly planed pine table in a kitchen with a new stove and refrigerator. "We need coffee. You just give me a minute here and then we'll talk. At least there's no more going down the hall for water." She slipped out of her jacket and plugged in the electric kettle that sat on the white tile counter.

"This is a big place," I observed, taking off my jacket. I was surprised by an unaccustomed pang of jealousy. "I imagine you must live here with somebody else."

"Yes. Four of us health students live here. We're sort of minding the place for the owners. They moved further north, up to a settlement on the shore of Hudson's Bay. They say it's just getting too crowded in Moosonee." I smiled but Queenie wasn't kidding.

In a few minutes the coffee was brewed and she set a steaming cup in front of me. "A woman, family, money or the law?" she asked abruptly. "Them's the only things — I mean those are the only reasons why people would be shooting other people. So which is it?"

I thought about it for a minute. "There is a woman — well, a very young woman, a girl really. She disappeared and because she had spent a lot of time on the street, Matt West asked me to try to find her."

"Like you helped me to find out what really happened to my girl, Moonstar?"

Queenie must think about her daughter all the time. The way I think about Jeffrey.

"The missing girl's name is Carrie Simm. She's —"

"The daughter of that bigwig movie guy. I read about her being missing and all. Plus I read they still didn't find out who killed her father."

I shot her a look of pride. "You mean you can read the newspaper now? Queenie, that's incredible!"

She kept her eyes shyly trained on her hands, folded around her coffee mug. Her words were low and almost gruff, but I didn't miss the sense of accomplishment that informed them. "You're paying good money for me to learn things and I'm learning them as fast as I can. We read the newspaper because it's up-to-date and because it's easy, seeing as the news in it matches what's on television. So, yeah, I read about the movie guy and his missing kid. But why do you think I can help?"

"Because you know how street kids think."

She didn't answer at once and when she did reply, her words were tinged with sorrow. "If I knew better how Moonstar thought about stuff, maybe she wouldn't have died."

"Queenie" — I reached out but she avoided my touch, instead moving toward the sink and leaning with her back against the counter and her arms folded in front of her.

"What do you know so far?"she asked, her brow furrowed in concentration.

Momentarily overcome at the enormous task of laying my current preoccupations out in a sensible way, I sat tongue-tied.

Queenie came back to the table and took both my

hands in hers. "It's begin at the beginning time, friend," she said.

I laughed softly. The phrase was one we'd used when we'd gone together to twelve-step sessions. It was like a talisman and it worked.

"You remember my landlady, Tootie Beets?"

Queenie rolled her eyes, "That kid with the black lips?"

"Dark red. The city expropriated her house in an agreement with a condominium developer. We all had to leave and before I could say good-bye, Tootie took off. Just disappeared."

"So?"

"She left me a note. It said, 'The Ferryman will be there'. I had no idea what she meant, but the name sounded threatening. Then it started to crop up again and again. The words can be made into a symbol — like this." I took a pen out of my pocket and on the back of my train ticket drew the cross made of six letters. Queenie studied it without reaction.

"So Tootie disappeared and the movie kid disappeared and you think it's connected?"

"I saw a photo with both of them in it. And Tootie started to act suspicious, too. Matt knew some things about Tootie."

"Matt knows everything," Queenie said, "he always does."

"Yeah, well whatever he knows or doesn't know, he asked me to talk to Tootie. He also told me to stay away from the Simm murder investigation but I ignored that. I found out Simm died bankrupt. That he was a drug dealer. That he had a lot of beautiful young women working for him hoping to make it into his films and become

202

world famous. I learned Simm had a business partner with whom he was involved personally as well as financially. She's a junkie, too."

"Had enemies, it sounds like," Queenie commented.

I found that just by the act of explaining the mystery to her, I understood it better. "And sometimes his daughter Carrie was one of those enemies, but not always. She was his best actress. And she seems to have been the only person in his life who stood by him to the end, despite his personal faults, his arrogance, his control and his indifference. Carrie was with him when he was shot. She was at his side when he was taken off in the ambulance, and she stayed with him until . . ."

"Until what?"

"Until, like Tootie, she disappeared." In spite of all that had happened with the girls in the swimming pool, I still hadn't accomplished the one thing Matt had asked. My frustration was clear to Queenie.

"And you been looking for her without luck?"she said. "Are you worried that this shooter is after her, too? Maybe he's the same guy killed her father."

"Yes, maybe. And Matt figured that if Carrie was afraid and needed somebody to turn to after her father's death, she'd go back to the street kids who were her friends. It seemed like a good theory. I did some more checking around and I found a gang of girls living in one of the catacombs, a squat they call the Marble Widow." What I'd just seen there came back to me in a flash.

Queenie put her hand on mine, calming me. "Yeah," she said. "I heard of that dump. They say it's a real slum. More rats than squatters. You didn't see this Carrie there?"

"No. But I did see Tootie's cat."

She screwed up her face, trying to assess the significance of that clue. I didn't think she was impressed. "One cat prowls, they all prowl." She said.

"What?"

"It's a Cree saying. There's a rude meaning and a polite meaning. The rude meaning is you can't trust men. The polite meaning is a lot of cats look just alike."

"No. It *was* Tootie's cat. And after watching those girls at the Marble Widow for more than a week, I found out they did know Carrie Simm, and I even bribed one to tell me where Carrie is. I was *that* close!" I held my thumb and finger in the air.

"And then somebody got shot?" Queenie asked, her black eyes on mine.

I told her about the limo and van Rijn and poor, doomed Sammy Lito, the idiot. A look of tenderness softened her features, "Thank God it wasn't you," was all she said.

"I was so frightened I had to run. I'm no hero, Queenie. But I had to warn the girls first. I went back to the Marble Widow, too late. The place was burned out. And one of the kids, the most helpless, is dead. I keep seeing her lying there. She was the most pathetic tiny thing. Skinny little stick legs. And crazy. They called her 'Legion'."

"Mark 5: 1–15."

"What?"

"Legion was the crazy man in the Bible that lived among the tombs. He had a million demons that tormented him and made him so wild that nobody could hardly hold him even if they put chains on him. One day Jesus came and the demons inside Legion seen him and knew who he was and they ran out of Legion and into a bunch of swine that drowned themselves in the sea. Then the man called Legion was clothed and in his right mind and not crazy anymore."

"Queenie," I said, "is there anyone in the Bible called the Ferryman?"

She wrinkled her nose again, such an endearing gesture that at the sight of it, loneliness stabbed me. I was realizing more and more how I'd missed her. "One person I heard of who runs a ferry in a story is that guy named Charon. He's the one you have to give a penny to to take you across the river of woe and into the underworld."

"Ah, yes. From the Greek."

Queenie took on that air of pride again. "Before you ask me how I know them old myths, I'll tell you. I don't know any Ferryman in the Bible, but I studied a book that said plenty of tribes and races and that have the same idea that a man in a boat could come and take you to a safer place. Is that what you mean?"

"I don't know. Maybe."

She pushed my coffee mug toward me. I took the cup and sipped the coffee.

Queenie sipped her coffee, too. "I'm sorry, Your Honor," she finally said. "I guess you come all the way for nothing. Unless . . ."

"Unless what?"

"Unless information isn't what you really come — came — up here for."

My face flushed and I was embarrassed to meet her eyes. But she simply reached out and touched my face. It was a brief touch. Her fingers didn't linger. But I could feel the warmth of her smooth, dusky skin.

"To me," she said, "this is kind of simple. If you know

where one kid is and you know she was friends with another kid, you figure where one is and then you know where they both are. I went through this all the time with my girl, Moonstar. I was always out lookin' for her. I was always findin' her with one friend or another. Young people are like that. They ain't crazy about being alone."

I thought about the solitary moment I'd observed with the Lynx. I wondered why she was so different from the other girls.

"Your Honor, look at it like this: A girl's father gets killed. She gets scared. She runs. First she's gonna run blind — anybody who'll take her. But pretty soon, word gets around. One girl talks to another. Friends take care of friends."

"Yes," I answered. "Tootie told me that a girl called Lynx helped her. This Lynx knows both Carrie and Tootie." Another thought occurred to me. "I checked that whole Marble Widow building and I didn't find Tootie or Carrie, but I did find a couple of sleeping bags in the . . ."

"So Lynx is your first person Carrie ran to. But probably there's a second person, who took Carrie to a safer place. Matt West thinks Tootie is that person." Queenie went on with a precision that would have pleased Matt, "You only got one thing left to figure out. Girls aren't dumb. They watch. They listen. They been on the street a long time and they're real used to looking out for the main chance."

"What do you mean?" I asked, leaning closer.

"To get exactly what they need." She leaned back, took a sip of coffee. "My guess is it's you gave 'em that."

"What?"

"They were looking for a safe place to stay. Safer than the Marble Widow. Carrie would run first to the squat because of Lynx. But then something better came up. Someplace Tootie knows about. Where would Tootie find out about a safe place?"

"Me."

"You got it."

But she wasn't finished. She sounded serious when she said, "Your Honor, you had a nice ride up here, a nice little chat with me. I'm real happy to see you. But you don't need me to tell you what's goin' on or to tell you your job, neither. You got to help them girls. If you don't and something worse happens to them, you're gonna be like a bum again, or worse." She looked at me as if rendering a judgment. "When the unclean spirit has gone out of a man, he passes through waterless places seeking rest and finds none."

"Cree or Greek?" I interrupted.

She didn't seem amused. "You can't go backward. You gotta go forward. Matthew 12: 43-45. She picked up the pen and the train ticket I'd left on the table. Laboriously, she wrote three Cree symbols.

"What's that?"

"My name. Look at it any time you think you ain't smart enough to solve a simple case like this."

I was flooded with gratitude, hope and a sense of relief. There were other feelings, too, which I decided to examine if I ever got a personal life.

I caught the Little Bear south that same day and the next evening I went straight from Union Station to Wigmore Ravine. There was no fast way down, so I had to take my time.

It had been winter in Moosonee. In Toronto, it was still autumn. The full moon, the Hunter's Moon, threw its

207

golden light into the vale of trees. Hunters named it because its rising immediately after sunset allowed them to stalk their prey into the night without interruption. I, too, worked by its light. The slippery leaves threatened to topple me with every step, but single-mindedly, I descended deeper and deeper into the wild valley.

CHAPTER THIRTEEN

Prickly branches of hawthorn and rough saplings of oak and maple scraped my face and fingers as I skidded down the steep incline of Wigmore Ravine to the rushing Don River. The moonlight shone through the trees, casting deep shadows in the forested hollows. I knew the place so well I could have negotiated the twisting path in total darkness. Had done so countless times.

On the river, the golden rays were scattered like tossed coins. I could make out the dark green flow breaking white where it hit a a low ridge of submerged rock, then smoothed again and raced toward its straitjacket in the downtown core. Walking was easier on the river bank than it was in the wild woods.

On the train back from Moosonee, I'd tried to reconstruct my final conversation with Tootie. I recalled how interested she'd been when I'd told her about my outdoor living arrangements. An older man flattered by the attention of a younger woman, I hadn't found her questions suspicious, her sudden fascination with nature a little odd for a street person.

I carefully traced the moonlit river upstream past the reforested meadow at the core of the ravine, and toward the deeply eroded cliff at the northern edge. The bank began to rise steeply on both sides as the river widened. One foot in front of the other, I followed a pebbled ledge perilously close to the water along the foot of the cliff until it took a sharp curve, then descended to a wide beach of pebbles.

The moon, more brilliant and more silver as it rose, illuminated the water with a clear metallic sheen. At the far end of the beach, I could make out a dark spot in the wall of the cliff. This was the entrance to my cave, my haven from the random cruelties of winter, my old familiar home.

There was no question of sneaking up on the cave. Between the light cast by the moon and the crunch of my boots on the pebbles, only a bullhorn would have been more effective in announcing my presence. Nonetheless, I stayed as close to the cliff base and made as little noise as I could.

I was only a few feet from the cave's mouth when a soft whimper, followed by the nearly inaudible sound of cloth being dragged across stone, met my hypersensitive ears.

I managed to get within a few feet of the entrance to the cave without attracting the attention of whoever was making that sound. I maneuvered myself flat against the cliff wall and peered in. I could see nothing but a few rags scattered just inside. The rags had definitely not been there when I'd last visited the cave. "Anybody here?" I whispered and in reply, I saw the rags move. I heard the whimper again, this time accompanied by the sound of scurrying. Compulsively, I darted through the opening in the rock as I blinked, momentarily blinded. All I smelled was coldness and moisture.

In a second, though, the apparent quiet of the cave revealed itself to be full of sound. From somewhere deep in the darkness came the steady drip of water on rock. And the river, too, lent its muffled rush to a medley of other noises: my own breathing, wind rising in the trees, the whisper of traffic in the neighborhoods far above. And then again, the scurry, the whimper and a new sound, the unmistakable tinkle of a small metal object being bounced against a hard, uneven surface.

I held my breath. A whimper. Silence. A tinkle.

And there in front of my dark-adapted eye, my friend Star, Tootie's orange-and-white tabby, gave a hearty swipe with its paw. A tiny object came to a stop at the toe of my boot, shining softly in the low light of the moon. At my feet lay a spent ammunition shell, a cartridge case the exact size and shape of the one Matt West had shown me. From the gun that had blasted a tidy hole in Charington Simm's skull.

I wrapped my handkerchief around my fingers before I picked the shell up. It was evidence in a homicide investigation. And I realized it was not the only evidence I had. I was no longer a homeless vagrant and an amateur detective, either. I was a responsible citizen and a sworn judge. Time to turn to the authorities. For me that meant only one person. I put the shell in my pocket and headed back downtown, ready to face his wrath.

"So did you think that a citizen could be murdered in the middle of town in broad daylight and the cops wouldn't notice?"

"Matt, I wasn't sure . . ."

211

"You've disappointed me, Portal, you really have. I thought we were perfectly clear on this. We were supposed to be working together." He rose, stepped out from behind his desk, crossed the room and stood behind the chair I was sitting in. I felt as though I were being interrogated. I made a motion to turn around but he stopped me by pressing down on my shoulder. I didn't know with what. I kept my eyes straight ahead. "Why didn't you come right to me?"his voice boomed. "I can understand being traumatized as a witness and fearing for your life. But to skip town?"

"Matt, give me a break. I'm not a professional like you. I intended to talk to you, but I got overwhelmed. First I see Lito shot. Then Legion's dead. Anyway, I'm here now. I don't know what the issue is, except timing."

"Timing is everything," Matt answered, "in this job like everywhere else. We stall on taking a witness statement, we fail to interview an informant in a timely manner . . ."

"What do you mean an *informant*? I thought I was engaged in community liaison."

"I'm using the term informant loosely," he said without coming around the front of my chair.

"No, you're not," I nearly shouted. I stood and faced him. His handsome, dark features were stern. He showed no surprise at my outburst. "You've never been a man to use words carelessly," I accused. "Or to use people without a well thought-out plan. You don't care that I didn't report Sammy Lito's death to you as if I were Mr. Model Public Citizen. You care enormously that your decoy got out of range. That's what I was, wasn't I — a decoy? Are you hoping whoever killed Simm will take a shot at me? Is that the only way you can catch crooks these days?"

Matt raised his left hand in a gesture of conciliation. "Calm down, Ellis," he said huskily. "This job only works if you forget you got any other life."

"At the moment, I *don't* have any other life," I answered miserably. "I'm starting to feel guilty that Tootie's involved."

"Is that what's got you so upset?" Matt asked.

"Yeah, and you?"

He rubbed the back of his neck. "I've seen William."

"How did it go?" I asked, not wanting to hear one more word on this topic.

"It went," Matt said and smiled.

He sat down. After a few moments' awkward silence, during which both of us struggled to gather our thoughts, he resumed. "We've always been sincere in our appreciation of your many contributions to the Police Service, Portal. We trust you. But even so, we can't fully disclose our undercover strategy to a civilian. I *can* tell you that for your own protection, we didn't send you out to look for Carrie Simm alone."

"You mean you tailed me?" I thought about the people I'd encountered during the past six weeks. Ducharme was no cop. She had a record. I'd given it to her myself. "Who was working for you? Tell me."

"You wanna drink, buddy?" Matt slurred.

I stared at him in astonishment. "You mean that filthy creep at the Marble Widow is a police officer? But he robbed me and attacked me with a bottle. And he's foul mouthed. One of the girls told me . . ."

"The officer was protecting his cover. He broke a bottle. He asked for and was given fifteen dollars. He taught a dirty word to a street kid. What would you like me to charge him with, Judge?"

"Why if you had a drunken bum, excuse me, an undercover officer, looking after those girls, did you need me, too?"

"Corelli wouldn't let you go it alone," Matt answered, "yet she wanted your connections and your expertise."

"I don't *care* about Corelli." I was starting to get angry again. "You didn't trust me! Not for a minute. Who else did you have spying on me? Lito? Is that why van Rijn shot him? Because he was a police officer?"

"Lito was all over the place," Matt answered. "When Simm died, he didn't know what to do with himself. He came to us six weeks ago. Said he saw you at a film event where you were asking questions about Simm. He said for a certain sum he would keep an eye on you. We told him to get lost."

"He did a pretty thorough job of getting lost," I said, remembering the sight of his slumped body. "That's another thing I've got on my conscience."

"Forget about him. He's not your concern. In fact, Ellis, none of this is your concern any longer."

"What do you mean?"

He kept his eyes down, as if he had a pressing need to examine the four paper clips he kept arranging and rearranging with his left hand. "You're done now. Go home and relax. Take a couple of weeks to think about things. Then come back and see me. If you are still willing to help us out, Deputy Corelli has a new mandate from the Board to —"

"What are you talking about? What about Tootie?"

"It's out of my hands, Ellis, so to speak. Corelli wants you off the case. We need to find Carrie Simm because she's a missing person. You tried to find her and failed. So you're dismissed. Simple." It didn't sound like Matt talk-

214

ing. It sounded like a marionette. Was that the tone he used when he had to convey orders he didn't personally believe in? Police or no police, I was going to find Tootie. But I couldn't ignore what I'd come to show Matt.

"This isn't as simple as you think," I said. I reached into my pocket. I pulled out my large white handkerchief and took my time unwrapping its folds so that Matt was leaning across his desk, vibrating with impatience as the last bit of fabric fell away from the shiny little shell.

His face lit up. "It's from a Raven — an ACP," he said softly. "How did you get that?"

"I could turn this over like a good citizen and let you and your boys figure out where it came from. It might take you a little time. Alternatively, you could really put some trust in me and tell me what's actually going on with the Simm case." Once or twice I'd found it necessary to pull rank on police officers in my courtroom. That had happened rarely. I didn't know what was emboldening me now unless it was my old refusal to fail. I used to be a man who wouldn't take no for an answer. Maybe I was becoming such a man again. "You tell me what you know, officer, and I'll return the favor."

Matt's jaw hardened and for a minute, I thought he was going to arrest me for obstructing justice, and forcibly remove the shell from my possession in a lawful non-warrant seizure of evidence. Instead, he shrugged his broad shoulders and began to lay the facts before me. "Van Rijn is what we consider a small player on the heroin scene. He supplies a few dealers here in town, businessmen, people in the arts, middle-class users with no street contacts. We could arrest these losers and haul them in, make a deal. We forget charges, they spill what they know about van Rijn. But right now, that's just not worth our while."

215

"You mean you left him alone hoping to nab someone higher up on the chain?"

"Not exactly. Van Rijn has been a hanger-on around Charington Simm's crowd for a couple of years now. On occasion, he's explained his occupation as a 'talent scout'. We live in a free country and we are not going to question landed immigrants about their occupations without strong legal reasons. One reason we might engage in such questioning is if we get an alert of some sort from immigration or from C.C.R.A."

The initials sounded ominously familiar. "Who?"

"Canada Customs and Revenue Agency," Matt answered.

"Oh," I said with disdain, "my enthusiastic friends in the tax department. They're after van Rijn? What for?" I was feigning ignorance.

So was Matt. "We don't know," he said.

I'd had enough. "Matt," I said, "I'm tired. I've been spying on young women for weeks. I've lost my home, my landlady, and I'm still carrying my personal effects around in a gym bag. I've been to James Bay and back in forty-eight hours. I've had to deal with Sammy Lito alive, which was just slightly worse than dealing with him dead. I've been almost reconciled with my son and now I don't even have a phone where he can call me. I'm going to tell you everything. Then I'm finished with this case." I slumped back in the chair exhausted.

It was like offering drugs to a junkie. Matt couldn't wait to hear where and how I'd found the shell. I also told him what I'd seen on the limo's TV. At the end of my narrative, he said simply, "We've got to get Carrie and the others out of that ravine now. We'll get warrants and stake out the whole area. You know that ravine better than anybody. You'll be our technical advisor. You're back in."

I thought about how frightened Tootie would be of a raid. "What do you need warrants for? We're not going to arrest the girls, just bring them out," I said. "But if we go down with personnel and equipment — lights, dogs, fire-power — we're telling the world we think somebody is in the valley. If the girls *are* down there, they probably come and go for food. What if you stake out the ravine while they're away? They'll see you and take off without ever returning to the cave. Besides, we have their mental state to think about. If they are in the cave, it's because they're terrified. At the first sight of police, they'll run and some-body will get hurt for sure. They're victims, after all, not criminals." Matt's dark green eyes were intent on my face. With what had I purchased such respect? With informa-tion, of course. The coin of the realm.

"What do you propose, Portal?"he asked.

"There's a better way," I answered. "Let me go down again and talk to them. Maybe I can persuade them we can protect Carrie and them, too. Once Carrie's safe you can interrogate her about her father and about van Rijn."

Matt shook his head. "There are too many unknowns here."

"We know van Rijn wants Carrie. We don't know what caused that fire at the Marble Widow, but if he torched it, if he smoked them out, then he followed the girls and they may have already led him to the cave, but he'd have to be fit and nimble to get down to the river."

"Or else know the ravine as well as you." He paused. "How do we know he hasn't got them already?"

"We don't, Matt. But if I go back down, I can have a better look around. I can —"

"You need daylight," Matt interrupted.

"I can go down in the dark. I can go back down now."

He thought about it for a long minute. "All right. But I don't know how much time I can give you on this, Portal. If there's a real chance Carrie Simm is down there, we're going to have to move in. I'm not the only one working this case, you know."

I nodded. We rose and I shook his hand. "I'm going to get something to eat and something warmer to wear," I said. "Then I'm going back to Wigmore."

CHAPTER FOURTEEN

I struggled back down into the ravine and lurked at a distance from the cave. Soon, the rising sun warmed enough to lift a thin layer of frost from the trees and rocks of the valley.

Stiff and sleepy, I wandered off into the bushes to urinate. When I returned, there was Tootie outside the cave, sitting on the pebbled strand and shivering. She and I jumped at the sight of each other. Her jet-black hair, white face and blood-red lipstick were as incongruous as the plumage of a penguin against the subtle mist of the river and its banks.

"Mr. Portal," she said, whispering. "How come you're down here? Are you, like, homeless again?"

I had spent the night thinking about what to say if I found her, how to convince Tootie and her friends to come along with me. I decided my angle would be that no one held them responsible for the fire or for Legion's death. If they were here together, I could tell them that Matt would find them a place to live. If Carrie was with them, I could counsel the girl that her father's killer would soon be found.

And Tootie — well, for Tootie, I had something different planned.

But now that I was standing face to face with her, all the carefully structured sentences that I'd rehearsed fled and instead I asked a stupid, obvious question. "You came here to stay — here in the cave?"

She kicked the rough beach with the toe of her boot. I saw that it was scuffed raw. For all her bizarre tastes in fashion, Tootie had always been impeccable in her grooming. I could smell her perspiration, unwashed skin, dirty hair.

"Yeah," she said sarcastically. "We had a whole lot of choices and we picked this." She swept the scene with her smooth white hand. But her dark red nails were broken and the polish chipped. "We coulda found a garage maybe or snuck around some park, but this location is, like, equipped with private accommodations, including cold and cold running water." She nodded toward the river and grinned. "By the way," she added, "we tried those toasted artichoke things. They were puke-o." She treated me to a demonstration of an index finger down her throat.

"Carrie and the other girls here with you?" I asked nonchalantly.

Tootie eyed me and looked away without answering.

There had been moments during the time I'd known Tootie when we'd almost approached a degree of tenderness. She had brought me some soup when I was sick. I had helped her with the household financial accounts. But since she was a "reformed" street kid and I was a "retired" judge, mostly we found it best to keep our distance. Landlady and tenant. Rent paid. Room provided. No questions asked. I felt that was different now.

"Tootie, would you be free to go for a little walk?"

"A walk?" She asked doubtfully. "What do you mean? Like where exactly?"

"Around the ravine. As I told you before, I used to spend a lot of time here. I could show you some nice spots. Looks like you could use a change of scene." I nodded toward the cave entrance. Smack in the middle of it sat Star assiduously licking her paws.

"What time is it?" Tootie asked, surprising me.

I glanced up at the sky, then over to where the spruce trees at the top of the ravine caught the dull light. "Not quite seven o'clock, I would say."

"I been sitting up all night. Without even any blanket." She glanced again at the cave. One good reason she'd be outside was that she was acting as a guard. I remembered little Shiv's comment about Lynx and Scotty working as guards. At the thought that Shiv was now missing, I shivered. Tootie shivered too and hugged herself. I took off my jacket and extended it toward her, but, "no thanks," she said. "I'm okay. I guess I could go for a walk if it doesn't take too long."

Amazingly, she held out her hand. I took her cool fingers in my own as we proceeded along the pebbled beach. It made me smile to think that Tootie, probably because of her grandmother, was kind to old people. We walked in silence, Tootie glancing around rather nervously. We reached the point at which the fast-flowing river broke into rapids not far from the boulder in the middle. The bank here was a treed slope on one side and a forest on the other. The mist began to clear. Sun skipped off the surface of the water and dappled our faces.

"Tootie," I said cautiously, "how would you feel about having a job?"

"A job?" She almost choked on the word. "What kind? I ran away when I was just a kid and I never really worked until I got the house a few years ago. That house was my, like, company, my first and only business. I don't think I could work for somebody else — you know, have a boss and all. I . . ."

She stopped dead, both in the middle of the path and also in the middle of her speech. "Wait a minute," she said, "this is a deal, isn't it? You came down here to make a deal."

I turned to face her. I had to be careful about my stance, my tone. I did not want to seem an authority figure. I wanted to be a friend. "I can help you, Tootie. All you have to do is assist me to get those other girls, especially Carrie, out of here. You're not criminals. Everybody knows that."

"You should be smarter than that, Mr. Portal."

I laughed, uncertain of her meaning. It seemed people always liked to tell me they knew something I should but didn't know. Lawyers do it to judges. Children do it to parents. "What?"

"A lot of times the one thing everybody's so sure they know turns out to be the one thing that isn't true."

"What do you mean?" I studied her face but her head was bent. It was no news that she was hiding something, but I was disappointed that she couldn't look me in the eye the way she had always done.

"Let's walk a little farther, Tootie," I suggested. "You can call my offer a deal, but I consider it more along the lines of a friend helping a friend to get on with her life." I wasn't sure whether she'd stay or flee, but when I resumed our walk along the river, she followed right behind.

The wood was silent and the path narrow and rutted. Once or twice I heard Tootie stumble, but I fought the urge to assist her. She needed to know I was confident of her ability to survive. I managed to make my demands heard without turning my head, sparing us the eye-contact problem.

"You know what the word 'villain' means, Tootie?" I began.

"Y-e-s," she drawled, sarcastically. "It means a bad guy. So?"

"So poor Carrie had a villain for a father."

"You didn't need to come here to tell me *that*," she sneered.

"I think she and your friend Lynx knew another villain, too, Tootie," I went on. "An Asian man, not from Belgium, but from Holland. Harmensz van Rijn."

I heard her stumble again, thrashing in the brush as though breaking a fall. I turned, reached out and grabbed her arm before she went down. She shook my hand violently away. "You're damn thick, you know that, Mr. Portal?" Now her dark eyes were locked onto mine, blazing. "I tell you and I tell you but you don't hear. Like all the other freaking relics. I *do not* talk about my friends. You *got* that?"

I took note of the temper tantrum. I'd thrown enough of them myself to know they are a cry for help. "Tootie, I've been to the swimming pool."

"What swimming pool? It's almost winter. Didn't you notice? Or are you getting blind, too, as well as deaf and stupid?"

Her uncharacteristic nastiness was a sure sign I was on the right track. She knew what I was talking about. "I've seen Shiv and Scotty and Lynx. I know about Legion.

And I think Carrie is with you. I want to make sure Shiv and the others get a decent place to live. And I want Carrie to get the counseling she needs. She saw her father shot in front of her. She'll be grieving. She —"

"You only *think* you know what you're talking about," Tootie shot at me. "You only *think* you know about Carrie. You don't know a damn thing about her. Take my word for it, Mr. Portal."

"Tootie, you have to listen. You're in danger down here."

"Yeah, yeah," she responded. "We could, like, get tetanus from a rusty can or a coyote could eat us. Oh, oh, oh . . . it's scary."

"This is nothing to kid about," I warned sharply. I had to fight the urge to give Tootie a good shake. "If you don't listen to me, the police are coming down here to force you out. That's if you're lucky, Tootie. If you're unlucky, van Rijn will get here first."

I saw real terror cross her young face. I couldn't imagine what was going through her head, but she had to be wondering whether van Rijn knew about the ravine, the river and the cave. "How do you know I'm not just here by myself, camping out like you camped out?" She asked.

"Because, among other things, I saw Star at the swimming pool with Shiv. Now Star is here. I think that means Shiv is here, too."

Tootie glanced back toward the path we'd traveled. Then she looked me in the eye and said, "You want to make a deal, okay. I'm listening."

"Look up there," I said to her, and I pointed toward the residential streets on the south edge of the ravine.

"Yeah? Grungy old buildings on Eglinton Avenue."

"It'll take us fifteen minutes to climb up to those buildings," I said. "If you come with me, I'll tell you exactly what I have in mind — or what the *deal* is, as you put it!"

"Either you're stupid or you think I am, Mr. Portal. First you tell me the cops are coming. Then you say that Dutch asshole is on the way. And now you expect me to follow you into a deserted building?" She shook her head as though there was no comprehending some people. But when I left the water's edge and kept right, winding up the treed slope to the top, she followed, stern-faced and silent.

Our feet scattered shards of glass as we crossed the cracked pavement of the Suburban's rear parking lot. A rusted metal door swung on a single remaining hinge. As if in mockery, an old padlock, securely fastened to a bolt, hung in midair, the bolt long rusted away from the door frame into which it had once slid.

"What happened to this place?" Tootie asked.

"I guess as the years went by maintenance was allowed to slide and it finally got ahead of the owner. Then the city stepped in and allowed the owner to evict all the tenants in order to completely renovate."

"How do you know all this stuff?"

"I know it was decent once because I lived here. And I know about the city's involvement because I have a lawyer working on a grant application to fix this building."

She laughed contemptuously. "Where would you get enough money to fix a big building like this?"

"Tootie, I'm not proud of this but the money comes from a divorce settlement with my ex-wife."

"Because she's so rich she has to support you?" Tootie asked in wonderment.

"No. We both had money. We invested it."

"Oh," she said knowingly, "you mean your judge money."

"Yes, I guess you could call it that." I smiled.

"And now you want to invest it again?"

"Yes."

Tootie slipped ahead of me. "I'll go first, Mr. Portal. I'm used to dumps like this. She led the way down a hallway lit only by the crisp autumn sun now spilling from windows visible through open or absent apartment doors. "It's creepy. Like people just ran away in the middle of the night or something," Tootie observed.

"I don't think the people left in a hurry," I told Tootie as we climbed up toward the fourth floor, from which I hoped to show her the view from the topmost apartments. "I'm sure they had many months' notice."

"It's depressing," she said, moving toward the rear of the apartment I'd ushered her into. A twenty-foot window stretched along the northern wall and looked out over Wigmore Ravine. From this angle, the valley was a mass of yellow and gold with the dark green river sliding through. Tootie's face filled with pleasure, but her expression clouded when she realized the lay of the land. "A person could spy on us," she said. "I get it. A person could come up here and watch what we're doing and figure out how to get us."

"Don't be afraid, Tootie. I'll help you." I moved closer to the window where she stood and gingerly stretched out my hand until my fingers brushed the scuffed leather of her jacket. I expected her to shrug me off, but she didn't. "To be honest, Tootie, it never occurred to me that a person could come up here and spy, but it's certainly possible. As for your being in danger, yes, that is something I want to talk to you about."

Though her words were harsh, her voice sounded weary rather than angry. "The cave is way safer than that freaking heap of crap downtown with that gummy-mouth clown in the underground. I don't know what was with that guy, anyway. He made like he was protecting the girls. What a villain!" She peered at me to see if I got the joke.

"Tootie, I'm not talking about a safe place to hide out. I'm talking about your life."

I was surprised to see her eyes fill with tears. She dragged the back of her hand across her face and sniffed, hard. "Now we're talking about that deal, right? I tell you where Carrie Simm is and you give me a job in this heap of shit." She glanced around the ruined apartment.

That was as good a way to explain it as any. "Yes," I answered.

There was a long pause as we both stared out over the ravine. A red-tailed hawk swooped from a nearby tree, followed the course of the river for a hundred feet, then soared away, disappearing into the northern reaches of the valley.

"Wow," she said sarcastically, "what a excellent opportunity for my big future."

"I have a plan for this building, Tootie," I replied. "All I want right now is for you to listen to my plan."

That bored look young people wear when they think a sermon or a speech is coming played over her sharp face. "This better be good," she said.

"If my grant is approved, I can hire contractors to turn this place back into a home for people such as your-self. We can mend everything that's broken: the rotten balconies, the crumbling garages, the pot-holed parking lot. Inside we can plaster and paint and fix all the

227

cupboards and closets and floors. And when we're done, we could find families — and single people, too — who'd live here because of their appreciation of the valley and their understanding that an apartment building can be a community."

Tootie glanced around. A piece of plaster the size of a garbage can lid had fallen from the ceiling, leaving a hole from which rusty water dripped onto a warped segment of parquet flooring. Maybe it was asking too much for Tootie to imagine what I saw.

"Would you keep the wood floors?"she asked. "I kept the wood floors in my house. My grandmother didn't let them rot, though."

"We could certainly keep the wooden floor," I said cautiously, not wanting to squelch this tiny flame of interest.

There was another long pause. Outside a ripple of wind swept the ravine, causing the leaves to shimmer.

"Who's 'we'?" Tootie asked.

"What?"

"You said *we* could fix the broken stuff and keep the floors and that. So, who do you mean when you say 'we'?"

I remembered Jeffrey's words about the Marble Widow and I felt a stab of guilt, as though my deal with Tootie were somehow disloyal to my son, but I answered anyway, "You and I, Tootie. We could work on this together. We can plan the renovation, decide exactly what should be repaired or removed, supervise the work. When the day comes, we'll find tenants. And we'll run it. You and I together."

She burst out laughing. She laughed so hard that a tear escaped and skittered along the white curve of her cheek. "You're out of your freaking geez mind, you know that? You expect me to buy that you'd trust *me* to be your partner in the big business of running a apartment building? How come you think I could do a job like that?"

I thought carefully before I answered her. "A Chinese philosopher once said that a king should rule a large country the same way he would cook a small fish."

Tootie wrinkled her nose and pursed her dark lips. "You mean if you do a small thing okay, like really careful and not too expensive, then probably you can do a big thing okay, too? That sort of thing?"

"That's exactly what I mean," I said, taking heart. She *was* interested. "You did such a good job running your rooming house that I am willing to take a chance and hire you to run our new palace."

"When would I start?"

"The minute the city approves my application"

"What if they don't — approve it, I mean?"

I didn't have the heart to think about that possibility. "Let me worry about that, Tootie."

She looked out the window and studied the scene for a long time. When she spoke, she kept her back to me. "What if I can't tell you anything about Carrie? What if I don't even *know* anything about her?" She turned and faced me. I saw defiance in her expression. A particular kind of defiance familiar to me as a parent and a judge, the defiance of one utterly convinced that even the most attractive gift is nothing but bait for a trap.

"I'm not bribing you, Tootie. If I get the approval for this grant, you have the job whether or not you tell me about Carrie. But if you don't help me out, I can't stall Matt West any longer. He will come down to the cave and get Carrie and he won't come alone."

"How will he know where we are? Are you going to tell him?"

I smiled. A look of shock crossed her face as she realized that her use of the word was as significant as mine had been. "*We?*"

"Leave me alone! Why should I care about this pile of crap? I had my own house, my own business. I don't want a job. I don't want to be somebody's assistant. Somebody's slave. Forget it." She pushed past me and fled into the unlit hallway.

She didn't get far. I found her sitting on the floor halfway down the corridor. I couldn't see her clearly, but I could hear her. She was doing something I'd once seen Queenie doing — sobbing almost soundlessly. Queenie told me that when she had to sleep in the women's shelters, the last thing she wanted was to be seen as weak and an easy target. She learned how to cry without opening her mouth. She said shelters, even in the middle of the night, were noisy enough to cover the sound of weeping with your mouth shut.

But the hallway of the apartment building was not noisy. Once I stood still there was no sound at all except the rhythmic suppressed sobbing.

"I'm so sick of it," she sniffed. "I'm cold. I'm starving. I haven't had a good shower since back in my house. I want my own house again. Or else I want my money now. I don't want to help Carrie hide anymore. I just can't do it."

She was weeping openly, and for a while, I just let her sob. Gradually, I moved closer to her and when I saw that she wasn't going to run again, I lowered myself to the floor beside her. The rug smelled as though animals had used it as a latrine. And Tootie smelled like an animal. No hint of lime and coconut now. Still I fought an urge to comfort her in my arms.

"Tell me what happened, Tootie. Begin at the beginning and take your time. I'll listen. I'm a good listener. I used to do it for a living."

She half sobbed, half laughed. "Yeah," she said, "I guess a judge does get paid to listen to witnesses. Is that what I am now?" The question was fraught with panic.

"No. No, Tootie. You're just a friend talking to a friend about other friends." I fought the temptation to badger her. I took a breath, calmed myself and began to assist Tootie in constructing a rational narrative.

"I lied in the note I left you the night I skipped, Mr. Portal. I'm sorry, but I thought you might be mad if —"

"Tootie, forget about me. Just say exactly what happened that night."

By now it was 9 A.M. In the dull gleam from distant windows, I saw Tootie draw her knees up to her chin and hug her legs in exactly the posture Jeffrey had always adopted when I'd told him a story in bed, around the campfire, beneath the Christmas tree. Had he listened? I listened now, my whole body bending toward the sound of Tootie's voice.

"No, Mr. Portal. My friends didn't call me that night. A couple of weeks before, Lynx *did* call me. She said she was helping somebody I knew and could the person stay in my house? I told her no because every room of mine had a tenant. Plus I already had a couple of those eviction letters I didn't tell anybody about. Then Lynx told me the person was Carrie. I got scared because I saw on TV that somebody killed Carrie's father. Lynx said that was the reason we had to help Carrie. In case the killer was after her. I still said no, but I was worried because Carrie hates Lynx. I felt real guilty.

"So where did Lynx and Carrie go?"

"To the catacombs. In the old days, Lynx knew the leader of the Spiders. They lived in the Marble Widow. That's why they call it a widow. But it wasn't safe either. The night you told me about the cave, I went to save Carrie. I had to sneak her away in the middle of the night and wait until morning to find the cave. It took us a long time. When we finally got there, I found out Shiv had followed us. With Star. I told Shiv to take Star back so a coyote wouldn't eat her. And I told Shiv I would kill her if she told Lynx where Carrie and I were."

I tried to say as little as possible. The information I had so long sought at such peril was spilling out.

"Carrie and me were only going to be here temporary. Carrie promised she'd go to her mother. But then . . ."

"Then, Tootie?"

"The police didn't arrest anybody for killing Carrie's father. We thought Carrie would be safe and could get back to normal real quick. Instead, she started getting sick."

"You mean she's ill?" I asked in alarm.

"I mean she's bananas," Tootie answered. "Wacko. Out to lunch. Like Legion, only worse."

"Worse? How?"

Tootie gave me an assessing glance, reluctant to say too much. She'd told me plenty already. "Violent," she said.

I parted my lips to utter the question, "Violent in what way?" But I didn't have time to form the words.

"There's more," Tootie said in a rush. "Lynx, Shiv and Scots sleep in the cave now, too. They came because Legion died. I know it wasn't their fault, but Scotty said we could all get blamed. We asked Lynx about it. She just said to shut up because she was figuring out what to do and we were distracting her.

"Who burned the Marble Widow, Tootie?"

She hugged her knees harder and rocked a little and kept her gaze away from mine, as if I could have seen her eyes in the dim hallway. "Legion set the fire. But not on purpose. She was so scared of fire! But it was getting colder and colder and Legion found where Scotty hid the lighters and lit all the damn candles at once. Something caught on fire and there was a whole lot of smoke and Legion, like, passed out. Lynx found her before she got burned and hauled her out, but it was too late and nobody could wake Legion up."

"If Lynx tried to save Legion's life, how could you all be blamed for the girl's death?"

"I don't know," Tootie said. "I don't know anything anymore. I think I should get out of Toronto. Maybe out of Canada, too." She ran her hand through her short, coal-black hair, causing it to stand on end. "I wanted to go to the cops from the night Lynx called me. But Lynx said no. She said Carrie would be called as a witness to murder and that if anybody knew we hid her we would be abstracting justice. It was just what you said, too."

"*Ob*structing. Obstructing justice." I was beginning to feel more and more responsible for the dangerous position Tootie was in.

She began to rock, the way I'd seen Legion rock, but Tootie seemed in full possesion of her faculties, even when she muttered, "I've got to take my trouble to the Ferryman. I've *got* to."

I sighed in exasperation. "Whoever this Ferryman is, he's not helping you right now. Who *is* he, Tootie?"

She gazed ahead as if she could see the man himself in the dark, reeking hallway. "When the Ferryman wants you to know him, he'll let you."

Anger triumphed over guilt. Stupid adolescents! I was sick of secrets and mysteries and other people's problems. And now I was contemplating spending all my money on a heap of rubble. *To hell with it and to hell with them.* I turned my back on Tootie Beets. I stood up and headed out.

I was about to board the bus on Eglinton Avenue when I heard running behind me and turned to see Tootie hopping over a low, straggly hedge. The moment's delay inspired the driver to close the door in my face and drive on.

So, short of running away, my only choice was to stand still.

"Look, Mr. Portal," Tootie struggled to say, her breath coming in gasping pants, "I didn't mean to be a smartass. Don't be mad. Don't go."

"Tootie, I'm tired. I'm old. Too old to be climbing up and down the walls of ravines. Too old to convince hardheads to act in their own best interests. Whatever you want to do about Carrie, just do it. Act responsibly, or not. As you choose. Leave me out of it."

"I want to make a deal. Please, Mr. Portal. I do."

I simply stood as if waiting for the next bus. The likelihood was that I'd be standing there for at least twenty minutes. She pretended I wasn't ignoring her.

"The deal is I accept your offer. I'll do it. I'll go down there right now and I'll tell Lynx that unless we turn ourselves in, the police are going to take us out."

"Nobody is going to 'take' you out, Tootie," I said with exasperation. "They're going to bring you out. It's not the same thing."

"And I'll make sure we stay there until you come with somebody to help Carrie."

I peered down the street as if expecting another bus to arrive momentarily.

"And finally," she said. "I'm offering to make a worthwhile investment."

I couldn't resist. I turned to look at her. "I don't want to be anybody's damn assistant. But I wouldn't mind being a partner. I can't go halves, but I don't think business partners have to be equal, right?"

"No," I said, intrigued.

"Okay, all the money the city is giving me for my house, over one hundred thousand dollars, I give it to you and you make me your partner. Then we do all the things you said, fix that dump up. Make decent apartments for people to live in. Run the whole thing like a small fish. Two small fish."

CHAPTER FIFTEEN

About noon, I called Police Headquarters. They said Matt was home waiting for my call. His home phone seemed to ring forever before someone finally picked it up. "Hello?"

Perhaps I shouldn't have been startled to recognize William Sterling's voice. "I'm *home!*" He sounded absolutely ecstatic. "And I owe it all to you, Ellis."

"But I didn't . . ."

"After I talked to you, I realized if you could seize the reins of your life and drag it back on course, I could, too."

I didn't have a lot of time at the moment to engage in philosophical analysis, but it did occur to me that sometimes a person does nothing and accomplishes more than when he strives mightily. "I'm glad I could help," I replied.

"Ellis," William said, "I've been trying to reach you. I wanted you to know I filed the grant application. The Suburban is available for purchase and fits the grant criteria. I proxied your signature as solicitor of record. No problem with that. There is, however, one unforeseen complication. There's a rival applicant."

"A rival?" I needed to talk to Matt right away, but my whole future seemed to be hanging on that grant. "Someone else wants the same building?"

"Not to worry. We'll do our best. With your housing experiences, I'm sure we'll have the edge." He laughed. I could just never be sure when William was mocking me. Maybe it was some strange way of showing affection.

"Thanks, William. Do whatever you have to." I would have added *and send me the bill*, if I'd had an address. "I have to talk to Matt," I finally got around to saying.

"He's at the Celtic Star with the guys from the pipe band. Yonge and Davisville. Need Matt's cell?"

"Thanks, William," I said, scribbling the number. But I didn't bother to use it. Instead I grabbed a cab.

The pub was roaring with talk and the clink and clack of food service. Every once in a while, there was a squeal as if somebody was gearing up his bagpipe — or had sat on it. It took no time to find the sole black Scot in the place. Matt wore a police sweatshirt over his kilt. As I pushed my way through the crowd, the thought foremost in my mind was that he'd have to put trousers on before he could catch the girls in the valley.

Working my way up to the bar until I was standing behind Matt, I was careful not to tap him on the shoulder. Instead, I shouted out, though I was so close, "Matt, I found Carrie Simm."

When Matt and I reached Sloane and Eglinton Avenues in the neighborhood of the ravine, it was dark again. The ETF, the Emergency Task Force, was preparing its ropes for a quick descent down the cliffs, the Youth Bureau social workers were at the ready and as many lighting technicians as Charington Simm used to shoot a movie were on standby to flood the ravine with illumination.

"We have to take it easy, Matt," I warned as we slipped out of a police cruiser parked with a dozen others on Sloane Avenue in front of a school. Behind the school a paved path led toward the ravine directly above the cave. "I think only you and I should go down there now and we have to take the long way. Once we get the girls out of the cave, we'll have to walk back along the river and through the woods. Your trained officers may be able to climb up and down cliffs, but the girls can't and neither can I. *Neither can you.* I almost added. "All we need to do is to talk to them."

"What if they're armed?"

"Armed?" The thought shocked me.

Matt gave curt orders to a crowd of officers, some of whom followed us to where the paved path ended and the forested approach to the ravine began. By the time we were in the center of the woods, however, we were alone, Matt following close behind as I led him past the old apple orchard. He asked, "How do you know where we are?"

I laughed sadly. "I'm like an animal, Matt. When it's dark I use my sense of smell. Halfway between the spot where we entered the ravine and the river, there's a derelict stand of apple trees. I can smell them now, can't you?"

He drew a deep breath. "I suppose so," he answered.

I could also smell the river and could tell exactly how close we were. The only sounds were the rushing of the water and the crunch of our feet on fallen leaves. It was a clear night and directly above us a few stars glimmered distantly. The moon had not yet risen. At the top edges of the ravine, the sky glowed with light reflected from street lamps, houses, apartments and parking lots. On the southern rim, the ghostly shape of the deserted building I'd been in only that morning rose up against the night sky. I thought I saw a flash of light, a pinpoint in one dark window, but decided it was probably a car's reflection.

But no light from fire, candles or flashlights marred the black expanse when we reached the flat beach in front of the mouth of the cave.

"Where is it?" Matt whispered urgently as we made our way over the pebbles. "I don't see anything."

I didn't either. Or hear any voices.

The detective shone a small but powerful flashlight he carried on his belt toward the mouth of the cave. There was no response to the light, not the slightest scrape or shuffle. Even Star, the cat, would have reacted to the burst of light. "Matt," I said, "they're gone."

He uttered a profanity that ended in a hiss. "Damn it, Portal. I've got a hundred people here. And you're saying I've wasted my time?"

Ignoring him for the moment, I walked slowly toward the cave. I tried to imagine Tootie returning there after we'd parted that morning. My hopes, my expectations for rational cooperation between the girls and the police, had obviously been unrealistic, but I *had* hoped they'd at least stay put until we could talk to them. Clearly, although I had expected little, I had expected too much. The cave had been abandoned in haste. Scattered clothing littered the beach. A dirty blanket wrapped around a pair of scuffed boots not unlike Tootie's lay on the sand. Cups, bottles, the white china bowl used to feed Star, were tossed in a heap outside the entrance.

Matt cast the flashlight's beam along the beach in an

arc that ran from the cave to the river and back again, as if he suspected the girls had swum away. In disgust, he shook his head. "Let's not waste any more time."

When we got back to the path up the eastern side of the ravine, I glanced at the spectral Suburban. "Wait," I said, stopping abruptly, causing Matt to lose his footing and skid off the path and into the brush. "Sorry. But listen, I think I know where the girls have fled."

Matt stepped back onto the trail and impatiently brushed his trousers. The ravine was full of thistles, some of which had found their Scot. "This better be good," he said darkly. Without answering, I led the way up the well-beaten track of this section of ravine.

The moon began to show itself behind the trees to our left. I could clearly see where we were going. I could also see an occasional metallic glimmer. Armed officers were hiding out around us.

In daylight, it was easily possible to climb from the middle of the ravine to the abandoned parking lot of the Suburban in less than half an hour. But in the dark it took twice as long. I hoped Matt's men wouldn't think that *I* was a suspect being led out of the ravine. My imagination worked overtime as I considered dying in a hail of friendly fire.

Where the path out of the wood opened onto the rear of the Suburban's parking lot behind the derelict garages, we stopped. I saw no indication of light in any window. I was just about to frame an apology to Matt, when he made a sweeping gesture with his powerful flashlight.

"Do that again, Matt," I whispered. "Swing the beam past the door there."

Immediately, he saw the same thing I'd noticed, for he stopped in mid-swing and held the light steady on the rusted metal door. In the center of the circle of light was a small square patch of bright red, clean paint, about the right size to have been covered for years by the broken bolt I'd seen attached when I'd been there earlier. Matt trained the light on the rough pavement at the foot of the door. On the ground lay the dislodged bolt.

Without a word, Matt handed me the light and I held it as he pushed the rusted door. As had been the case that morning, the only light inside the building came from the exterior street lights. On the building's north, which faced the ravine, all lay in total darkness. On the south, facing Eglinton Avenue, the interiors of the apartments we passed were dimly visible through doors ajar or missing, lighted by the poles on the busy thoroughfare outside. Intermittently, the headlights of a car would flash on an apartment's walls. I jumped in alarm each time, but Matt led me up two floors, where we found nothing but rubble and the occasional rat.

On the third of the building's four floors, we saw a quick flick of light coming from the end of the hall. When Matt swiftly extinguished his own flashlight, a split second passed before the light at the end of the hall went dark, too. Matt reacted instantly. He dove over the threshold, me stumbling behind him. We crouched in tense silence when, echoing in the quiet like cannon fire, came the sound of feet running up a metal staircase. We were doomed. An Uzi-toting special police officer was about to open fire behind us. Involuntarily, I pasted myself to the wall.

But in an empty building any noise seems closer than it is. The runner was on the other side of the building, on the northern stairwell. Without warning, another burst of sound sent Matt diving for the floor again. A heavy object dropped on an uncarpeted fourth floor above us. The rasping scrape of metal being dragged across wood assaulted our ears, followed by a few tentative footfalls, then a staccato march with a purposefulness that could only be human.

"Let's go," Matt said, his lithe spring the result of his powerful build. It took me longer to get up and for an instant I was eye-level to his waist and the dark outline of his holstered gun. The presence of the Glock startled me. I'd had a lot of experience with firearms in my court-room, but on my knees in a dark hall nose-to-nose with a handgun was not one of those experiences.

I gathered my wits. "I think I know which apartment they're in. I was here earlier today," I whispered. I thought Matt nodded, but he was obscured in shadow. On the fourth floor I saw a replica of the floor below, with the door to apartment 417 closed. At its base a bar of light dimly flickered.

Why didn't Matt use his radio to call for backup? But he did nothing of the sort. Without drawing his Glock, his flashlight stashed, the one-handed cop went it alone, except of course, for me, his tentative and frightened shadow. The scraped, cracked door of 417 surprisingly swung open at his touch. Matt slipped into the apart-ment. I stood behind him, holding my breath. In the rear wall of the ten-foot-square dining area beyond the galley kitchen, the window Tootie and I had looked out of that morning reflected the strange scene within.

An old metal cookie pan teetered atop an upended wooden chest on the floor in the center of the room, hold-ing two dozen votive candles in the sand that filled the pan. Each candle seemed to dance in its own indepen-dent breeze, the flames flickering in all directions and casting an eerie light on the faces of four young women on one side of the pan and a fifth on the opposite side. Tootie, Lynx, Scotty and Shiv stood watching Carrie Simm, all so absorbed that not one of them noticed Matt and me.

"Now they know where I am," Carrie accused. "Thanks to your stupid moves, I'm a dead person. Either they take me or he does. I'm dead." As she spoke, the once-adored young movie star fluttered her hands and tugged frantically at her hair, the wild blonde spikes framing her face like a dirty halo. A cross-shaped series of red scratches on her forehead, I realized with horror, were not random but the Ferryman cryptogram. The letters writhed in the uncertain illumination. Carrie herself seemed to weave into and out of the flame as if she were a moth. She wore one of the long-sleeved black T-shirts I'd bought. Its newness contrasted sharply with the stained, tattered jeans she also wore. Her movements continued in spasms and she seemed to be raving. But despite all this, she was still hypnotically beautiful, her haunting eyes wide above her high-boned, flushed cheeks, her lithe body sometimes wholly visible in the golden glow, sometimes half obscured by darkness.

Nobody moved toward her. Nobody argued with her. Nobody spoke. Long moments passed before I realized her audience was captive. She was not merely waving her hands, she was waving a tiny handgun. The Raven in flight. The ACP picked up at the scene of her father's death. The missing murder weapon. The smoking gun.

Matt saw it at the same instant I did. Silhouetted against the scene, he reached for the Glock at his waist, restrained himself, curved his fingers away from the holster, dropped his hand to his side.

I gasped.

The gasp echoed in the apartment, bounced off the walls, shocked into stillness even the dancing candle flames. For a split second there was no sound, no motion, not even the exhalation of a breath. And then, in an action so swift that I didn't even see it happen, Carrie Simm grabbed Tootie with one hand and held the gun to the nape of Tootie's neck with the other. "Okay," Carrie screamed, "I hear you. I see you there by the door. I see him, too. I saw him in the hall before. But I'm not going. I'm not going alive. Nobody's going to make me go away with him. Get him out of here or I'll shoot." She brandished the gun toward the three girls huddled on the other side of the box. Then she gave Tootie a hard shake.

Seeing Tootie terrorized, helpless, jarred a long-lost paternal indignation. I didn't stop to figure it out. I might be inept, but Queenie was right. I had to go forward.

"I'm the one you need to shoot," I said in my sonorous judge's voice. The voice that could reach to the last person in the last row of any courtroom in the Province of Ontario. The voice that had once had the power to tell a prisoner he was going away for life. The voice that had set the innocent free. "I'm the one who brought us here tonight. Shoot me." I brushed past Matt and strode into the circle of light. I was quaking with fear. I prayed that my gamble would pay off. If it didn't, I, too, was a dead person.

Carrie stood still. She stared at me with complete clarity in her eyes. She was not drugged. She was not mad. "Who the hell are you?" She inquired, still holding the Raven against Tootie's neck.

I had to improvise, swallow my own terror. "I'm the enemy of your enemies: Stalton. Lito. Your father. I'm the man who told the police that someone evil is after you. That's true, isn't it Carrie? You have to protect yourself, don't you? The only way was to hide out, wasn't it?" I tried to keep my eyes directly on her face, though that was hard in the failing light. "But now we're here and you're safe."

"We? Lito's here?" Carrie's hand shook and Tootie flinched. "Lito's dead, Carrie. Matt West is with me." She looked puzzled. "Solomon," I risked adding.

"I can't go with Solomon," Carrie cried. "It's no good. Everybody knows Solomon is a cop. I want the cops out of here. Get the cops out of here!"

"Okay." I glanced out of the corner of my eye for some signal from Matt, but he wasn't looking at me. He was watching the shadows on the wall behind Carrie's back. I had the uncanny feeling that Matt had asked for and received somebody's permission to let me remain in charge.

I kept improvising. "Carrie," I said, "This cop will leave, I promise. But you have to do something for me first, okay?"

Stillness. Silence. Then slowly, she nodded.

"Let Tootie go. And the other girls, too. Let them walk out of this apartment with Solomon. Then you and I will talk things over about the person who killed your father."

It was a wild shot, but this statement had an immediate effect on Carrie. Her eyes widened, her face showed puzzlement, then a strange sort of relief. Most dramatically of all, she swung the gun away from Tootie's neck and pointed it directly at me! I swallowed hard and forced my quivering voice to sound calm.

"Good, Carrie. You understand. Tootie and the others will go with Detective West and *I'll* be your hostage."

245

Tootie slid away and sprang toward the other girls, eliciting no response from Carrie, who now seemed to see me only. In a few more seconds, I felt a rush of air at the back of my neck, as the four girls eased past me and toward Matt and freedom.

"Carrie kept her fingers curled tightly around the grip of the little semiautomatic. Despite the gun, I felt this girl was no Legion. She was alert, controlling. Violent, as Tootie had said, but not crazy. Still, the fatherly sympathy I'd felt in those hours of video-watching vanished now that she had a gun in my face.

"Carrie," I said, daring to move a fraction away, "do you think you could give me the gun? I can't help you if you're pointing that thing at me."

"Give me a break," she spat with contempt. She giggled and waved the gun at my throat.

"Just put it down, Carrie," I said in a voice only a little above a whisper. I was afraid to talk any louder. I stood still and we stared at each other. I started to remember prayers I knew when I was her age. Prayers for the dead.

"I'm not crazy," she finally said. "Just scared. I can't stay here. He's coming." She glanced up at me with an expression that I'd seen before. On the screen in the Fu Manchu limo. I chanced stepping a little closer. The candles flickered violently and a few went out. I did not relish the prospect of continuing this dangerous conversation in darkness. "Give me the gun, Carrie. If it's van Rijn that you're afraid of, this gun isn't going to help. Your only hope is to come with me. I can protect you."

She ignored my suggestion. "Legion's dead, isn't she?" Carrie asked softly. "Legion got burned to death."

"Carrie," I said as gently as I could manage, "Legion

didn't burn. I think she breathed smoke or fumes and just closed her eyes and —"

"Sometimes people just have to die, don't they?"

Did she mean me? I strained to listen for any sign of Matt. Carrie raised the gun and I flinched. "This is a nice little piece, don't you think?" She ran a finger along the lip of the barrel, then put the same finger to her lips and kissed it.

"Carrie, put it down."

She studied the ACP in her palm. "I got it off my father, actually," she said. "It's a pocket gun. Lots of people have them for their personal protection. I went with my father to that big party on opening night."

"I know," I responded. "But we can help you with that. If you come with me, we'll get help. Together, we can catch your father's killer. Even with your fingerprints on it, the gun is still valuable evidence."

"*Especially* with my fingerprints on it." And she flashed me a grin that would have struck me as evil even without the dramatic shadows and dancing light, even without her incongruous fair beauty that was evident still. "You just don't get this, do you, you old relic?"

"What, Carrie?" How much longer would we stand like two alley cats at a face-off?

"My father sold me. I don't mean as a hooker. I mean as a wife. He sold me so he could make more freaking movies. But I'm not going to do it. So I wait until I'm just close enough. There's a crowd around and everybody's looking at Daddy and his friends, the big stars. I open my purse. I take out the gun. I hide it in my sleeve and I shoot. Nobody can hardly hear the gun. All they can hear is me screaming. Because I'm like, 'Help! Oh, God!

247

Somebody shot my father!' Of course I've got blood all over my white dress. Nobody in the world is going to think the shooter is me. I keep the Raven on me. I throw myself on my father's body. Everybody's thinking killers always run away. So if somebody stays, they're not the killer. Right?"

I had studied Matt's video thoroughly, had run it and stopped it and run it again so many times that I could picture every move Carrie was describing. It fit. It fit perfectly.

"Carrie," I said softly, "you're a victim. You've been a victim for a long time. Whatever happened, there's help."

All I needed was for us — both of us — to keep calm a few seconds more. I glanced at the sputtering little candles wondering how much light was left. Then, without warning, the dim shadows were pierced by the beam of a flashlight, the same flashlight I'd seen in the window and the hall. It held Carrie and me frozen for a moment. Then it shifted purposefully. Framed in the doorway was Harmensz van Rijn.

"No!" Carrie shouted, springing toward the door. "I won't. Not ever!"

She swung the gun toward the man on the threshold. After the second or third shot, the flashlight fell to the floor and went out. Van Rijn toppled, his face a bloody mess, his hands splayed and empty.

But there was no other shot.

Carrie stepped away from the body in the doorway, the gun held loosely at her side. She walked past me, not touching me, though the kitchen was only a few feet wide. She slumped down on the floor near the wooden chest where a single candle flickered in the metal pan. Defeated, I sat down beside her.

Carrie opened her lips as if to speak but all that came out was a garbled sound that I thought might be "water".

"There's no water here, Carrie," I said, gathering my wits a little. "But if you give me the gun, I'll see you get gallons."

She seemed not to hear me. She began to rock back and forth, uttering the same sound over and over.

"'Bought her'? You're not saying 'water', you're saying 'bought her'?"

"Her father sold her. The pervert bought her. She shot Daddy. Then his daughter." She laughed softly as if the rhyme pleased her.

"Carrie, please, give me the gun. I'll take you to a place where you won't be alone or afraid or cold."

She smiled at me, a smile that for one small instant revealed again the angelic, wise face of the movie videos. "I'll get there by myself," she said. "I always do." I felt a blast of air and heard a shot so close it deafened me. Carrie hadn't lost track of the rounds in her gun. With the one left, she blew a large hole in her lustrous curls.

CHAPTER SIXTEEN

E ight days later, after a week of sleep in a hotel near City Hall, I remembered my promise to Tootie. I knew *I* would never enter the Suburban again, but my reluctance did not release me from my vow to help Tootie. I would instruct William Sterling to make a deal. I would withdraw my application on the property if my rival agreed to give Tootie a decent job on a site project.

And I had to see Matt West. I showered, dressed, ate a huge meal and walked a few blocks up to Police Headquarters.

Matt, ever the stone-faced cop, pretended not to be pleased to see me, but I could detect a smile teasing his face. He was dictating to his computer. The softwear seemed to understand every word of his clear, unaccented English, free of the speech patterns of a Scottish father and a Jamaican mother. I was surprised, but I remembered that long ago I'd worked hard to erase all hint of my Italian ancestry in my own speech.

"Be with you in a minute," Matt said, then had to delete those six words from his report. Modern technology sometimes doesn't allow for spontaneity. I poured myself a coffee and reached for a doughnut, double-chocolate glazed. But I recalled that Queenie had found me pudgy, so I left the treat sitting in its box. I'd received a letter that morning, with the envelope printed in large, carefully formed capital letters. I hadn't given my address to anyone. But Matt West knew where I was staying and he might have given the address to the writer. The minute I saw the labored printing on the envelope, my heart leapt.

> *Dear Your Honor:*
>
> *This is the first letter I ever wrote by myself. I used the dictionary to copy words I already know how to say. Phonetics. See how fast I can learn?*
>
> *I am enjoying school very much. But mostly I like it because I am learning good things to help people when I come back to Toronto.*
>
> *When somebody helps you the best thanks is to do the same for a stranger.*
>
> *This is how I am going to thank you, by helping homeless people with their health.*
>
> *Here are two Cree words to go along with my English writing.*
>
> > *Wah pah kay (tomorrow)*
> > *Ne tay he (my heart)*
>
> *Your friend,*
> *Queenie*

I wasn't sure what "tomorrow my heart" meant, but it made me feel that I didn't want to be fat or unattractive to Queenie in any way.

"Okay, Portal, here's the story," Matt said, breaking rudely into my thoughts. "Van Rijn was known to us for some time. On occasion he supplied small-time dealers

251

like Charington Simm but the drug trade was just a sideline."

"Skip the details, Matt," I interrupted. "I got most of this figured out. Van Rijn presents himself as a talent agent. He gets close to people in the movie business. But he's not providing beautiful girls. He's hunting them. He bribes them when possible, kidnaps them when necessary. Then he uses his international connections to ship them out to ready markets, China, for example. He sees Carrie. Like everybody else, he understands she's something special. Deluxe. He knows her father is a desperate man, so he makes a deal. What he doesn't understand, however, is Carrie's wilfulness, her spirit, the fact that she would rather kill her own father than live like a captive. She was Charington Simm's captive all her life. But that was her limit."

Matt nodded.

"How did Lito and Stalton fit into this?" I asked him.

"Junkies and small-time losers," Matt spat out. "We got nothing on Stalton yet, but sooner or later, we will. She helped Charington turn over girls to van Rijn in exchange for her daily fix. Then she helped Lito and van Rijn. She'll attach herself to some other piece of garbage and we'll move in. Matter of time."

Matt took a file from his drawer but left it unopened. As I leaned forward to read the label, Matt put his wrist stump over it. I jumped back. "Portal," he said, "Corelli's got you up for a citizen citation for bravery."

"Give it to somebody who deservs it, Matt."

"The way we see it," he answered, "you saved four people, including a fellow officer."

"Fellow officer? What now?" Suddenly I remembered.

"Matt, when Carrie had that gun on me, I could see shadows behind her. Somebody making a hand signal. And you responded, as though you were getting an okay to let me take control. Who — ?"

Matt opened the folder on his desk and handed me a letter on the stationery of the Toronto Police Service. I could feel his eyes on me as I read. The document stated that I had assisted the police in a difficult witness protection case, had diffused a hostage-taking incident and finally, that my actions had resulted in solving a homicide. The letter was signed, "Monica Davisville, Constable First Class," with a badge number. I put the letter down in front of me and just looked at it for a while. "I *wasn't* ever alone on this, was I, Matt? The Lynx was with me. Just the way she was with Tootie and Carrie and the others. She's the 'fellow officer.'"

Matt put the letter back in the file. The tab had my name on it. "The Lynx took over from Solomon. Her cover's still good. So keep your mouth shut, Portal."

"If you had *her*, Matt, why did you need me?"

He got that crafty look in his eyes. "At first it was because Corelli was on my back and I thought it couldn't hurt to have you on board as an extra."

"Window dressing?"

"Big time. Then Tootie vanished and so did Carrie. That meant Lynx had lost her target. We figured we had to get to Tootie and that you were our best bet. We thought it would be straightforward. We weren't on the homicide, remember. Our assignment was witness protection. Obviously matters turned out a little different than we anticipated."

"Matters often do." I thought about the agonizing

moments I had spent with Carrie, waiting for Matt to rescue me. "Why didn't you come back, Matt? Why didn't you intervene before Carrie killed herself?" If I had really been deserving of a bravery citation, I thought, I would have been able to save *her*.

"I *did* come back," Matt said. "But van Rijn was there before me. Short of a hail of gunfire, there was no way we could have got you and Carrie out."

"So you saved me by allowing Carrie . . ."

"Let it go, Portal. If you were a cop maybe you'd understand these things. As it is, you're only a judge."

He didn't smile but I did. "And Tootie keeps calling," he added. "She wants to hear from you."

"I know I should see her but I need more time. I —"

"And William wants you to call him, too."

I hadn't meant to walk to the neighborhood where I'd first met little Legion, but I found myself on Wellesley and then at the Marble Widow. It was being prepared for demolition. The fence the children had painted was gone and in its place stood a sturdy metal one bearing a metal sign that read: "A Community Project Sponsored by the Far Sun Bank of Eastern Commerce."

I'd had enough of buildings and their mysteries. I was suddenly glad that I was living in a hotel. It made it easier to pull up stakes. Now that I'd decided not to pursue the renovation grant for the Suburban, I could go anywhere in Canada — in the world — if I felt like it.

By the time I got to the Marble Widow, it was dark. But not so dark that I couldn't make out the figure in a long black coat leaning against the frame of a destroyed window.

"Tootie, I cried. "What are you doing here?"

She looked as if she could ask *me* the same question, but instead she said, "A deal's a deal, Mr. Portal. And the deal is we're going to work together. We're going to fix up that Suburban building.

"But Tootie," I replied, remembering the horror, "how can we ever forget what happened there?"

"We never will," she answered. "We'll, like, put up one of those memorial things. And we could change the name. Call it the 'Carrie Simm' or something like that." She stared down at her hands. I noticed her nails were perfectly manicured and dark red again. "I know Carrie did a wrong thing. Killing is always wrong. But her life was so bad . . . We tried to tell her there was another way, but she never would listen. Her problems don't make what she did right, but they do sort of make you understand. You know what I mean?"

I looked into her sad eyes. "How long did you girls know it was Carrie who shot her father?"

"I'm the only one," she answered. "Not even Lynx knew, except she probably got suspicious. Sometimes I see Carrie dying as my own fault. But she scared me. She liked to wave the Raven in my face."

She sounded so guilty that I quickly comforted her. "Three people died in front of me and I didn't do anything," I said. "I was frightened for my own life, too."

Tootie put her flawless white hand on mine. "Maybe we have to, like, forget the past and just think about the future. That's why we have to be the winner when they pick who gets the grant. We don't want people living in caves and swimming pools, right?"

"Right, Tootie." She gave my hand a squeeze and I

leaned over and kissed her dark, straight hair as I had once kissed the hair of my own daughter. "But Tootie," I said, "if we're going to be partners, I have to know who the Ferryman is."

She stared into space for a minute. "Mr. Portal," she said, "behind Juvenile Hall, there's this garage made into a church. It's not really part of the hall because no, like, religion is allowed when the government pays, but a lot of girls from the hall go there. That's where we hear about how when you need to cross a river of trouble and there's no bridge and you can't swim, the Ferryman will be there."

"Tootie, you put your faith in God, the Ferryman? How can you say God helps in time of trouble after all that's happened?"

"I could understand why you say that, Mr. Portal," she answered. "But you could look at it different, too. You could look at yourself. You helped poor people. You shared your money and brains. You forgave people who did wrong. You got into things you were afraid of so other people could be safe. Sometimes the Lord is the Ferryman, true. But sometimes, if we believe, it's *us*. *You're* the Ferryman, Mr. Portal."

The next Friday morning, William Sterling advised me that both the city and the owner of the Suburban had officially declared a draw between my offer and that of my rival. The first bid to be signed by a judge would be the winner.

"Did you look at this carefully?" William asked, as he pointed to the signature of the rival bidder. The name was neatly printed beneath the blank signature line. I adjusted my reading glasses. The name came into focus. "Jeffrey Portal."

"Jeffrey?" I asked, incredulous. "My son is my rival?" I saw what I had to do. "Give me your pen," I demanded of William. "Jeffrey needs a judge to sign his application. *I'll* sign it. And you get it to City Hall." William looked about to refuse. But he had to honor my request. He owed me.

To live in Canada is always to hear winter breathing behind you. *Kee way tin.*

The flakes flew, making the ravine look as though it were veiled in bridal gauze. The bridal wear that nuns of my youth put on the day they took their vows and relinquished forever the temptations of this world.

"Goodbye," I whispered to Wigmore. I intended never to come again.

I heard a rustle behind me, a bird or a squirrel. I didn't bother to check. I stood still and let the cold wind cool my heated face. Then I turned to go back to the city streets.

I heard the rustle again. My son was standing in front of me.

"I came to say goodbye to this place," Jeffrey said. His blue eyes scanned the valley. "I've loved it here since I was a boy."

I felt my heart soar. "You don't have to say goodbye, Jeffrey. The Suburban is yours. I signed your application. You have the grant!"

He gave me a quick smile of satisfaction.

"The Suburban is *yours*, Dad. When I saw that you were the rival bidder, I got Stow to sign *your* application!"

I began to feel a wild hope rising. Either way the

winning bid belonged to one of us. My eyes swept across the valley: the forest where the meadow had once been, the fragrant old apple orchard, the cliff, the smooth green river itself. Why couldn't Jeffrey and I work together? It was a simple idea but the courage it took to propose it was almost greater than I could muster.

Ask him, my inner voice insisted. *Just ask him.*

So I did. Which is how my son and I and my partner, Tootie Beets, got into the business of saving the Suburban *and* the lands on the rim of the valley, and, some would say, ourselves.